THE ATOMIC WEIGHT OF SECRETS

OR

THE ARRIVAL OF THE MYSTERIOUS MEN IN BLACK

— Book One —

Eden Unger Bowditch

bancroft
press

ISBN 978-1-61088-002-2 $19.95 (cloth)
ISBN 978-1-61088-006-0 $14.95 (paper)

Published by Bancroft Press ("Books that enlighten")
P.O. Box 65360, Baltimore, MD 21209
800-637-7377
410-764-1967 (fax)
www.bancroftpress.com

Cover design and author photo: Steve Parke
Interior design: Tracy Copes
Chapter illustrations: Jason Williford

Printed in the United States of America

FOR MY CHILDREN,

JULIUS, LYRIC, AND CYRUS, WHO SHOWED ME WHERE

"MAGIC" FALLS SHORT AND THAT REAL MAGIC

IS SOMETHING WE CAN TOUCH.

AND TO THE LOVE OF MY LIFE,

WITHOUT WHOM I JUST WOULDN'T BE—NATE.

NOTE TO READER

Dear Reader,

If you wonder whether you have walked into the right book, ask yourself whether you have ever had to tie a shoelace to a light switch in order to create enough force to pull it open from your bed...or if you have ever put vinegar into baking soda and created a volcano...or if you have ever had to use your formidable brain to invent something to help you or those near you, if not mankind. If so, then you know how important invention can be.

For some, tiny moments of invention can lead to bigger and more powerful uses of brainpower, unleashing something mystical within. This, good reader, is the secret to where the real magic lies.

But be wary of what magic you bring into this world, because sometimes we cannot undo the magic we create.

—Eden Unger Bowditch

Table Of Contents

The Strange Round Bird

Strange round bird with three flat wings,

Never ever stops when it shivers and sings,

Never to be touched even if you are bold,

Turns the world to dust and lead into gold.

Three are the wings, one is the key,

One is the element that clings to the three.

Turns like a planet but it holds such power,

Clings to itself like the petals of a flower.

—the poet Muhibbi (1494—1566), unpublished

ONE DROP FROM DISASTER

OR

SCIENCE INTERRUPTED

There were two things the scientist knew for certain. One, he had only seconds to change the world. And, two, if he took too long, all his efforts might be for nothing.

As beads of sweat on his forehead threatened to rain into his eyes, he thought to himself, *Not now.* With only a handful of moments to achieve the correct ratio, he could ill afford the time or movement to wipe away the perspiration.

His hand twitched ever so slightly, his fingers motionless, as he clutched the burette. Trying not to blink, he hooked his elbow on the edge of the table and leaned in to brace himself. The corner of the table cut into his arm, but he had no choice. He had to prevent his hand from shaking any way he could—his right hand, anyway. His left, holding the beaker, continued a slow, circular spin, to be sure that the resin, when released, would not settle at the bottom, and that the other liquid remained in constant motion. With so much resting on an action so small, he could not make even the tiniest of mistakes.

The scientist took a deep breath and let it out slowly. This eased the fog beginning to cloud his glasses. One droplet—one golden droplet from the burette's long, slender glass tube—was all he needed. The golden resin in the burette had to be released into the rotating beaker and captured in the clear, viscous liquid. Any more than one droplet, even a fraction more, and, after months and months of computations, he would have to begin everything all over again. That is, if he survived the catastrophe.

His thumb ever so gently touched the rubber bulb at the end of the burette. This light pressure pushed the resin down the glass tube, a small golden bulge appearing at the bottom.

The sound of a creaking door suddenly filled the silent room. His breath caught in his throat. *Careful. Concentrate. One droplet.*

The scientist could hear the footsteps moving closer—long, slow, deliberate strides, stepping over the threshold and down the aisle behind him. Even as his heart pounded against his chest, he kept his breath intensely slow. Though he tried to ignore it, he could feel the warmth of the hand even before it came to rest on his shoulder.

His breath caught.

His elbow slipped.

The droplet released and fell, inert, to the ground.

"Is this how you clean the blackboard, Wallace?" Miss Brett asked.

"I . . ." But Wallace bit his lip. He looked at the ground where the tiny droplet had soaked into the wooden floor of the classroom. The resin had left a shimmering residue Wallace knew could never be removed. Already, the chemical structure of that spot was different from the rest of the wood surrounding it. The stain would be there, forever, hard as stone and smooth as glass. Wallace could visualize the equation in his head. He was, after all, a scientist, and the fact that he was two days shy of ten years old did not mean he was anything less. He was a scientist, as surely as his father was—and as his mother had been—and all who had come before them. This experiment was as important as anything on which any of them had ever worked.

Not that Wallace had ever known much about their work. All he knew was that his mother believed in him. She told him she firmly felt that one day, perhaps that very day, Wallace would do something that would change the world. She knew it, and she made him believe it, too.

In any case, the fact that this polymer—this molecular compound, this chemical concoction—could change the world was clearly not going to get Wallace out of blackboard duty.

"It's lunchtime," said Miss Brett, "and I know you must be hungry. Everyone else is outside finishing sandwiches and taking exercise."

Wallace's small brown nose was simply not big enough to hold his large glasses in place. He pushed the stems up against his sweaty round cheeks and looked out the window, where his four classmates sat under an oak tree in the middle of the schoolyard. They looked like any ordinary group of school children, taking a break from study while innocently basking in the afternoon sun. That had been the plan, after all—to appear innocent. It had been the plan to look, for all the world, as if they had not a care, not a worry, no concern other than who would get to hold the jump rope or who got the last cream cheese and jelly sandwich.

However, these children were neither ordinary schoolmates, nor, unbeknownst to Miss Brett, were they simply having a picnic. Wallace caught sight of each of his colleagues as they played by the tree.

Faye, the oldest at thirteen, was tall and slender as a gazelle but, Wallace considered, infinitely more like a python in temperament.

Noah looked gawky and gangly, even comical, with his wisps of reddish-blonde hair waving like wheat in the wind, but Wallace had seen that twelve-year-old boy work feats of engineering magic (not to mention what he could do on a violin, to which Wallace had listened in secret).

Jasper, who was the same age as Noah, was always at attention, keeping guard over little Lucy.

Lucy, who was all of six years old, might have been the most brilliant of them all.

Yes, they all looked like children enjoying the day. But they were not ordinary children. Nor, Wallace sensed in the pit of his stomach, were they innocent.

———⟶✦⟵———

"Well, young man?" Miss Brett said.

Wallace's pleading face softened Miss Brett's features. Not so much skinny, but small and a bit frail for his age, Wallace seemed even younger than his nearly ten years. Miss Brett's heart so obviously ached for him. She saw a sad little hungry boy eager to join his friends, but she didn't know the real reason why.

Wallace did not like deceiving Miss Brett. Miss Brett was

very kind. Over the weeks that he and the other children had been together and in her care, she had conducted her classes with foresight and imagination.

And to Wallace, she gave something he had not had in many years. She gave him something that would remain secret even from his classmates—something he shared only with her. This made the deception all the more painful.

It was one thing to not explain the nature of their work to their teacher—how could she understand it anyway? But to keep such a secret, and plan such an escape behind her back, was another thing entirely.

In fact, they all longed to tell her. They wanted Miss Brett to know all about their brilliant creation. But the dangers were too great right now. For her. For them. For it.

Wallace reached into the pocket of his trousers. The pocket, he knew, was empty. Not generally prone to fancy, Wallace wished he still had his lucky coin. The thought of his empty pocket reminded him of a bigger emptiness. He hoped his father had not lost the coin. And he hoped his father himself was not lost.

In his other pocket, Wallace felt his magnifying glass. He corked the vial and slipped it into the same pocket, leaving his other empty, awaiting the return of the coin. He took the burette and placed it, along with the clear liquid, into a basket that hung outside the window, on the ledge. Miss Brett wanted to keep poisons outside the classroom whenever possible.

Miss Brett pulled back her sleeves and picked up the bucket of wet rags that sat, as yet untouched, near the blackboard.

"Come on. I'll help you."

Wallace bent to dip the rag in the bucket again. Right now,

the main objective was finishing this chore and getting out of the classroom. He looked out the window as he rose to face the blackboard. *They* would be coming, maybe any minute, and he would be too late.

"Come on, Wallace," Miss Brett urged gently. "I'd like to get started on the gardening shed. I want to clean it out before dark."

Wallace knew his brown face had suddenly turned pale. Miss Brett wanted to clean out the gardening shed. Wallace already knew this and tried not to panic as she reminded him.

He looked over by the road at the edge of the field. He could see the back of the truck. It was still there. There was still a chance.

CHAPTER TWO

MINDS OVER MATTER

OR

 A VIEW FROM THE SCHOOLYARD

"He's cleaning the ruddy blackboard," groaned Faye.

They were facing life and death and Wallace was cleaning the blackboard.

"Cleaning the blackboard?" Jasper asked, his voice cracking as he tried to remain calm.

"At least Miss Brett is helping him," Noah said, trying to find the bright side. "As long as she's in there with Wallace, she can't be cleaning the shed."

All things considered, Noah could not help but see the irony in their predicament. They needed to get to the shed before Miss Brett, and they needed Wallace to be done with his chore. However, Wallace being done with his chore meant that Miss Brett would be headed for the gardening shed.

Faye harrumphed. "We shouldn't have agreed to let him finish his useless—"

"It is not useless," Jasper declared firmly. "It's a brilliant piece of chemistry and …" Jasper gulped down the words he wanted to say but couldn't. "It couldn't wait."

"You've been saying that, Jasper," Faye said, stepping closer to him, "but you haven't explained. Why can't it wait? Why is it so—"

"What's going to happen?" Lucy asked, interrupting Faye and slipping her hand into Jasper's.

This *was* the question. As scientists, Jasper, Lucy, Faye, Noah, and Wallace knew more than most people about a lot of things. They knew more than most about the power and the magic of science. As scientists, they knew the power they held in their hands.

But as for what was going to happen, they hadn't a clue. So much of their lives here remained a terrible mystery. But Jasper knew two things the others didn't. First, he knew that this experiment, in fact, *did* have something to do with an upcoming event. And, second, he knew that Wallace had no choice but to finish this experiment. And if that meant forgoing the plan, Jasper knew in his heart that Wallace would not have a quick decision on his hands.

So little made sense right now. For one thing, it had been over two months with no real word from their parents. Without warning or explanation, the worlds of the young scientists had been turned on their sides. Their parents had simply disappeared. A dark shadow loomed over them all. There had to be a way to find their parents and to help them escape from their captors.

Now, the children had formed, and meticulously laid out, a plan to free their parents, themselves, and Miss Brett from the clutches of—and there were really no better words to describe them—the *men in black*. In truth, this was not their first plan. Or second. Or ninth. The five young scientists had been working on escape plans since their first days at Sole Manner Farm. But over these last few weeks, while they worked on their most brilliant invention, the children had all agreed, and hoped desperately, that this was the best plan yet. It was, without a doubt, the only plan they had left.

And there was Wallace, stuck in the classroom.

Faye shook her head. "He shouldn't have risked it."

"This is his life's work, Faye. He's been working on that polymer for ... well, years," Jasper said. "He had to do it now, or ... it would have been for nothing."

"Whatever use it may be in the future," Faye said, "it's of no use to us now. We can't use it to save our parents. It isn't going to magically answer all our problems. Is it going to save the world? I don't even care. I'm too busy trying to save our parents, or have you forgotten? If it wasn't for Wallace's—"

"Don't," Jasper warned.

Although Faye might have disagreed, each child had been vital to the creation of this plan and to the invention at the heart of it. So much was riding on everything they did.

Back in the days before the men in black, when the children saw invention as nothing more than pleasure, in the days when the young scientists' minds were not shadowed by fear and the presence of mysterious strangers, back in their own homes, their own countries, their own worlds, they each had worked hard on various inventions. Now, they could see how all these inventions fit together—they were parts of the same, much larger and more important invention. Before they were all brought here, to Sole Manner Farm, there was already something uniting them. Each child had provided a piece of the puzzle—except Wallace.

But they had been brought to the farm against their will.

Even though they were glad to be together, they had been ripped from their lives, and from their parents. This was their mutual condition. This was their bond.

Now, it might well be true that the children had never actually suffered torture, torment, or bodily harm. And there was an obvious effort, on the part of invisible hands, to make them comfortable in their captivity. But harm was felt in a different way.

They were haunted by the sinister men in black, and they hadn't the faintest idea what was going on around them. And they did indeed feel like captives, or castaways, trapped on an island of sorts. The farm was totally isolated, there in the fields outside Dayton, Ohio, in the middle of America. And the fields, like the sea, held them apart from civilization.

"There's just no way Wallace completed his polymer," said Faye, wiping the crumbs from the handkerchief she had used as her personal tablecloth for lunch. She climbed up, joining Jasper on the rock at the base of the old oak tree, and peered in the direction of the schoolhouse. The tree was huge, with broad, spreading branches that were great for climbing and shade. It had knotty, lumpy roots that served as steps, seats, or just something to lean on. This was the tree under which Miss Brett read, and under which the children played or sat or lay in the grass.

"He would have needed twenty-seven seconds more," said Lucy, peering through the small spyglass she had made from the hollow wooden dowel she had found in a closet in the farmhouse, and the two glass discs she had found under the classroom microscope.

Faye held her hand out expectantly and muttered, "What a waste of time."

Lucy handed the spyglass over.

"I wish he had cleaned the blackboard first, then finished the experiment," Jasper said, almost to himself, trying to sweep a lock of darkish blonde hair from his eyes. "We all know Miss Brett would have let him finish if he'd done what she'd asked."

"But then she'd probably be following him right now with a bucket and a broom, ready to sweep out everything we've hidden in the gardening shed," Faye said. "And then where would we be?"

Jasper drank the last of his milk and wiped his cup before placing it back in the hamper. He took Lucy's handkerchief, shook out the crumbs, and collected the napkins from the rest of the group, placing them in the hamper as well. Jasper handed out small apples to his schoolmates. He put two back in the hamper. He realized he might not get a chance to give one to Miss Brett.

"It's his own fault he didn't do it earlier," said Faye. "It's going to be all his fault. If he couldn't be part of this invention, then the least he could do is not prevent us from—"

"Don't blame Wallace," Jasper said, facing Faye. "He's doing his best, and it had to be done now, or it would have been . . . well, he couldn't. The world needs that polymer as much as Wallace needs to finish it."

"One of you will still have to distract Miss Brett and keep her from the gardening shed." Faye felt a twinge of remorse she did not want the others to see. This was a time to be strong—a time to get out while they could.

"One of us?" Jasper tried to keep his voice from breaking.

"It certainly can't be me," Faye said, as if this were a matter of fact. "I've got to make sure I get on the truck. As if we don't all know I'm the most important. Not that you others aren't needed.

But let's be honest."

When he first met Faye, Jasper was so nonplussed, so overwhelmed by her exotic and stunning beauty that he blushed whenever he looked at her. Her voice, with its delicate hint of India, had distracted him from hearing what she said. As the days passed and turned into weeks, then months, her brash rudeness and thoughtless outbursts stunned him the most. He opened his mouth, but Noah beat him to it.

"I'd like to see your bits and pieces make it on their own, Lady Faye," said Noah, looking at her with sly amusement. "A horse's rear may be where the kick is, but it can't go anywhere without its head."

"Are you..." Faye was fuming. "Are you calling me a horse's bum, Mr. Gangly Oh-I'm-Afraid-Of-My-Violin Canto-Sagas? Or is that you back there following my lead?"

"Lady Faye, you amaze me. But you certainly do have a whole heap of kick in you," said Noah, smiling and bowing in mock reverence. "And I await your command, as do we all."

Faye opened her mouth to lay it on him but, realizing this would constitute a kick, backed down, taking that deep breath Miss Brett had taught her to take before saying something that would only make things worse.

"The carriages will be coming to fetch us," said Faye grumpily, trying to appear unflustered. "*They* could be here any minute, for all we know. And we have no idea when *he* plans to leave. He's always unpredictable." She pointed her thumb across the field to a gawky man sitting in a tree—a birdwatcher who, according to the sign on his vehicle, was from the Daytonic Birdwatchers' Society. With his binoculars and his notebooks, he had been visible out there more and more over the last few weeks, but not every day and at no exact hour. Luckily, he always managed to drive off before danger came around the corner. And today, he and his Knox truck would be the children's means of escape.

Lucy felt sorry for the birdwatcher. Not only was he clumsy but, from the view through her spyglass, which Faye had returned to her, he had apparently shaved off half his moustache.

But then she saw something else.

"Oh, no!" shouted Lucy, pointing in the other direction. "Look at the road!"

It took but a second look to see what Lucy saw. The trail of dust winding through the fields, headed in their direction, was from the one road that led out of the farm and to the city. The dust was the familiar warning that *they* were coming. Every Friday afternoon, the carriages (and twice, motorcars) came, as if riding a great serpent of dust.

It was the men in black, coming for them. The men in black, the strangely sinister men who haunted their lives.

The men who took their parents away.

"I say we go now," said Faye.

"What?" said Jasper.

"They'll be here any minute!" Faye said. "It's too big of a risk. We can't wait any longer!"

"You mean leave Wallace behind?!" Jasper cried in disbelief, numb from the lash of Faye's tongue. Abandon Wallace? Never.

But, as he turned, hurt and angry by the very sight of Faye, Jasper also saw the trail of dust. They all knew the men in black were coming for them.

And soon it would be too late.

CHAPTER THREE

A Modest Proposal

OR

 HOW LUCY CAME TO BITE HER NAILS

Only a few months ago—before the men in black, before Dayton, Ohio, and before their secret invention—life had been so very different for Lucy and Jasper. Indeed, it had been somewhat normal. Considering that both their parents were important scientists and nothing was normal about that, life was normal.

The Modest family lived in a comfortable house in a comfortable neighborhood on the west side of London. Lucy and Jasper ate their breakfast together every morning. They had supper with their parents, when their parents, Drs. Isabelle and Tobias Modest, were in town. And had the time. And chose to join their children for a meal. Their mother and father were frightfully busy. But they assured their children that their work was helping to make the world a better place and, therefore, their children were (almost) always in their thoughts during the long hours…days…weeks that Isabelle and Tobias Modest were away. Jasper and Lucy knew they were loved because their parents had told them. How this love worked, however, was rarely shown.

Approximately one Sunday per month, the whole Modest family would spend time together, as a family. They would sit together quietly in the salon, reading to themselves from their scientific journals. Or perhaps they would listen to recorded lectures on the phonograph. They would even take the occasional walk in the park, on weekends when both parents were in town. And they had the time. And they chose to spend that time walking in the park. Often, this meant that their parents would walk together, deep in conversation, and Jasper and Lucy would follow behind.

Sometimes, Jasper would bring a small boat he'd built, with a little propeller—he was very keen on designing propellers. He'd place the boat in the pond and let it run. Or sometimes, he would make a helicopter and let it whirl, the string-triggered propeller keeping it aloft. Jasper had designed a slow release that still allowed a strong twirl. He also designed a reverse-pull mechanism so that the propeller could maintain power for a very long time.

During their walks in the park, Jasper saw other families walking together. The other families often held hands or flew kites or walked dogs. And these families did these things, all of these things, together—mothers, fathers, children, dogs. Other families had a slightly different concept of *together*, he noticed. But still, walking in the park was surely a normal thing for a family to do, and it was something the Modest family did as well. This made them somewhat normal. Somehow, this was important to Jasper. He liked to think his family participated in things that other families did.

Jasper's sandy blonde hair was like his father's, and Lucy's thick dark hair was like her mother's. Both children had freckles on their noses that didn't seem to come from anyone in particular.

Their house was nice. Jasper and Lucy had comfortable rooms, wholesome food and, most important, each other. On the whole, home life did not present any hardships.

School life was a different story, though. Clever as the Modest children were, no teacher had ever cared much for either one. Yes, at a very young age, Jasper had discovered that teachers—at least all teachers Jasper had encountered—were not terribly keen on being shown how to do things by undersized little boys. He also learned that teasing, cruel pranks, and bullying were part of everyday life, in the classroom and out.

Jasper was always prepared to run at a moment's notice. He was good at running and found many opportunities to practice. When he tried to explain the physics of a marble in motion, all while making an excellent shot, he had been pelted with marbles by the boys in his class. The boys hadn't a clue what he was talking about and hated him for it. Jasper had been forced by a very large and nasty girl to eat an earthworm he'd brought to class to show how the creature could turn and fertilize the soil. The girl did not understand a word he had said, except, finally, "fertilize." When a group of older boys tried to get him to drink mercury after he'd explained it was the only metal that retained its liquid form at room temperature, his teacher did nothing.

Jasper had gotten into trouble when three boys in his class had chased him up a tree and then smashed a Chinese puzzle box he had opened. The teacher had been quite upset with the boys, but also with Jasper. All four of them were given detention. The boys were in trouble for breaking the Chinese puzzle box, which belonged to the teacher. Jasper was in trouble for opening it.

The teacher, as it happens, had brought the box to show the

students a puzzle that could not be done. The lot of them had ruined the lesson, and were to write lines to the effect that they would not ruin lessons in the future. Jasper's ability to run came in handy that day as he raced around the classroom, deftly weaving around desks, avoiding chalk pelted at him by the three other boys.

Jasper got extra lines for running in the classroom.

At twelve years old, Jasper may very well have been small for his age, and may not have been able to lift a school desk above his head or pull the door out by its hinges, but he could run faster than anyone.

Lucy was rather petite herself. She wore her hair long, and she had the most enormous brown eyes. She had a sweet round face and a crooked smile and delicate hands that were often busy creating something rather fabulous.

And Lucy had a magical memory. She could remember anything and everything.

But the fact that she was cute, and sweet, and a very good listener, and brilliant, plainly did not help her at school. She found that memorizing great swaths of text did not impress her teachers. Making clever things with her hands only made her classmates resent her. Pointing out that Napoleon became emperor in 1804 and not 1408 made her teacher furious, especially because the mistake was in the book itself and the book belonged to the teacher. A glare that shot daggers was her reward for informing her teacher, who was trying to translate from the French, that *mouton* meant *sheep*, not *banana*. And when Lucy showed her teacher the correct way to say "Kalamata," while also explaining that it was not a species of tree frog but both an olive and a city in

Greece, she earned herself time in the corner for her trouble, after being made to write lines such as "I will not be an ugly horrid little know-it-all," or "Lucy Modest is not modest."

At the very least, Lucy's cleverness made her teacher and her classmates uncomfortable. Once, a particularly nasty teacher stopped the whole class and said, to growls from the students, "If you're so clever, why don't you teach? The whole class is going to listen to Lucy. Oh, dear, she'll have to stand on a chair because she's too small for anyone to see. Oh, but that is against the rules, standing on chairs. Because of Lucy, the whole class is going to write 'I will not stand on chairs,' so you can thank her for that, class. And Lucy, you had better start remembering that you're the child and I am the teacher. If you're so clever, how come you didn't figure that out, missy?" Tears had fallen on Lucy's paper as she wrote, "I will not stand on chairs."

Eventually, teachers took to making her sit in the back of the room, and ignoring her when she raised her hand in class. It was easier for them and much less disruptive. One teacher went so far as to make Lucy sit in a corner and wear a gag over her mouth (which prevented the little girl from chewing on her charm bracelet, which she did when she was excited, anxious, or unhappy). The teacher made her don a dunce cap as well. Sometimes (and this, too, prevented the little girl from chewing her bracelet), the teacher would tie Lucy's hands together to prevent any "unrequested and unwanted creativity" that might originate in that corner. On Lucy's chair, the teacher placed a placard that read, "I am Lucy and I am not as clever as I think." The other students found this quite entertaining. They thoroughly enjoyed anything that brought Lucy down a notch or two.

But in general, they, like the teachers, usually ignored her—the exception being when they had something unfriendly to say.

Lucy's classmates had devised ugly little rhymes in her honor, such as, "Lucy Modest thinks she's the cleverest / but she's the shortest and makes us the boredest." Fortunately, Lucy had the decency and foresight not to correct their grammar. Sometimes, the other children were less clever but more to the point: "Lucy Modest stinks."

Lucy usually obliged with tears and a swift departure.

Lonely as life was at times, Jasper and Lucy had each other. And they had their parents, too. Often. Or, at least, occasionally. The Modest family, on the whole, had no extraordinary problems. They never quarreled or bickered. It was the way their family worked. No family was perfect, Jasper reminded himself. Most families had mums who were home for them when they returned from school. Most children had mums waiting, open-armed, with warm biscuits and loving kisses. Jasper would have liked his mum or dad to be there when he and Lucy got home. But he also knew that his parents worked long hours or traveled a great deal for work. Parents worked because they had to. It was necessary. They did it for their children.

———◦———

Everything changed with the arrival of those men. Those men in big black hats and long black coats and matching black boots, wearing dark spectacles that hid their eyes, speaking in whispered tones with strange and indistinct foreign accents. They seemed to move as one, all seven of them, as they came knocking on the door.

Almost as if the men were expected, the Drs. Modest opened the door. The strange men lined stone steps like so many footmen and stood in total silence. Then, the doors of the coaches opened and two more men in black descended. They walked past their comrades and into the Modest home. Isabelle and Tobias Modest did not stop them—they did not, in fact, react in any way—but Jasper and Lucy certainly did, hiding on the landing at the top of the stairs.

The two men in black who had invaded their home were, without a doubt, the most bizarre men the children had ever seen in their entire lives. There would have been something funny about the whole thing, too, if it all didn't feel so sinister.

The first man was not remarkable in build, nor was he remarkable in stature. He was average, you might say. He was totally average in every way, except for the fact that he was wearing a black satin fully-ruffed ballerina tutu around his middle and had a large black Mexican sombrero pulled down to his nose. He wore a long black silk scarf wrapped several times around his neck and up above his mouth, so all you could see were the dark glasses perched at the end of his nose, upon which the sombrero rested.

The other man was taller, and was dressed simply in a black furry suit that covered his hands and feet. His face was bearded and, upon his head, he wore large fuzzy bear ears that matched his suit.

The two men disappeared into the locked study with Jasper and Lucy's parents. The adults all spoke so softly that Jasper and Lucy could not hear what they were saying, even when the children placed teacups against the study door to listen.

After hours of mysterious discussion, the strange men in black left without a word. Jasper and Lucy saw the concern on their parents' faces, but the children were afraid to ask why. Lucy sat on the hearth rug, chewing on her bracelet as she watched her parents whisper back and forth, standing in the doorway long after the men had gone.

Nothing was said at supper. After eating barely a bite, Isabelle and Tobias Modest left the dining room table. Jasper and Lucy continued to pick at their own plates in silence. They really didn't fancy eating, either.

That night, Jasper and Lucy were left to their own evening preparations when it was time to go to bed. They undressed and put on their nightclothes slowly, in hopes someone would come to talk. But no one did. Although they both lay awake for hours, no one came to tuck them in or say goodnight, or offer any words of comfort or explanation.

The next morning, the children found the cupboards in the nursery empty and those in their bedrooms bare. A set of clothes had been laid out for each of them. Jasper and Lucy dressed in silence and gingerly descended the stairs.

Instead of their normal breakfast on the table, Jasper and Lucy found their parents waiting by a large black carriage at the end of the drive, filled with steamer trunks containing what looked to be all of their clothes and other possessions. In the night, while they slept, the effects of the Modest children had been packed away. And still, Jasper and Lucy hadn't a clue as to why. The children tried to get their parents' attention, but muffled whispers and deep incomprehensible looks passed between the adults, so there was never a chance to ask.

Clinging to one another, hunger falling unnoticed behind fear and confusion, Jasper and Lucy were shuffled into the waiting carriage, where silence prevailed. Within an hour, the family was on a train to Dover and, by that evening, on a ship headed for America. Still no words had passed between parents and children. No explanation. No comforting assurance that all would be fine.

Lucy had that charm bracelet in her mouth throughout their days at sea. Jasper was sure that, had the bracelet and charms not been made of something seemingly indestructible, Lucy's nervous nibbles would have mangled it beyond recognition. She sometimes seemed to be getting awfully close to her wrist. This horrified Jasper, bringing to mind a story about his grandfather, who had once found, in a bear trap, the leg of a raccoon. The creature had found it preferable to chew off its own leg than be taken prisoner into some terrifying unknown.

With a simple, soft touch, Jasper had taken to gently urging Lucy's wrist from her mouth. This worked, but only temporarily, so he began holding her braceleted hand in his as they walked. Their matching bracelets always seemed to interact oddly with each other, making an interesting tinkling noise as they jangled against one another, sometimes becoming entwined. The two siblings had tried at times to fit the odd-shaped charms together. Jasper, who loved puzzles, was convinced that whoever had made the bracelets had done a rather poor job. The charms never really fit.

⟫●⟪

After a week at sea, the family arrived in New York City, where they were met by another big black carriage with shaded windows and gold trim around all four doors. It had an oversized top, which made the inside seem huge and cavernous. It was driven by a big coachman dressed in a black suit with gold trim, who wore an oversized coachman's cap and dark oval glasses. The coachman, in fact, looked very much like the carriage he was driving.

The carriage driver took them to a train station in the middle of Manhattan. New York City was enormous—almost as big as London—and at least as crowded, but Jasper and Lucy didn't get to see much of it before they were hurried into the station and onto a waiting locomotive by a man in a long black dressing robe with a big black babushka on his head.

As on the ship, Lucy and Jasper had their own compartment. Their parents' compartment was the next room over, connected by an adjoining door. The children's room had bunk beds, a washbasin, and a table. Both children had been on trains in London, but neither had ever been on a sleeping train.

Together, Jasper and Lucy climbed to the top bunk and watched out the window as the train began to move from the station. If it had not been for the fear of what lay ahead, the ride would have been wonderful. But worry hung like thunder over them, rumbling with promise of something unwanted.

Lucy took the bracelet and wrist out of her mouth and clung to Jasper with both hands. They felt the rocking of the train get stronger as it sped into the night. In the moonlight, Jasper could see fear in his sister's eyes.

"What's going to happen?" she asked.

Jasper didn't have a clue, but he couldn't tell her that.

"Well, different things, surely," came Jasper's weak offering, "but everything will be all right."

"Will it really be all right?" she pleaded. Lucy's wide eyes showed utter trust in her brother. Jasper didn't want to let her down, and knew he had to tell the truth. She remembered absolutely everything and she'd never forgive him if he lied.

Not that he ever would. Not to Lucy.

"I certainly hope so, Luce," he said. "If not, we'll make it right." Just how he planned to do that was beyond his ken at that moment.

That night, they made a rather big puddle on the floor of their cabin. The puddle was water that splashed from the wash basin. First, Jasper spilled as he poured the nearly cold water into the basin. Pouring water on a train is not a simple task. Next, Lucy splashed her face and most of the cabin in her attempts to wash up. Needless to say, after they washed, the children had to change into a second pair of nightclothes.

No one had come to help them. Lucy and Jasper could hear their parents' voices through the wall, but they could not hear what was being said. When Lucy pulled open the door to ask if Mummy or Daddy could tuck her in, she could see that someone else was in the compartment with them—someone with a voice that Lucy had never heard before, because, surely, if she had heard it, she would have remembered.

It was a man wearing what looked like a fluffy black wooly

jumper and a floppy black hat he wore pulled down to his nose. He had on a pair of dark shaded glasses so Lucy couldn't see his eyes.

Lucy's father stood and walked to the door. Lucy opened her mouth to say something, but Tobias Modest closed the door without a word, flipped the lock, and nearly pinched the tip of Lucy's nose. He hadn't even said "goodnight."

Climbing into her bunk, her charm bracelet between her teeth, Lucy stifled the tears that threatened to fall. Jasper climbed down and tucked his sister in, kissing her on the nose and on the forehead. This is what their mother did when she was not away from home and not busy with something else, and when she remembered to come and tuck in her children at night. Then, Jasper climbed back into his bunk.

They could still hear the voices next door, but they were much more muffled. Lucy got out of her bunk and climbed up into her brother's. Neither Modest child fell asleep easily that night, even though the train trundled along like a great cradle, rocking from side to side.

Later that night, it was Lucy, in the upper bunk with Jasper, who noticed the crack of light coming through the top of the doorway. Jasper had begun to doze in earnest when someone turned the lock. Pressing close to her brother, Lucy shut her eyes quickly so whoever was coming through the door would think she was asleep, too.

Lucy felt soft lips upon her forehead and realized it was her mother. "Bonne nuit, ma chére petite fille," Isabelle Modest crooned softly. Lucy didn't notice as her mother unhooked the clasp on the bracelet that the little girl had worn as far back as she could remember—and that was very far back—but she did notice when Isabelle Modest slid the bracelet off her wrist. Then, she did the same with Jasper's. "Je les en ai besoin, mes chers," she said softly, explaining that she needed to take them, speaking to what she believed to be her two sleeping children. "Mais . . . j'espére . . . je souhaite . . ." Isabelle Modest began, but what she hoped and wished was not expressed aloud.

Tobias Modest stepped into the cabin and walked over to the bunks, placing his hand on his wife's shoulder. The two walked out, the crack of light bending, then disappearing, as they closed the door behind them.

Lucy turned over and clung to Jasper. Her wrist went instinctively to her mouth, but there was nothing to chew. It was then and there, for the first time, that Lucy brought a finger to her lips, and she began to nibble at her nail. She buried her face into her brother's back, and slowly fell into a fitful sleep.

<hr />

In the morning, Jasper and Lucy lay together in Jasper's upper bunk, looking at the rolling countryside from the window. They both waited to be fetched for breakfast, but no one came. They knocked on the adjoining door, but no one answered. The door was still locked. They could hear no voices from the other side.

Jasper and Lucy thought that their parents might still be asleep. The children dressed and left the cabin, thinking to try the hallway door. They knocked and the door fell open. The room was tidy, as if no one had been there. Neither their parents nor their parents' belongings were anywhere to be found.

"There's nothing under the table, then?" Jasper asked, helping his sister out of the tight space.

"Not even a crumb," said Lucy.

"Not even a crumb?" asked Jasper, amazed. "On a train?"

They searched the room thoroughly, including behind the closet door, and in the water closet. They even checked under the bunks. Nothing—not even a speck of dust or dirt. The beds looked as if no one had ever slept in them. The carpet looked as if it had never been trodden upon.

The children walked down the hallway in hopes of finding their parents or someone who knew where to find them. They even hoped to find that odd man Lucy had seen, or the others who had come to their house that fateful evening. They went up to the observatory, back to the caboose, and all the way to the engine. Along the way, they peeked into the dining car, which smelled of breakfast and coffee, and the lounge car, where well-fed travelers reclined in well-stuffed chairs, well-stuffed themselves with breakfast. To the great displeasure and dismay of several inhabitants, the two Modest children peeked into private compartments that were unlocked or ajar. Unable to find either their mother or their father, Jasper and Lucy shuffled toward the smell of sausages, eggs, and coffee.

They sat themselves down at a dining car table for four in hopes their parents would arrive with an explanation. After waiting a half an hour, they ate breakfast on their own. They had ordered eggs, but when the man in the black apron brought the food, Lucy found she couldn't eat them, because they jiggled too much as the train bumped along. She nibbled on the corner of a piece of toast, tearing bits from around the edges. If nothing else, this kept her from crying. Jasper, on the other hand, ate four eggs, sausage, bacon, tomatoes, and three scones smothered in strawberry jam and clotted cream. For later use, he placed two more scones in his pocket, not knowing what might happen next. He and Lucy thanked the steward, who looked at them sadly. He hadn't seen either of their parents on this journey, he had said when they had asked him. Jasper and Lucy walked back from the dining car to their cabin.

The two leather cases that held all their personal things were now packed and sitting at the door of their compartment, which was otherwise completely empty. Like their parents' cabin, theirs had been scrubbed top to bottom, as if no one had ever been in it. Even the big wet spot on the carpet where Jasper had spilled from the pitcher was gone. The two Modest children sat in silence, gazing out the window, wondering where this train was taking them and what was happening to their lives. They sat and watched the countryside change as the sun moved across the sky.

"My bracelet!" Jasper said suddenly. He startled Lucy, who was deeply involved with a hangnail on her third finger. "Lucy, where are our bracelets?" It was not until this moment that he realized the bracelets were gone.

"Mummy took them," Lucy said, her face sad and her voice resigned.

"When?"

"When we were asleep. Well, you were asleep. I was almost asleep, but you were totally asleep. I was more like pretending."

"Why didn't you tell me?" Jasper tried not to shout, but suddenly, for the first time, it truly, deeply, painfully felt like his entire world was crashing down around him, and he was helplessly watching.

"We were so busy, investigating." Lucy's eyes were frightened. "I didn't think it would help find them. I'm sorry."

Jasper opened his mouth to scold, but stopped. What difference did it make now? Lucy was right.

"Why," he said, swallowing, "why did Mummy take them, Lucy?"

"She said she would need them."

This, to Jasper, seemed utterly absurd. "Need them? For what? Grandmother gave them to us when we were small—so small we don't even remember. They were ours, we always had them, they . . . they were ours." Jasper found himself crying. Lucy was crying too now, right into his shirt. "She didn't say anything?" Jasper said, wishing he hadn't gotten so upset in front of Lucy.

"Just that she wished..."

"Wished what?" asked Jasper.

Lucy sat up a bit and cocked her head to one side. Then she shook it. "She didn't say. Just that she would need them both, but not for any particular thing."

"What could she need a charm bracelet for? Two children's charm bracelets? It's not like they're made of gold, or belong to King Edward or something. They don't do anything. They're ours." He noticed Lucy chewing on her torn fingernails. "Stop that!" Jasper said grumpily.

How could his parents leave him to take care of Lucy, let alone himself, on a train, in a foreign country, without his charm bracelet? This was not right. He put his arm protectively around Lucy's shoulder.

Well, he would take care of her. Clearly, no one else was

going to do it.

The train ended its journey in Dayton, Ohio in the early afternoon. No one came to fetch them from the cabin. No one let them know where to go. Jasper and Lucy took their bags and walked to the exit at the back of their train car. They looked out at the sea of people, waiting to greet their long-awaited arrivals. Among the coaches and horses and carts, Jasper and Lucy saw the one they knew had to be theirs—a big black carriage, like the ones that had taken them from their home to the ship, and then from the ship to the train. Gingerly, the two children stepped down from the train.

As soon as they descended, a man grabbed for their bags. Jasper cried out and struggled to keep a hold of them with both hands. With a flick of the wrist, the man yanked the bags from Jasper's grasp and, with one hand, held them well above Jasper's reach. With the other hand, the man hustled the two children along the platform. Jasper turned to shout and, for the first time, got a good look at the man.

Wiry, dressed in a black linen jacket and trousers much too large for his skinny frame. His hat, too, seemed much too large, and his face was invisible in the shadow it cast. It was precisely because of this strange black attire that Jasper knew this man was there to fetch them, and was not some nefarious stranger out to do them harm. Well, he might well be a nefarious stranger out to do them harm but, if so, he was their own personal nefarious stranger, and Jasper knew they had no choice but to follow. The man placed their bags next to the black carriage and disappeared into the crowd.

"Where are our parents?" Jasper asked of a second man—this one in a black brimless hat bent at the very top and dark thick triangular glasses the same shape as his hat, as he heaved their bags up onto the carriage. The man did not answer, but he ushered the children toward the open coach door. Jasper stopped and Lucy bumped into him.

"We're not going anywhere with you until you tell us where our parents are," Jasper said. "What have you done with them?"

The man simply grabbed the children, one by one, and placed them bodily into the carriage. Jasper fought burning tears of anger and humiliation as he sat like a prisoner. Lucy clung to his arm, the little fingers of one hand digging deep into his flesh, the other hand poised against her chin. As she nibbled her nails, Jasper pulled Lucy's hand away from her mouth. Lucy looked down, feeling a bit sheepish for having been nibbling unawares. She placed her hand firmly in her lap. Within seconds, however, once again without realizing it, she put her fingers back into her mouth. Jasper did not say a word, but simply took her hand into his and held it.

<hr>

The carriage drove them for what seemed like hours. It felt as if they went back and forth, zigzagging throughout the city. Lucy began to recite addresses as they passed the same ones periodically, first going one direction, then another. Finally, the carriage turned onto a lovely street lined with big elm trees.

They pulled up in front of a grand house that stood alone on the west side of the block, no neighbors on either side. There was an expansive lawn on either side of the house, and a stone walk that led to the front steps. "One Elm Street" was written in gold letters on a sign by the gate.

Gingerly, and with great trepidation, the children slowly descended. The driver stood by the open carriage door. He then walked around and took their bags from the trunk, set them on the pavement and then, without a word, returned to his seat on the carriage. With a flick of the wrist, he pulled the horses into a trot, and the carriage was off, the children standing alone in front of One Elm Street.

At once, they both noticed a short round woman wearing a white apron standing at the door, waving enthusiastically. It was clear she was waving at them, because no one else was around, but neither Jasper nor Lucy had ever seen her before. As she approached, they could see that the woman's face was rosy and jolly, and she smiled at the children, arms opened wide, welcoming them. It was as if she had been missing them, as if they were returning and not arriving.

"My dears, my dears," she said, waddling down the steps to meet them, wrapping her arms around them both. Immediately, Jasper, smothered in a giant bosom, had to catch his breath. Her arms were like a vice. "Let me look at you. I bet you're hungry after a journey like that."

"Who are you?" he gasped. Lucy, too, was struggling to find air. "I mean, I'm sorry, but—"

"Oh, Jasper, it is me who should apologize," said the woman, pulling them back from her embrace and looking intently at both children. "I'm Rosie. I'm your Rosie. I'll be taking care of things here at home. I'm the cook and the nanny and the nurse. And whatever you need, just ask." She smiled again and winked. "Give me those heavy bags, my darlings," she said, picking up their bags as if they weighed nothing. For such a short, round woman, she certainly seemed to have arms of steel. With powerful arms around the two children and a bag in each hand, Rosie walked them up the path.

When they stepped over the threshold, both children let out a deep breath. They had been traveling so long, it was a pleasure to step into a house that really looked like a home. What they felt was an invitation to come in and be welcomed. And this house was filled with the most delicious aromas two hungry children had ever smelled.

"I've got a pot of mutton stew waiting for you two," Rosie said to Jasper and Lucy as they stood dumbfounded in the doorway. She gave each of them another hug and shuffled them into the entrance hall. Rosie's round, squat body, as well as the clucking sound she made with her teeth, reminded the children of a mother hen rounding up her chicks.

"Where is Mummy? And Daddy?" asked Lucy.

"They'll be along," Rosie said. "Here we go. Come this way." She clucked, flapping her arms as she guided the two children into the kitchen.

"She really is a mother hen," whispered Lucy to Jasper.

"Cheep cheep," whispered Jasper to Lucy.

"Cheep cheep," whispered Lucy back.

The house was lovely, with umbrellas in the umbrella stand and hats on the hatrack. The walls were clean and freshly painted in yellows and blues and warm creamy whites. And the house was full of windows, though not many facing the front. Only on the second floor did the children see sunlight shining through glass.

The rooms were furnished with comfortable chairs and sofas, nothing fussy or delicate.

Upstairs, the nursery was full of games and toys. There were blackboards covering one entire wall and, in the corner, a small, but fully functional, science laboratory. Beakers and test tubes were lined neatly in one cupboard, and goggles, aprons, and rubber gloves placed, just as neatly, on shelves in another. Stone basins, candles, and burners, and long lengths of rubber tubing and several mortises and pestles in various sizes, were on shelves as well. In short, it had everything a nursery science lab should have, if a nursery other than this one had ever been equipped with a science laboratory.

Down the hall was a bathroom. Next to the nursery were three bedrooms—one for Lucy, one for Jasper, and a small one off the far side of the nursery that belonged to Rosie. Down past the bath was a large master bedroom that clearly belonged to their parents. Peeking in, the children saw their father's slippers and mother's robe. This was reassuring. Surely it meant that their parents were planning to come—that is, if they had not been here already.

Rosie, they quickly learned, was a wonderful cook. She could, and would, make any of their favorite dishes—roast beef, Yorkshire pudding, roast potatoes with gravy. She could make puddings, cakes, and custards, and anything chocolate. Over the following days, the very well-fed children became very fond of Rosie indeed.

That was a very good thing, too. It was good because their parents had not yet appeared.

"Sorry, darlings, but your parents have gone to the laboratory early this morning," Rosie would say when the children came down for breakfast. "I think they should be home tonight in time to tuck you in."

And then, at night, she'd say, "Well, your parents had wanted to be home before you went to your beds, but it looks like they've been detained. Perhaps you will see them in the morning." Rosie would tuck the children in their beds. Then, she'd sit in the rocking chair in the threshold between Jasper and Lucy's bedrooms, humming and knitting until the children fell asleep.

———◦◦◦———

Life at One Elm was, all things considered, quite pleasant. The children found their laboratory to be very well stocked. The nursery had building blocks and puzzles and toys. Behind the house was a lovely and rather vast meadow that seemed to open only onto the four houses that made up their block. There were never any other people around, and the trees and the houses blocked the view from the street, so Jasper and Lucy could play for hours, undisturbed. They would imagine a ship that could take them to the moon, and ponder how many layers of metal sheathing they would need. Sometimes, Jasper would make propellers from the long grasses, and he and Lucy would experiment by dropping them from different heights. And of course, every meal was delicious. Days were spent doing what they liked, and evenings were warm and cozy. It went along like this for quite a while, until Lucy realized something on the way to breakfast one morning.

"It has been seventeen days since we have seen Mummy and Daddy."

Jasper was stunned. He knew it had been a while, but over two weeks? He couldn't believe it.

"Sorry, darlings, but your parents have gone to the laboratory early this morning," said Rosie as she prepared hot porridge with sweet cream, brown sugar, vanilla, and butter. She dribbled maple syrup over the whole thing before she scooped it into the bowls and placed them in front of the children. "I think they should be home tonight in time to tuck you—"

"It's been seventeen days," Jasper said, cutting off the familiar morning announcement.

Rosie gasped. Clucking her teeth, she gave the children a quick half-smile. "Must fetch the juice," she mumbled as she scurried off to the kitchen. It seemed to take forever for Rosie to return. In fact, Rosie still hadn't returned to the dining room by the time the children finished their porridge. They could hear her banging around in the kitchen, clucking and squawking to herself, but about what, they could not discern.

After their juiceless breakfast, Jasper and Lucy went back upstairs to the nursery. As they passed their parents' bedroom, they both stopped at the door and looked inside. Everything was perfectly neat and orderly. The bed was made without a wrinkle. Daddy's slippers were placed neatly next to his bedside table. Mummy's glass jug of water sat, full, on hers. In fact, everything was so neat and orderly that it looked as if no one had been there for days.

Maybe even seventeen days.

The rest of the day was a busy one for the Modest children. All afternoon, Jasper and Lucy formed a plan. Lucy found some copper wire in the carriage house. She cut a length of it using Rosie's sewing shears. Jasper used the musket from an old tin soldier he had found in one of his pockets. He uncoiled the tin thread that made up the barrel, tying it to the lock on the door. Lucy stole into the pantry and took a thimble of vinegar and salty brine. Jasper cut the end of his leather shoelace. Before lunch, they had made a working battery. It wasn't a terribly strong battery, but it would nonetheless serve their purpose. It only needed to be strong enough to ring a very small bell.

⸻

"What time did Mummy and Daddy come home last night?" Lucy asked Rosie when they were seated at the table for lunch. Jasper gently caught Lucy's hand as it headed, fingers extended, toward her mouth.

"Oh, I wouldn't know," Rosie said as she placed a plate of kippers in front of Lucy. "I was long asleep myself, I'm sure."

"What time did you go to sleep?" Jasper asked, taking a bite of his lunch and trying to sound casual, as if this was an inconsequential, everyday question.

"Well . . ." Rosie looked up as if to remember, but then shot a glance sideways at Jasper, who dodged it by examining his kippers. "Let's see, then . . . Must have been by ten o'clock. Had a bit of darning to do last night. Might have been a bit later."

"Just wondered, that's all," Jasper said when Rosie gave him an inquiring look. "Lovely kippers, Rosie. Yum."

After their meal, Jasper and Lucy attached the end of the copper wire spool to the doorknob in their parents' room. They ran it under the carpet in the hall and between the table and chest in the nursery and up along the side of Jasper's bed. Jasper wrapped it around the bedpost and attached it to a small bell.

"Let's test it," Jasper said.

Lucy ran down the hall. Jasper waved from his doorway. When Lucy closed the door of their parents' bedroom, which completed the circuit, she squealed with delight. With Jasper's door open, she could hear the tiny tinkle of the bell on his bedpost. Their device had worked.

That night, after a supper of roast quail and parsnips, a savory tart of sautéed potatoes and leeks, then vanilla custard topped with candied oranges, Jasper and Lucy got into their nightclothes as usual.

"Well, your parents wanted to, well, it is a fact that they wanted to be home before you went to your beds, but it looks like they've been detained. Perhaps you will see them in the morning," Rosie said as she settled into the rocking chair and began to hum.

Within moments, Jasper snored loudly, and Lucy let her breath become even and repetitive.

"My, the little darlings must have been exhausted," Rosie said to herself. She went to their beds and tucked them in, giving them each a peck on the forehead.

As soon as Rosie's footsteps had clip-clopped down the stairs, padding along the marble floor below, Lucy climbed quietly out of bed.

"Jasper?" she called in a whisper.

"Quick! Come in!" he said.

Lucy scrambled into Jasper's room. The two hid under Jasper's blanket and looked at his pocket watch. He had painted the numbers with phosphorous, which glows, so he could read them in the dark. It was 8:57 in the evening.

By 9:43, Lucy was yawning at regular intervals.

"It's all right, Luce. We've got the alarm," said Jasper. "Maybe you should go back to sleep in your bed. I'll wake you when—I mean if—they come home."

Yawning twice again, Lucy went back into her own bed and fell quickly to sleep. Jasper yawned, too. His eyes itched and he rubbed them. He shut them, just to soothe the itchiness. It felt much better to have them closed.

<hr />

Suddenly, Jasper awoke with a start. He looked at his pocket watch. It was 4:26 in the morning. He checked the alarm. Everything seemed to be in place, but the alarm hadn't gone off.

He tiptoed into Lucy's room. She was fast asleep. He decided not to wake her. He tiptoed down the hall to their parents' room. He peeked inside.

Everything was exactly as it had been. The bed was made without a wrinkle. Daddy's slippers were placed neatly next to his bedside table. Mummy's glass jug of water sat, still full, untouched, on hers.

Jasper went over to the glass jug. It had a matching cup that sat on top as a cover. He ran his finger across it. A very thin layer of dust had settled there.

Dust? Jasper knew what that meant. Mummy's water jug hadn't been used in, oh, probably about seventeen days.

Jasper walked back to his room. He climbed into bed, too worried to rest, too exhausted to sleep. But he decided he would just close his eyes.

Sleep came anyway.

In the morning, Lucy came running in.

"Well? Did it never ring?" she asked, with anticipation.

"It never rang, and Mummy and Daddy never came home," said Jasper. "We were right. They haven't been here in days."

"Eighteen days?" Lucy asked.

"Eighteen days," Jasper said.

At breakfast, Rosie served warm butter cake and apricot jam with fresh pears from the tree in the garden. On a tray, she brought in a pot of sweet steaming milk that smelled of vanilla. Rosie dropped lumps of chocolate into the milk and stirred as the chocolate began to melt.

"Sorry, darlings, your parents have gone to the laboratory early this morning," she told them as she poured hot chocolate into their cups. "I think they should be—"

"They haven't been here for seventeen—no, eighteen days now," Jasper said accusingly. He could see tears trailing down Lucy's cheeks. This made him even angrier, but also braver. "Nothing was touched in their room. There was dust on Mummy's water."

Rosie spilled the hot chocolate.

"Oh, dear!" she exclaimed, rushing into the kitchen, teeth clucking loudly as she went.

She came back with a rag to wipe up the spill. Her eyes, too, needed wiping. Like Lucy's, they were very wet.

"We don't think it's your fault that Mummy and Daddy have gone," Lucy said, sniffling, "but we want them back. We want our mummy and daddy."

"Oh, child, I am sorry. But your parents have been so very busy they don't always come home, and I…I—"

"They never come home, do they?" Jasper said.

"Never ever," Lucy said.

Rosie put the rag to her lips to stifle a yelp and rushed into the kitchen again. This time, she did not come back out, so Jasper and Lucy excused themselves to no one and went up to the nursery.

They sat quietly by the nursery window, looking out at nothing in particular, not speaking, and not wanting to. Just before noon, their eyes followed a shiny black motorcar as it pulled up to the house. They were excited at first, thinking it might be their parents, but out stepped a man with a large black cloak, dark glasses, and a tall black woolen hat with a very large pompom on the very tiptop. He hurried into the house. From up in the nursery, the children could hear voices. One was a mumble, and the other was Rosie's anxious clucking. Within minutes, the man rushed back into the car and sped off.

At supper that evening, Rosie smiled nervously. The meat was slightly burnt and there were no vegetables. Rosie gave them each two pieces of apple pie with cream. She didn't say a word.

After supper, the children climbed into their beds.

"Well, your parents..." Rosie put a handkerchief to her lips. "They wanted ... they really truly ... they had hoped ... truly hoped ... to be home before you went to your beds." Rosie blew her nose loudly. "Perhaps you will see them in the morning." Clearing her throat, she began to hum, but her humming was punctuated by the nervous clucking of her teeth.

Jasper and Lucy fell right to sleep. The worry and exhaustion had just been too much for one day. But for the two Modest children, the day was not quite over.

———

At 3:17 in the morning, the little bell rang on Jasper's bedpost. Jasper sat up with a start. It took him a moment to remember that he had not disconnected the bell. Something was happening. Something was definitely happening right then and there, he thought as he ran into Lucy's room.

"Wake up, Lucy. The bell—it's ringing."

Lucy shook off the sleep and beamed at her brother. "Mummy and Daddy! They're back, aren't they?" Lucy jumped up with excitement and flung her arms around her brother. "Oh, Jasper, they're back!"

"No, Lucy—"

"They're not back?" Her face fell.

"I don't know." Jasper hated the disappointment in his sister's face.

But Lucy nodded, stoically. She understood. She got down, reached, and pulled something from beneath her bed. The two of them ran back into Jasper's room and unhooked the bell. He had left it ringing because if it stopped, they'd know the door was open again.

Now, as silent as could be, they tiptoed toward their parents' bedroom. The door was still closed. Jasper and Lucy could hear shuffling from within. Lucy tapped Jasper on the shoulder. She showed him what she had brought—a wooden spoon, upon which was attached a small mirror. It looked like an oversized dentist's tool. In her pocket, she had a second mirror and some wire. She hooked the second mirror to the wire and attached it to the spoon, facing the other mirror.

Carefully, they slid the spoon under the door. The first mirror reflected what was in the room. The second reflected what was in the first mirror so Lucy and Jasper could see. Both of the children hoped it would be their father, putting on his slippers and pouring their mother a glass of water, and their mother, brushing out her long brown hair. Instead, they saw nothing of the sort. What they saw sent chills down their spines.

In the room was a very tall man, dressed all in black, with a black velvet top hat perched high on his head. His suit was black velvet—trousers, vest, and jacket. A black scarf covering his chin, he wore big dark glasses that seemed to wrap around his head. With a hand caressing the rim of his hat, he walked casually around the bedroom. Was he looking for something? As the children watched, riveted, the man went over to their mother's dressing table. The children half-expected him to tear open the drawers and search their contents, but instead, he placed their mother's brush in the middle, moving it from its position on the right-hand side.

He then went to the bedside table. Was he going to inspect

the drawer? No. He first removed a black handkerchief from his breast pocket and wiped the dusty rim of the water jug. He proceeded to simply pour water into the glass that sat beside it on the bedside table. He then returned half of the contents back into the jug, inspected the glass, swirled its contents, and replaced it, now half-full, on the bedside table.

Then the man walked to the other side of the room, stopped, bent down, and disappeared behind the bed. He reappeared holding their father's slippers. Jasper's neck tingled as the hairs stood up in silent protest. He threw a glance at Lucy, and he could see, even in the dimness of the hall, that she was not happy about this either.

It was difficult to see, but with a slight adjustment to the mirror, Jasper and Lucy could observe the man as he carried the slippers into the bathroom, apparently placing them beside the bath. He stood back, inspecting his handiwork.

Lucy and Jasper could not believe such bizarre behavior, nor could they believe that this most bizarre man was puttering around their parents' room, moving things around as he pleased, making himself, in some bizarre way, at home. Whether their parents had been there or not, it still housed their things, and the man was still an intruder.

The children took calming breaths and watched as the black-clad intruder went over to the bed and sat upon it. Checking its firmness, the fellow began to bounce. Furious, Jasper and Lucy watched as he bounced four or five times in a quite restrained manner, and not very high at all. He stopped to set his hat back straight on his head. The children looked at one another in disbelief.

The man then bounced five more times, getting a bit higher with each bounce. Even with his face hidden, and even though the children could only imagine a dour expression hidden beneath his hat, scarf, and glasses, he appeared to really enjoy himself. He bounced and he bounced and he bounced some more, getting quite high, with his arms and legs flapping as if he was trying to fly.

Then he bounced and bounced and bounced right off the side of the bed and fell flat onto the floor.

He jumped up quickly, looking around as if to check that no one saw him tumble. Jasper and Lucy instinctively squeezed together, though there was no chance the man could see them outside the door.

The man then brushed himself off and looked at himself in the mirror. He adjusted his glasses, which had gone askew, fixed his hat again, and pulled his scarf higher onto his nose. Leaning over toward the bureau, the man seemed to be counting the drawers, of which there were only five. When he got to the fourth, he opened it.

Lucy stifled a gasp. It was her mother's nightdress drawer. How awful! This strange man was peeking into her mother's private things! Worse than that, the man reached in and very deliberately picked up a pink flannel nightdress. But the man did not stop at the nightdress—he looked beneath it. So he was searching for something.

The man removed an old green leather-bound book—only it wasn't really a book, because it didn't seem to have many pages, if any at all. It had a leather binding, with loose leather straps hanging from its spine. Perhaps it was not what the man had hoped would be there, and perhaps the real thing was well-hidden and protected by their parents, and this was merely to put the man off the trail.

But the man did not seem disappointed. He simply wiped the empty green binding with his sleeve, then leaned over. To Jasper and Lucy's astonishment and disgust, the intruder leaned over and kissed it. He gazed upon it as if it were something to revere and adore. He looked at it in awe, lowering his head as if in prayer. Then, treating it as if it were the Crown Jewels, he gently replaced the book, wiping off some speck of dust that may or may not have rudely settled upon it. Then, with careful neatness, he returned the pink flannel nightdress to its place, covering the green leather thing, and closed the drawer with care.

To the horror of the children, it was at that moment when he whipped his head around and looked directly at the door.

Jasper and Lucy pulled the mirror back, ran as fast as they could to their bedrooms, and jumped into their beds. Down the hall, they could hear that door creak open, though it was quite remarkable that they could hear anything over the loud pounding of their hearts. They both held their breath until the pitter-patter of the man's feet disappeared down the stairs.

For the rest of that night, neither Lucy nor Jasper could sleep. Alone in their own beds, they watched the sun come up in the morning.

On the way down to breakfast, Jasper and Lucy passed their parents' room. The door was wide open, the bed was rumpled, and their mother's brush and father's slippers were out of place. The water glass, half full, sat, as it had the night before, on their mother's bedside table next to the dust-free jug. For all intents and purposes, it looked as if their parents had been there, slept there, and left in a hurry that morning. And if Jasper and Lucy hadn't seen otherwise, they would have believed it.

"Come on," Jasper said to Lucy, the heat rising in his face.

"I'm coming," said Lucy, who stood in the doorway for a moment.

"What?" Jasper asked, turning to his sister.

"I . . . I need to go potty," she said quickly. "I'll meet you down there."

"Lucy? What are you thinking? What are you up to?"

"I just don't want to leave the green thing in Mummy's drawer," Lucy said. "I want to take it."

"Well . . ." Jasper thought about it. "I suppose. I'll keep a lookout while you get it."

Lucy hugged her brother and stole into the room to get the green leather book. Then, together, they ran back to Lucy's room and placed it on her bed. Upon quick inspection, it was nothing but two covers and a spine. There were signs that it had once held pages—more than just the one—but those were reduced to flakes and torn edges. Now it had only one blank page, made of linen. From the green leather cover fluttered petals, crumpled and faded, of long-dead flowers.

Hiding the book under Lucy's bed, they hurried from the room, stopped to take a few calming breaths, and continue on their way down for breakfast.

"Sorry, darlings, but your parents have gone to the laboratory

... early this morning," said Rosie, calmer and more comfortable than she had been in the last couple of days. She spread raspberry jam on the crumpets and served chilled honeyed milk and bowls full of blueberry compote and cream. A bouquet of Sweet William stood in the middle of the table.

"Do you think they'll be home to tuck us in?" asked Jasper, trying to keep the anger from his voice.

"I, well, I—"

"They didn't come home last night, did they?" said Lucy, plucking a stem of Sweet William.

"You can look in their room, I haven't had a chance to—"

"He did it," said Lucy. "The man in black."

Rosie gasped and ran into the kitchen in a flurry. Jasper and Lucy, leaving their breakfasts untouched, got up from the table and went straight to the nursery.

They said very little that morning, but they did a lot of thinking. They decided to remain cloistered in their rooms and in the nursery for the rest of the day. They looked at the green thing but could not understand its significance. Jasper built two towers with blocks and Lucy connected them with a bridge of pencils. Then Jasper worked on his propeller designs and reconnected the bell in case someone returned to their parents' room.

Lucy took out the green leather binding again. She looked at the faded petals as they turned to dust between her nibbled fingers.

Around midday, hunger overcame the children's resolve. When they snuck down to steal bread and fruit from the kitchen, they found the dining room as they had left it that morning. Finding it hard to resist Rosie's breakfast, they quickly nibbled the cream-covered compote grabbed a glass of milk and handfuls of cold crumpets, and dashed back up to the nursery.

They refused to let Rosie into their rooms when she knocked, and did not respond when she asked them down for tea. At bedtime, they pretended not to hear Rosie sing to them from outside the door. They could hear her clucking and sniffling, and both Modest children felt sad for her. But both were adamant about finding out what had happened to their parents, and if hurting Rosie's feelings was involved, it simply had to be done.

In the morning, the house was very quiet. Still determined and still upset, Lucy and Jasper were not hungry, so they did not go down for breakfast and, instead, spent the morning making plans for what they would say to Rosie and how they would get their answers. But again, around noon, they were famished, so Lucy and Jasper dressed and came down for lunch.

To their surprise, the table was not made, and Rosie was nowhere to be found. The children went into the kitchen and found, left on the table, what was clearly their uneaten breakfast.

As they were about to eat the cold eggs and sausages and pour the lukewarm juice, they heard, once again, the sound of a motorcar pulling up in front of the house. They ran out to see who it was. Rosie stood in the doorway, blowing her nose.

A short heavyset man with a thick black overcoat and a tall black pointed hat with a wide brim, which flapped down in the front and back, climbed out of the car. Another man, not thin but not fat, of medium height, with a short jacket, a wide hat, and thick woolen gloves, all black, was with him. Both wore dark glasses, and their hats were so low on their faces one could not see them well at all.

The men took Rosie gently by the elbows and escorted her back into the house.

"Bring us the children," the short man said in the same odd accent as the first strange men in black—the ones who had come to their house in London on that awful day that seemed so long ago.

Unable to run, the children just stood their ground when the men entered the room.

"Oh," said the medium man upon seeing the steely faces of Jasper and Lucy. "They are already here."

The two men sat down at the table. Though the fire was lit and the room was quite warm, neither man removed anything from their persons that would have given the children a better look at them. Still, Jasper and Lucy were sure that neither man was the one bouncing on the bed the night before.

"Where are our parents?" said Lucy.

"Your parents are at their laboratory."

"I want to know where their laboratory is!" said Jasper, sounding more fearsome than he felt.

"We cannot tell you," said the short man.

"What have you done to them?" cried Lucy from behind Jasper. "You've taken Mummy and Daddy and you won't give them back! Oh, what have you done? Have you hurt them?"

"Of course not," said the medium man, who seemed honestly surprised.

"Your parents are very important to us," said the short man.

"We must have them," said the medium man.

Lucy gasped in horror. "*Have* them? Are you going to eat

them?"

"What?!" Both men stared.

"Lucy!" said Jasper.

"What is such a question?" the short man grumbled. "What is such nonsense? No more questions. We are here to tell you that you will be going to school."

"Tomorrow," said the medium man.

"A car will come for you. Pack what you will need," said the short man.

"You will be boarding at the school," said the medium man. "You may come home for weekends and holidays, as long as schedules, well, schedules permitting."

"Schedules . . ." Jasper struggled to overcome his shock. "Holidays . . . how long are we expected to be here?"

"Long, perhaps," said the medium man.

"It is forever or not," said the short man.

"What?" Jasper was utterly confused.

"Or not. Long, short, or not," said the medium man.

Both men stood and walked to the front door. The short man turned back. "Ah, this is for you," he said, handing an envelope to Jasper.

With that, the men were gone, leaving a cloud of smelly smoke behind them as the motorcar sped down the drive.

The envelope was addressed to Jasper and Lucy. It was in their mother's own familiar handwriting. Lucy tore the envelope and pulled out the letter.

Chers enfants, Darling Jasper and Lucy, our wonderful children—

We must be brief and cannot say much. However, we understand you have been worried about us. Rosie was very concerned for you. We want you to know that we are fine, except that we do miss you. Our work is forcing us to remain here at the laboratory. It is very important work and we cannot be with you right now. As much as anything, you must stay safe. Do not make trouble for yourselves or for us. Vous comprenez? Do not make yourselves stand out in a crowd or seem to be doing anything odd. Do nothing that appears out of the ordinary. Be invisible, if you can.

Please know that we love you and we will see you soon, aussitôt que possible.

N'ayez pas peur, nos chers. Do not be afraid. You must never forget that a treasure is the bird in the hand, not something else, n'oubliez pas.

Nous vous embarassons très très fort.

Love,
Mummy and Daddy

P.S. Remember Lewes Castle.

Jasper and Lucy read the letter once, twice, and three times.

"It's Mummy's handwriting," said Lucy. "See the curly Ms, and the twist in the Fs? I'm sure it's Mummy. And only she would know that we would remember Lewes Castle."

"I don't remember Lewes Castle," said Jasper. "I mean, I remember the castle in Lewes, but what does that have to do with anything?"

"When you were eight and I was two, we went on holiday to the south of England, to Lewes."

Of course, Jasper thought, *only Lucy would remember something that happened when she was two.*

"You know Lewes, Jasper," said Lucy, mistaking his incredulity for forgetfulness. "It's in Sussex. It's where they have the biggest Guy Fawkes bonfire in the whole world. Remember we went down there for Bonfire Night?"

"I remember that," Jasper said.

"Well, we went to Sussex for the Lewes Bonfire Night, and stayed at Thomas Tree House Lodge on the High Street," said Lucy. "The next morning, we went to the castle. It was November, so there weren't flowers that I could put in my hair or throw at you for you to catch, but there were trees. And the flags were so colorful I pretended they were for me and I was a princess and I asked you to play, too, but you wanted to pretend you were a knight in battle and you found a stick and you said it was a sword and you wanted to reach the flags and you climbed up, up and out on the edge of a turret. I ran after you and I found a stick and I ran up, too. Then, a very big man grabbed you by the shoulders and pulled you in.

"We thought he was a villain and was trying to kidnap you. He looked like a big horrid scary bad man, too, with a scar on his nose and a rough fuzzy black beard, and I was crying and I was hitting him on the bum with my stick because I couldn't reach any higher. He plucked you off the edge and carried you, kicking and screaming, and me hitting his bum the whole way down the curly, twisty flights of stairs. Mummy and Daddy were across the courtyard and didn't even see us. He asked me where Mummy and Daddy were and I pointed my stick at them. He told Mummy and Daddy what had happened, about climbing on the turret. He thought you might fall. He didn't even tell on me for hitting him."

"And? Does 'Remember Lewes Castle' mean someone is trying to save us?" asked Jasper.

"I don't know," said Lucy. "That's the funny thing. I don't know what it means."

Jasper and Lucy, still unsure of the meaning, but without many options, went to their rooms to pack for school.

CHAPTER FOUR

THE SCHOOL AT SOLE MANNER FARM

OR

JASPER AND LUCY FIND THEIR PLACES

Jasper and Lucy systematically took their clothing, piece by piece, and placed the lot into travel bags. They didn't even have the emotional strength to tell Rosie they did not want her help, so she busied herself refolding and brushing off everything they had packed.

Jasper's silence was simply because he could not find the words for protesting yet another departure. But Lucy had a ghostly quality to her, a kind of dark sadness that hung about her like a shadow. Her silence worried Jasper. She had been so eager for answers.

"Lucy." Jasper touched her hand. Rosie had just left the room to fetch clothes hanging on the clothesline in the garden. Lucy, while refolding her yellow nightdress, had slowed to a stop. She simply stood there, mid-sleeve, looking up at her brother, then quickly down at the floor, neatly placing the sleeve of the nightdress in a fold.

"Lucy," Jasper repeated.

Lucy slowly raised her head. Her eyes were full of tears.

Jasper put his arm around her and she fell onto his chest in great shuddering sobs.

"Oh, Jasper!" she cried, unable to say anything else for nearly a full minute. Taking a deep breath when she finally could, Lucy looked up at her brother searchingly. "It . . . it's our fault, isn't it? It's all our fault."

"What do you mean, our fault? Of course it isn't our fault."

"It's our fault they're sending us away," she said. "It's our fault they're taking us away from Rosie. It's our fault they're taking us away from where Mummy and Daddy might come and . . . and . . . and . . ." But she could not continue.

"Oh, Lucy," Jasper said, taking his sister by the shoulders, "don't be such a silly thing. It's never been our fault. Those men were planning to take us to school all along."

"But they came right after we rang the bell. And we did it and we made them angry and we shouted at Rosie and the men came right away and we made them come because we shouted and made Rosie sad and—"

"Hold on there, Luce," Jasper said. "No one knows about the bell but us. And we have been shouting at Rosie, but . . ." Jasper swallowed hard and felt the pang of guilt in his belly. "Well, they've obviously been planning to send us to school. I'm sure of it. Rosie may have even mentioned it to us."

"To you? She never mentioned it to me, Jasper."

"Well, no. But she never sent for them, I bet. They just . . . had to set it up. That's it—they had to find the right school for us to attend." Jasper didn't know what he was really saying. He just didn't want Lucy to blame herself.

"But now we've lost Rosie." Lucy's eyes were full of tears.

"Nonsense, my precious girl," said Rosie, standing at the door with an armful of clean laundry. She dropped her bundle onto the bed and pulled the children to her. Rosie was a strong woman and, in her arms, they would have been hugging her whether they had wanted to or not, which they did. "My sweet children, my darlings, my dears, my sweet *clann*," she said, "never for a moment can you think I'd deliver you into the hands of harm. Upon the weekends, I shall be here, with treacle tarts and Yorkshire pudding and clotted cream and cakes and roasts and pies and everything this old pair of hands can make to fill your bellies. I'll be here to sing you to sleep and to sing you to wake. You'll be back in my arms, right soon…" She kissed them both and they could each feel the tears falling onto the tops of their heads.

"Will you make hot chocolate and honey biscuits?" asked Lucy. She hadn't had an appetite for days, but suddenly she was famished.

"Well, we don't have to wait for the weekend," said Rosie. "Let's have some hot chocolate right now." Rosie hurried off to the kitchen to prepare a late hot chocolate for the children.

———

The morning came and found the children with renewed fears. This time they were not afraid that they would not be returning to Rosie. This time they were afraid of what lay ahead. Neither Modest child could think of a single pleasant school experience, other than the end of term and the subsequent departure. No, the idea that they were going to be sent to a school in which a new set of children were at this very moment preparing to hate them was not an idea they looked forward to.

It was with that weighing on their shoulders that Jasper and Lucy walked solemnly out of the house at One Elm Street, the sound of Rosie's clucking right behind. As she left, Lucy bent and picked a small flower growing between the paving stones and waved it at Rosie, who, in turn, waved her hankie at the children.

Jasper and Lucy climbed into the waiting carriage. Actually, there were two waiting carriages, one driven by a man wearing dark glasses, a black cape, and a bullfighter's hat that appeared to have actual horns coming out of either side, the other by a driver who seemed to be so short that he'd have a hard time seeing over the knee guard on the coachman's seat. That said, his hat was so tall it seemed it would stretch higher than the man himself, if they were placed side by side. Like his fluffy jumper and ballooning trousers, the hat was black. His glasses, or rather goggles, were black, too.

The children were led by the bullfighter who, unlike the other driver, stepped down from his perch and took their satchels.

"Where is this school?" asked Jasper, as the bullfighter coachman opened the carriage door.

"Yes," said the coachman, who closed the door behind them.

Jasper did not ask anything else.

Once the carriage began to move, Rosie waddled out to the street and waved them away with her hankie. Lucy climbed up to the back window and waved until Rosie was out of sight. Then Lucy slid down into her seat and clung to Jasper's arm.

Jasper looked down at his sister and gave her the most forced smile he had ever had to muster in his life. He looked out of the window so she wouldn't see the tears in his eyes.

———◦———

Jasper was startled awake. He was in the carriage with Lucy who, asleep, had been drooling from the corner of her mouth onto Jasper's shirt, which was wet where the drool had pooled.

For a moment, Jasper could not remember where he was. For a moment, he thought everything had been a dream—the move, the boat, the train, the house, Rosie, the men in black—and he was in a carriage with his parents.

But then, he blinked, and it all came back to him in a giant leap. It was real.

Outside, the city had become more countryside, and the other carriage was no longer following. He wondered when they had separated and why there had been two when it had only been Lucy and himself.

Without warning, the carriage turned. Jasper caught sight of a rusted old gate ahead, standing in front of a long drive through fields and an orchard. There was an old sign, half hidden by a willow tree. The hinges on one side were broken, having rusted away. The sign said "Sole Manner Farm." It may have even said "Sole Manner Farm School" at one time, but it was impossible to tell because that part of the sign had broken away and what looked like an "S" may just have been an impression on the wood. And there was some other kind of writing on the sign, too, or perhaps it was the only remains of a pattern running along the bottom edge.

Whatever it said didn't matter to Jasper when he saw the

farmhouse at the far side of the field. Lucy stirred.

"I think we're here," Jasper said, allowing his sister to wake of her own accord.

"Where's here?" asked Lucy with a yawn. "Are we lost?"

"I think it's the school," Jasper said, "or the farm. I think we're on a farm, but we've definitely come on purpose. I doubt we're lost."

Lucy clambered up to see through the window.

"It's lovely," she said, admiring the orchard and watching the birds drift on the breeze.

Jasper saw the birds, too, and the fields, and he understood what Lucy was seeing.

"It *is* lovely," he said. And it was.

———⇒•←———

"Lovely" was an excellent description. The smell of apples yet to ripen and late berries at the end of their season filled the carriage. Lucy pulled down a window so they could breathe in the fresh air. There were none of the dirty smells of the city. Here, you could fill your lungs without smelling smokestacks or tanneries or glue factories. Here, there was nothing but air to breathe.

As they pulled up to the farmhouse, Jasper could see that there was a classroom. The farmhouse had a second building, and Jasper guessed that was where they would sleep. Farther back, he could see this place really was a farm, a working farm, with a barn, a henhouse, acres of green, a potting shed, and an old silo that had fallen into rubble,

Lucy pointed and gasped. Jasper followed the line of her

finger. There, standing in the doorway of what was clearly the schoolhouse, was a very lovely young woman.

"She's beautiful," Lucy said, practically breathing the words instead of speaking them.

Whether she was beautiful or not, Jasper could not tell, but the woman's smile made him agree. It was a smile that said everything was going to be all right. Jasper wished he could believe it.

The woman approached the carriage, and her smile broadened as she saw little Lucy struggling to keep her eyes above the bottom of the window ledge.

"You're like a princess," Lucy said.

"Well, thank you, sweet angel. I'm so glad you've come," said the woman. "And this is your brother? Welcome. I'm Miss Brett. I'm your teacher." Her fair hair was pulled back into a braid, but several strands had escaped and framed her face as they fell. She had eyes the color of the darkening summer sky.

She did not wait for the coachman to open the door. Instead, the coachman threw her an indistinct look and went to fetch the baggage.

Jasper and Lucy stepped down from the carriage with Miss Brett holding their hands. Once they were down, Miss Brett knelt to meet Lucy's gaze, eye to eye.

"I'm Lucy," said Lucy.

"I'm Jasper," Jasper said.

"Yes you are," said Miss Brett, smiling, standing now and guiding the children to the schoolhouse. "We've been waiting for you…"

———⟫●⟪———

The classroom was marvelous to behold. There were microscopes and telescopes and, on one table, all manner of test tubes, burettes, and burners. On opposite corners of the ceiling, there were also paper flowers and a great paper sun and moon. There were shelves of books and rows of puzzles.

And also there, in that room, were two children around Jasper's age.

At a desk, looking over a set of blueprints and comparing them to sketches in a notebook, was a girl the likes of whom Jasper had never before seen. The moment he saw her, he understood fully how beauty could take your breath away. He had seen portraits and photographs of beautiful women and girls, but never in his life had he seen one in real life. The girl had warm skin that looked not as if the sun had darkened it, but as if the sun had entered it. Her hair, almost a dark red with wisps of gold, was long, down below her waist, plaited into one thick braid.

As Jasper approached, the girl looked up from what she was doing. Her eyes were the greenest green, but at the same time, the goldest gold. Jasper reached out his hand automatically and tried to speak.

"I…me…I…my—"

The beautiful girl did not take his hand. Instead, she opened up that beautiful mouth of hers and, in a sultry voice that carried with it an essence of an Indian accent, she said, "Are you an idiot? What is this? Are there more of them? And this one doesn't even know how to talk."

Stung by her bite, Jasper was stunned and shaken. He looked down at his hand as if it was a traitor.

"I can speak," he said, his voice squeaking. "My name is Jasper, and Lucy there is my sister."

"Well, you should know your ruddy name, *Jasper*," she said, pointing to a folded paper on one of the five desks. It said "JASPER." "You've got some help now, so you can practice saying it. Now don't disturb me."

"Faye," Miss Brett said, Lucy still at her side, "I told you that all the classmates were arriving today. Why don't you go fetch the lovely biscuits we made this morning?" There was no scolding in her voice.

Her face lighting up, Faye ran across the classroom, opened the door on the far side of the room, and rushed through it.

"Faye arrived this morning," Miss Brett said, "as did Wallace."

The small boy sat at a desk on the far side of the room. He was writing in a small notebook.

"Hello," Jasper said as he approached the desk, cautiously. Did this one bite, too?

"Hello," the boy responded shyly. He extended a hand, as Jasper had done to Faye.

"I'm Jasper," said Jasper, taking the hand gladly. "How long have you been here?"

"I arrived about an hour—no, two hours ago," Wallace said, taking a look at the clock on the wall of the classroom.

"I helped Miss Brett make these, as I was the first to arrive," said Faye, returning to the room with a tray of biscuits.

Jasper grabbed a biscuit and took a bite. "These are delicious,

Faye," he said, smiling at her.

Faye looked up, then blushed. "Well, I . . . well, don't eat them all." To Jasper's disappointment, the sulk seemed to take over Faye once again, so he walked back over to Wallace, who had returned to his seat after taking a biscuit.

"Are there only five students?" Jasper saw there were only five desks and, so far, four children. Wallace's desk was dead center, Jasper and Faye in front, and Lucy and someone named "NOAH" in back.

"He should be coming, too. Today, like the rest of us," said Wallace. "That's what Miss Brett said."

"Does Miss Brett run the school? Is she the headmistress?" Jasper asked, finishing his biscuit.

"Well, I suppose," Wallace said. "She lives here in the farmhouse, as will we, I imagine. She seems very pleasant to me. She's certainly the nicest teacher I've ever come across. Well, except my mother."

"Your mother is a teacher?"

"Um, well . . . she taught me. But Miss Brett seems very capable. She really is very, very nice. So far, this is all I've been able to conclude. Anything else would be guesswork." Wallace looked up at Jasper through his thick glasses.

Jasper smiled and felt that, for the first time, he was speaking to a child who would have no interest in torturing him, no desire in hurting Lucy, and no reason to resent either of them for their intelligence. He looked at what Wallace was writing. It seemed to be an equation of sorts.

"Would you like to see my calculations on this chemical variant?" said Wallace. "I think I've worked out a kink in the

design of this polymer. I'm trying to complete it and test it before
... well, I only have a few weeks. Would you like to see?" Jasper
leaned over as Wallace began to explain.

Lucy was still having trouble looking at anything but Miss
Brett.

"Well, come on, Lucy, let's bring your bag into your room, and
then I'll show you the kitchen," Miss Brett said.

"Can I sleep with you, Miss Brett?" asked Lucy. "I'm very cozy,
or so I've heard."

"I'm sure you are," Miss Brett said, trying to keep her smile
from turning into a laugh. "But you'll be sharing the big bed with
Faye. Her bags are already in the room."

After Miss Brett led Lucy to the white room, where Lucy
placed her bag on the bed, she took Lucy by the hand and led her
into the kitchen.

"Do you like butter biscuits?" said Miss Brett. "We have a
batch about to come out of the oven, and we'll need to put another
batch in. I like to butter the top of each biscuit before I put them in
to bake. Did your mother ever make butter biscuits?"

"Make them? You mean in the laboratory?" Lucy said,
confused. "Butter biscuits sound like something lovely to eat. I
thought they were something to eat."

"Yes, they are, sweet angel," Miss Brett said. "I meant did your
mother ever bake them ... in the kitchen ... in an oven?"

"No, Mummy doesn't know what an oven is," Lucy said.
"Hortensia the cook did everything in the kitchen."

"I see," Miss Brett said, smiling. "You'll learn all about kitchens while you're with me. Then you can teach your mother when..."

But Miss Brett did not know when.

"Everyone keeps saying 'when,'" said Lucy. "I suppose that is much better than 'if,' and if it was 'if,' I would be so sad I would be crying, but I'm not crying, Miss Brett, because I am a big girl and I would only cry if the 'if' was bigger than the 'when' and the 'when' went away and there was only an 'if' and I thought Mummy and Daddy were gone forever and I...I...I..."

Lucy began to cry, and Miss Brett folded her into her arms and sat with her until the sobs eased into a tiny snoring noise. Then she picked up Lucy and brought her to the bedroom she had selected for her own. As she placed the little girl on the bed, she decided to wait until Lucy awoke to make another batch of biscuits. Miss Brett returned to the classroom, where she worried she might be needed to prevent Faye from biting the head off any of the new arrivals. She made sure to leave the door open between the kitchen and the classroom. The biscuits already in the oven needed only a few more minutes.

———

"Look, Miss Brett," Wallace said, pointing through the window at the dirt road on the far side of the field. "A black carriage is approaching. Do you think it's Noah?"

"I do believe it is, Wallace," she said, wiping her hands on her apron. "Let's greet our new classmate."

Miss Brett stepped outside as the carriage pulled up. A lanky boy carrying a violin case stepped out of the carriage. Miss Brett escorted him into the classroom. He got as far as the door before Jasper and Wallace appeared to show him in.

Leaving them to their greetings, Miss Brett moved toward the kitchen. She had to take the biscuits out of the oven and she wanted to check on Lucy, but then she glanced over at Faye, who was writing in her notebook, ignoring the others gathering at the door.

Miss Brett walked over to Faye and placed her hand on Faye's shoulder. "Faye? Come join us, won't you?"

"You don't need me over there. You've got the others." Faye's face felt hot, but she refused to look up at Miss Brett.

"But I won't have you," Miss Brett said gently.

"It's already too crowded," grumbled Faye. She didn't look up—she couldn't. In a few short hours, Faye had lost her place as the one and only.

"Want to help me with the biscuits?" Miss Brett said.

Faye shook her head, and Miss Brett walked away. Faye snapped her pencil in half, then bent under her desk to retrieve the fallen piece. She wanted nothing more than to run and run and run all the way home, back to the world she knew, back to her perfect home and perfect garden and perfect life.

CHAPTER FIVE

Faye's Absolutely Perfect Life

OR

LITTLE MARMELO FINDS AN OVEN

Faye may have spoken in an Indian-tinged upper-class English accent, but she was only half-Indian by birth—the other half was American. She had lived her whole life in India, had traveled through most of it, and spoke many of India's twenty-some languages. Her Hindi, as well as her Tamil, Bengali, Urdu, Marathi, and Punjabi, was flawless, like everything else about her—as perfect as she imagined her life to be.

Faye's father, Rajesh Vigyanveta, was born in New Delhi, but went to college in America. It was there that he met Faye's mother, Gwendolyn. Gwendolyn was from America—Ohio, originally. While Faye's father, on leave from Cambridge, was becoming a star at Harvard, Gwendolyn studied at the Annex, the new college, where women could study using Harvard University facilities. Since Harvard instructors taught there, study groups were formed, and Faye's parents fell in love over a pile of textbooks. By the time they left so her father could finish his studies at Cambridge, they were famous.

Although they had had offers from every university in the

world, the Vigyanveta family moved to New Delhi several years before Faye was born. Her mother wanted to live abroad, and her father wanted to go back home. Faye's father accepted a post as head of science at St. Stephen's College, teaching chemistry and physics. He had been urged to take the job by Dr. Samuel Allnut, with whom he had studied at Cambridge. Faye's mother was hired as chief chemist for a large British company.

And soon, Faye Vidya Vigyanveta was born.

Two things about Faye were quite clear early in her life. First, she was, without a doubt, a striking beauty. She was always tall for her age, long and lean, with her father's olive skin and her mother's apple-green eyes. She looked like she might have stepped out of a painting or sculpture. She was not only considered beautiful, but exotic, her bright green eyes and dark auburn hair standing out in any New Delhi crowd, her beautiful dark skin setting her apart within her mother's family.

She might have embraced such attention. It might have made her feel like a queen. However, at thirteen, beauty was wholly unimportant to Faye. It had never been important, except when it got in the way. In fact, at an early age, she had found it terribly annoying when people pinched her cheeks, gawked, or otherwise displayed untoward interest in her appearance. As far back as she could remember, she resented the fact that people were impressed with something that was not her own doing. She didn't create her beauty. She was merely stuck with it.

The second thing evident from a very early age (and this was the one that actually mattered to her) was that Faye had a brilliant mind. And she had an extraordinary knack for building things. It was amazing what she could build—mechanical things, engineering things, architectural things. She was—and she would be the first to admit it—a genius. From her earliest moments, Faye loved to experiment with devices. She loved to make things with gears and pulleys and springs. When she was three and a half, she took parts from her father's bicycle and built an electric fan.

(By coincidence, seven thousand kilometers away in London, a boy named Jasper Modest had done the same thing from parts of his toy boat.)

At the time, Faye had been given full reign of the family laboratory. This did not sit well with her father's assistants, but they never complained or fussed, for two reasons: One, it was an honor to be chosen as an assistant to Professor Vigyanveta, and two, there was a long line of would-be assistants waiting to replace those who chose to complain about conditions.

That said, there were reasons why the young lads working in the laboratory felt disgruntled. A woman, let alone a little girl, was an odd and unwanted sight in a science lab, and this particular girl was arrogant and annoying. After all, her mother was not only a scientist, but also an American, and everyone knew what those Americans were like. Still, they put up with the fact that a gorgeous little girl was measurably more intelligent than all of them put together.

At the age of six, Faye created a contraption that had many gears and pulleys and springs, all attached to an assortment of different-sized hooks. (The myriad items that were sacrificed for this invention are too numerous to be mentioned individually, but their loss in the name of science is duly noted.) The invention could pick up beakers and move them around the laboratory by the mere touch of a lever. Admittedly, this particular invention was not one of Faye's most successful. Her parents had been quite encouraging before they knew the quantity of things that would be cannibalized for the creation. After several mishaps in which lab assistants were hauled around the room at the end of assorted hooks and a rather nasty explosion that was the result of improperly combined chemicals tipped accidentally from a flying beaker, the Vigyanvetas had to lay out a new set of rules.

Faye's parents wanted to give their daughter every opportunity to exercise her talents. They also wanted to protect their belongings from overly capable little hands. So, they had a special table, just her size, built for their daughter, placed on the far, far side of the lab so she could do her own work and, more important to them, not interfere with theirs. Faye was no longer provided unlimited access to her parents' equipment, but she was still allowed to wander around, taking notes and observing the work going in the laboratory.

Though not everywhere in the laboratory. In the back, there was a room with three very large locks. This room was off-limits to Faye, and it had always been so. Faye could always tell when her parents would be headed to the secret room. They would either begin to speak in whispers, or suddenly receive some missive that they would read, heads together. Then would come the double nod, and off they would go, disappearing behind the great wooden door. Her parents spent hours every day in that room. The answer was always "no" when Faye wanted to follow them in. It was perhaps the only insurmountable "no" that had ever come into Faye's otherwise perfect life. And life had otherwise been perfect. It really, really had...

The Vigyanveta family laboratory was connected to the Vigyanveta family house that sat on the Vigyanveta family estate. The Vigyanveta family house was a magnificent mansion that had been in the Vigyanveta family for eleven generations. It was surrounded by meadows and orchards full of mango trees and bael trees. There were virtual forests of bamboo and wildly colorful gardens bursting with rhododendrons, ginger, begonia, balsam, clematis, lilies, blue poppy, and orchids brought from the northeast and tended to in greenhouses and beautiful glass bells. There was even the Vidya Vigyanveta orchid, developed by Faye's great-great-grandfather. And of course, there were the most beautiful roses, like the Viveka Vigyanveta rose—known as the most elegant, stunning rose in India—developed by her great-great-great grandmother. There were vegetable and herb gardens full of cabbages, tomatoes, brinjal, tulsi (basil), mint, and fenugreek. There were groves of banana and tangy pepper trees, and all around, little waterfalls that fell into clear pools on which lotuses and water lilies floated. Huge green and red and blue macaws, toucans, and peacocks (including her favorite white peacock) roamed freely around the land, as flamingoes bathed (before the monsoon season) in the numerous ponds. There was so much property that Faye could walk for an hour and still be on the Vigyanveta family land.

Faye lived, for all intents and purposes, like a princess. There were servants and assistants to attend to her every need. She had only to ask for something—or sometimes, just look as if she might possibly ask—and it would be in front of her before she could get upset about not having it. There was just one thing nobody seemed able to provide.

———>•<———

"I would like a friend," Faye declared one day, standing beside her father's desk.

"You have many friends, my little *marmelo*," her father said, distracted by his work.

"I have no friends," she said, fiddling with her silver chain, which held an old family heirloom. She had worn the necklace for as long as she could remember. It had been in the family for generations, she had been told. When she felt insecure, she held it close. It had, after all, survived a very long time.

"Mali is your friend," said her father.

"He is not. Mali is the gardener."

"Play with his son, little Surya. He can be your friend."

"Little Surya is thirty-seven years old, and he's been the head gardener in Ootacamund since I was five," said Faye. "There are no friends here, Father. There are only servants."

"Well, I will tell them they must entertain you," her father said. "I will insist they be your friends." He gave her a quick smile, then dashed into the back room. She could hear the locks turn, one by one.

———>•<———

Faye never had any problems in school because she never went to school. She had always been tutored. When she was small, she had a series of teachers from France and Spain, and one from Germany. For the last couple years, she had been taught by her father's students.

When she came down to the library for breakfast one morning, she thought that the very round man in the black trench coat and black turban, who also wore a monocle with a very dark lens, was her new tutor.

"Are you here for me?" she asked as she was served sweet tea flavored with honey, cardamom, and vanilla.

"Am I..?"

"Are you?" Faye said, sipping her tea.

"Am I what?" asked the man, indignantly.

"Are you my tutor?" Faye knew she was wrong before she asked, but she thought he might tell her what he was actually doing in her library.

"Tutor a child?" He almost spat out the words. "I will have you know that I am here on business, and it is most certainly none of *your* business."

When Faye's parents came in, they were immediately and obviously quite agitated, though Faye couldn't tell whether it was by her presence or the man's. Her mother pulled Faye close as if to protect her somehow.

Faye clutched the silver chain that hung from her neck.

"Go to your studies, Faye," her father urged, dismissing her with a sweeping wave of his hand. "We must speak of things that are not of your concern."

As the three grown-ups left the room, walked through the door of the lab, and into the back room, Faye followed. She listened as the door closed behind them and the three locks turned. Even then, Faye had suspected there was something important about the meeting, but she had had no idea then how that meeting—the meeting that she was not, in fact, even allowed to attend—would so change her life.

———◦———

Though Faye Vigyanveta had taken a ferry several times to go from the continent to England, she had been on a real ship only twice before. Faye had been only three months old at the time, and now had no real memory of the experience. This time, she told herself, she would never forget.

The ship they took went from Glasgow and crossed two continents over several days, and Faye quickly discovered that she loved the sea. Though she had always dreamed of flying, and being what felt like miles above the water on the premiere deck of the *Astoria*, she could imagine herself soaring over the ocean, so high she could not even feel the spray on her face from the crashing waves. The train that followed was another exciting ride. She was treated like a queen by the staff of the dining car, who brought delights for her tongue that she happily devoured. Faye enjoyed every minute of the journey to Dayton, Ohio in America.

Well, not every minute. She was moved to extreme grumpiness when she thought how she had been forced into this trip without even being consulted. She had been given mere hours to pack a small bag of anything she wanted. She packed some of her sketches and her favorite notebook, an old birthday card a cousin had sent her mother which had her favorite painting on the front, a small glass hummingbird that she kept on her desk, and a miniature silver spoon that had been hers as a baby. She was sad when she thought about the elephants and the monkeys and all the secret places that belonged only to Faye in India. None of the servants came with them—servants she had known her whole life, servants whom her father had known his whole life, too. Faye wondered what life would be like without them. Would new servants be provided?

"I wouldn't mind doing things for myself," she had told her mother. As soon as she said this, she felt her throat close around the words, but not in time to stop them from coming out. It was as if her body was trying to prevent her mouth from saying anything that might cause her more hardship. Wasn't it enough that she would have to become accustomed to new servants? That she would have to tell new servants how she drank her tea and how warm she liked her bath?

"Well, we'll have to see," her mother had said. Faye could see her mother was distracted and worried. By her mother's faraway look, Faye guessed that she didn't know what to expect in America, either.

———✦———

At the harbor, in the crowd of welcoming onlookers, Faye immediately recognized the man in the black hat and black suit with dark glasses. She waved, and then realized it was not the man she had mistaken for her tutor. That man had been very round, but not very tall. This man was both round and tall. In fact, the reason she noticed him among all these people was that he stood at least a head above everybody else. That, and his hat.

Instead of the black turban, he wore what appeared to be a

woman's bonnet. The hat was lacy, and had a large, black, gemmed, rose-shaped brooch in the front. The hat was tied in a large bow beneath the man's chin.

"Is that a style here in America?" asked Faye. From the look of the crowd, she thought not.

"In style? In America?" Her mother suddenly smiled. "I don't let you out enough, do I?" The two of them shared a laugh, the first in a long, long time.

Faye looked at the funny-looking man again. This one didn't have a monocle. Instead, he wore what looked to be the kind of protective eyewear one uses when welding metal with a torch, only the lenses were very dark.

The family climbed into the carriage driven by the floral hat-wearing man in black. "Our home will be at One Chestnut," Faye's father said to the driver. "Oh, but I suppose you know that."

The driver seemed to make turns at every block. Faye could have sworn they were traveling in ever-widening circles. All of the streets seemed to be named after trees, which fit the many trees scattered everywhere.

"My Aunt Susan and Uncle Milton lived down that way!" exclaimed Faye's mother as they drove through a pleasant neighborhood. "Uncle Milton still does. Right down there on Hawthorn Street." She spoke of how much she loved summers with her cousin Katharine, an only girl with four older brothers. Faye imagined she must have really loved having Faye's mother there, too. She certainly loved it when Katharine visited them in India.

"Can we stop for a visit?" Faye asked hopefully. Her mother gave her a weak smile, then looked back out the window.

They drove for well over an hour, and then stopped right behind another black carriage.

"The girl stays," the driver said, adjusting the bow beneath his chin. "The doctors descend. The other carriage will take you to the laboratory."

Faye's father cleared his throat. "Oh, well, it is not as I had anticipated. I thought we'd be going to the house first. It's so close—"

"The girl stays here."

"But I don't want to stay," said Faye, clinging to her mother. "I want to go to our house. With you."

"Rajesh," Faye's mother said, turning to her husband.

"The girl stays," the driver said again. "The doctors go to the laboratory."

"It will be fine, dear," her mother said, peeling Faye's fingers from her arm. "You go with the nice man—"

"What nice man?" Faye asked.

"You go with our driver, Faye," her father said. "There is much preparation we need to do."

Faye's mother kissed Faye on the forehead, then looked down at the silver crest Faye had around her neck. "I'm going to take this, Faye—"

"But it's mine! Father gave it to me!" she said. Her mother unhooked it from the chain.

"You keep the chain," her mother said, "but I'll need to take the amulet."

Faye was miserable. "Am I going somewhere so unsafe you're worried about family heirlooms?"

"You will go to the schoolhouse," the driver said.

"Schoolhouse?" Faye repeated in disbelief. No one had said anything about school.

"Oh, yes, we thought you'd enjoy a bit of school," her father said, cheerfully. "Perhaps you will find some friends."

"Can't I just get tutored at home?"

"The girl stays at school," said the driver.

"Oh." Faye's mother appeared confused for a moment. "Well…" She looked at her daughter, offering nothing more than a limp impression of a smile. "That will be a nice experience for you, Faye dear."

"Mother, I don't want to stay at school. I don't want to go to school. I want to—"

"Descend immediately, please," the driver said. Faye's parents looked at her apologetically, but, as far as Faye was concerned, clearly without any real remorse. Faye could not believe they were just leaving her, abandoning her to a fate unknown. She felt a bit ill and most definitely unhappy about the whole thing. More unhappy than she had ever been in her whole life.

"I'm not going!" shouted Faye.

"Young lady—" her father began, but Faye did not wait to hear the rest. She grabbed the handle to the car and threw it open. Her mother reached for Faye's shoulder, but missed. Falling out of the carriage, Faye scrambled to her feet and began to run.

She ran faster than she ever had, tears streaming from her eyes and blinding her. They spilled into her ears like cold wet fingers, muffling the sound of her own breathing.

It didn't matter. She had no idea where she was, where she was going, or what she would do when she got anywhere. She just ran, as if her life depended on it, which, as far as she knew, it did.

She ran and ran and ran.

She ran for perhaps all of twenty seconds before she was lifted bodily from the ground.

"Let me go, you big, stupid, ugly lunatic!" she screamed, knocking the floral hat askew and kicking the coachman in the shins. He simply threw her over his shoulder and, without a word, carried her back to the coach.

Her parents were no longer in the first carriage, and now sat in the other one. Hidden somewhat by the high-backed driver's seat, the other driver seemed to be wearing, from her upside-down, wholly undignified position, something remarkably like bunny ears. This did not amuse. *These idiotic maniacs*, she thought. *I hate them all.* Slung like a potato sack over the man's shoulder, she felt as if she was choking on a stone that had grown in her gut, and now rolled down into her throat.

As the second carriage drove off, Faye watched her parents as they waved. She flapped her hand limply back at them, clutching at the crest that was no longer there. She tugged at the chain. School? She could not imagine.

———◆———

Still, she certainly spent the carriage ride doing so. The images she conjured up were nothing less than horrible. By the time they arrived at the schoolhouse, Faye was full of dread. She looked around. The big ugly carriage, driven by Mr. Crazy Lady's Hat, was clearly in the middle of nowhere. Dayton had not been much to look at, but at least there were people. With the exception of the occasional tractor being pulled by a team of horses, there was nothing anywhere around here. And now Faye was being guided to some old farm. They stopped in front of what seemed to Faye like a storage hut or a servant's house. She looked around and did not see a proper house, or what she imagined to be a proper school.

"This is it," said the driver, pulling on the reins as the carriage came to a stop. He got down from his seat and removed Faye's trunk.

Faye did not climb down. She remained in her seat, hoping to be taken back to her parents, back to the ship, and back to her home. Instead, the driver opened her door and stood aside. When she didn't move, he picked her up as easily as before and placed her on the ground. He closed the door, got back in, and drove off, leaving Faye sitting on the ground in a cloud of dust from the dirty road.

"Are you all right, dear?" asked a very lovely woman who seemed to appear out of nowhere, kneeling down so she was on face level with Faye.

Faye opened her mouth to complain, but the anger, the fear, and the humiliation finally merged, and the stone in her stomach dropped and hit bottom. She burst into tears. The woman held Faye in her arms until the sobbing eased. Then she helped Faye to stand, and the two of them dragged Faye's trunk into the little barn which, Faye quickly realized, was her new school.

"I'm Miss Brett," said the woman, "and you must be Faye. Come, help me take the biscuits out of the oven."

Faye's eyes lit up. She followed Miss Brett into the house. For the first time in her life, Faye was going to see the inside of a kitchen oven.

The kitchen, as a whole, proved to be a laboratory of discovery for Faye.

"Goodness," Faye had commented as Miss Brett broke the eggs into the bowl, "your American eggs are quite different from ours back home. Are you sure these eggs are all right?"

Miss Brett sniffed the eggs before she began to whisk them.

"Yes, dear, they're fine," she said. "I collected them this morning."

"Only ours in India, the albumin, the whites, see, they really are white and quite a bit firmer than the ones you have here."

Miss Brett stopped whisking and looked at Faye. Gently, she said, "These will be, too, sweet angel—they just haven't yet been cooked. The whites of the eggs are clear when the eggs are raw."

Faye was stunned. "All eggs?"

"Yes, all eggs."

Miss Brett caressed Faye's head before handing her the bowl to pour into the batter. The girl had never seen a raw egg before. How remarkable.

And so the afternoon began. Faye and Miss Brett made a batch of butter biscuits, and it was Faye's job to add the slabs of butter to the top of each one. At first, Faye had feared that, in America, biscuits would be globs of wet goo, until she learned that the globs of disgusting pastry batter would be baked into delicious biscuits.

"Just by heating them in the oven," Faye said, amazed. She

had been familiar with heat being the catalyst of change in the laboratory, but nothing she had ever created there would have found its way into her mouth. Faye smiled as she placed remarkably even dollops of butter on the top of each glob.

"Now," Miss Brett said, turning to Faye as she wiped her hands on her apron, "let's take a look at the rest of the house." She reached for Faye's hand and Faye gladly took it. Right then and there, Faye decided that if being kidnapped meant she would stay with Miss Brett, then the whole thing would not be as terrible as it might have been. Miss Brett, Faye decided, was a lovely person, and Faye felt safe and cared for. Certainly, she would be well fed.

"This will be your room, I believe," said Miss Brett. With the sun nearly at high noon, the white bedroom was bathed in light. There was a bouquet of fresh flowers in a vase on the dressing table. Faye smiled. What a lovely room. She'd enjoy making it her own.

CHAPTER SIX

IN A CLASS OF THEIR OWN
OR
MISS BRETT DISCOVERS THE GAP

After she got over the fact that there was nothing she could do about where she was, Faye settled into the comfort of Miss Brett's company. That first morning, she had Miss Brett's undivided attention. If her parents didn't care about her enough to stay with her, or bring her with them, she would simply have a new life with Miss Brett. Everything here was quite lovely.

It was lovely, that is, until the others arrived. Then Faye dug out her pouting face and tried it on again. However, wearing the frown became more and more difficult as the afternoon grew. Although Miss Brett was dividing her attention, Faye could not help but find the other students rather interesting. They were, she decided, quite nearly as brilliant as she. They all had a great deal to share.

"You know, Faye, Jasper has been working on propellers," Lucy said cheerily, having awoken from her nap. "I saw some of your sketches of wings. Maybe the propeller can make your wings glide across the air like they make things glide across the water."

"What?" Faye felt like cleaning out her ears.

"Jasper can make things glide across the water with his propellers," Lucy said.

"Propellers?" Faye was interested enough that she forgot to say something mean to Lucy about being nosey. She looked over at Jasper.

"I've made a few boats that used propellers held by elastic strips," said Jasper. "And I made an aerial screw that can fly—"

"It can fly?" Faye was standing now.

"Well, it can propel itself up and float across the air. It comes down when the propeller stops, but I've found a way to slow the release of power from the twisted rubber band."

As the children began to investigate the classroom itself, Miss Brett called things to order. She showed them the maps and the books and the supplies. Clearly, she didn't need to explain the laboratory. Before she'd met her charges, she thought a fully equipped science laboratory an unusual thing to have in a classroom for children—she considered volatile chemicals and dangerous equipment were strictly the domain of knowledgeable adults—but now she understood why these items were there, and why they were appropriate. However brilliant their parents might be, these children could be no less brilliant themselves.

But being nursemaid, caretaker, and nanny to a class full of amazing prodigies was not in her job description. She had only been told there would be five children from the ages of six to thirteen.

"These are jolly good biscuits, Miss Brett," Lucy said as she wandered over to her seat. And that, it seemed, was the last thing Miss Brett understood.

"My calculations always resulted in a more viscous liquid,"

said Wallace to Noah, both in the middle of a discussion, standing next to the blackboard.

"I think you'll need more than that to create real propulsion capacity," Faye said to Jasper as they looked over something on his desk.

"I don't think that vinegar is a good substitute for sulphuric acid," said Noah, "but we can experiment and compare."

One thing Miss Brett *did* know was that sulfuric acid happened to be a very dangerous, even deadly, substance. She made a mental note to herself that under no circumstances would she allow sulfuric acid in the classroom.

That afternoon, Miss Brett overheard her students discuss the creation of at least three ingenious inventions, equations for five different experiments (one of which would have to be done without the sulfuric acid), and the initial draft of blueprints for two intriguing projects, one with wings. And to think, Miss Brett had only hoped they would be able to finish the first chapter in *Alice's Adventures in Wonderland*.

After Noah tried to explain to Miss Brett, unsuccessfully, how the automobile engine worked, and Faye tried to explain the concepts of aerodynamics, Miss Brett realized that trying to follow what they were saying, let alone teaching them something they didn't know, outside the kitchen at least, might be nearly impossible.

"You all know so much," Miss Brett finally said. "It's a bit daunting for me. Has anyone else ever felt like Alice trying to chase the White Rabbit?"

To this, she received a sea of blank faces.

"Alice who?" Jasper asked, wondering if Alice had been

perhaps a zoologist or small animal veterinarian.

"Why, Alice in Wonderland, from the stories of Lewis Carroll," Miss Brett said.

"Maybe we didn't get that story in England," Jasper said.

"The story comes from England, Jasper. I'm surprised that your parents never read it to you."

"Read it to us? Our parents?"

"Well, what kind of stories do they read to you?" Miss Brett asked.

From the empty expressions on those intelligent faces, Miss Brett knew something was amiss.

A hand went up in the air.

"I read to my mother once," said Noah.

"I don't think stories were ever read to us," said Jasper. "Sometimes, if it was a topic of interest to us, our parents read aloud from journals."

"Well, my parents were terribly busy," said Faye.

"What about you, Wallace?" Miss Brett asked.

Wallace looked down. "I would have remembered. My ... my mother, she ... well, maybe when I was small but ... but if she had read to me, I'd remember, wouldn't I?"

"Well, I don't know your mother, Wallace, so I can't ..." Miss Brett could see immediately that the little boy was in pain. Perhaps, if his mother had gone away when he was very young . .. or if she had gone ... "Of course, you would have remembered," Miss Brett said firmly. "Of course."

But then, this meant that Wallace's mother had not read to him.

Then she looked at all of their expectant faces. They all

wanted to understand. They all wanted to know.

"Come with me, children," she said. Gathering up the biscuits and handing the jug of milk to Noah, she picked up the hamper next to her desk and marched all of them outside onto the grass.

"We haven't done anything wrong, have we, Miss Brett?" asked Lucy, trotting alongside, concern written all over her face.

"Of course you haven't," Miss Brett said. "It's just time we did some sharing."

Miss Brett removed from her hamper a beautiful book that looked quite worn—not from abuse, but from use and love.

"This was my mother's copy of *Alice's Adventures in Wonderland*," said Miss Brett. "She loved it and read it over and over. She brought it over with her from England when she moved to America. She read it to me when I was small. I loved it and read it over and over, too."

"Did she read it to you?" asked Lucy.

"Yes, she did," said Miss Brett. "And her father read it to her."

"My mother never read the story to me," said Lucy. "Maybe her father never read to her. She's French, you see. Daddy's English, and he never read it, either."

"Well, shall we get started?" Miss Brett opened the book. "The book begins with this poem," she said.

> "All in the Golden Afternoon
> Full leisurely we glide;
> For both our oars, with little skill,
> By little arms are plied,
> While little hands make vain pretence
> Our wanderings to guide…"

The children sat, mouths agape, beaming. They were riveted by the poem, and then by the first chapter, with Alice and the White Rabbit.

"Oh, how lovely," said Lucy very quietly, so as not to disturb Miss Brett. Lucy was excited to learn stories and songs and rhymes written especially for children. It was like discovering a box filled with gifts that had always been in plain sight, but had somehow gone unnoticed.

"Does anyone know another poem? Perhaps a nursery rhyme?" said Miss Brett. "Who knows 'Humpty Dumpty'?"

They all looked at one another. No one seemed to have heard of it.

"'Hickory Dickory Dock'…?"

"Is that on the coast of America?" asked Jasper.

"No, I would have heard of it. It sounds like it might be Indian," said Wallace.

"No, then I would have heard of it," said Faye.

"Children," Miss Brett said, "it's a rhyme sung to children! You must know 'Rock-a-bye baby / on the treetop. / When the wind blows—'"

"How horrid!" said Lucy. "Why is the baby on the treetop? It might fall when the wind blows, if it blows hard enough."

"How about 'Jack Be Nimble,' or 'This little piggy went to market—'"

"Whose little piggy?" said Lucy, concern returning. "Why would he go to market?"

"It's a little rhyme for counting toes," said Miss Brett. "Didn't anyone ever call your toes 'piggies'?"

"Why would anyone do that?" said Noah. "They're toes, after all, not pigs."

"It's only a little rhyme meant to . . . look, all of you. Didn't anyone tell you rhymes or sing to you when you were small?"

"My mother is an opera singer," said Noah. "She sings all the time."

"I mean especially for you."

"She sings especially to me. She sings arias from operas and—"

"I mean songs especially for children, written especially for children." Miss Brett felt flustered. Was it possible they knew not a single lullaby among them?

Noah could see what he thought to be disappointment in her face. He tried hard to think of something—something that wasn't by Mozart or Verdi, something that could have been a lullaby.

"There was the 'Strange Round Bird' song," Noah said, tentatively. He wasn't sure this song was the kind she meant by poems or songs especially for children. "It's like a poem."

"That's impossible. I know a song by that name!" Faye said excitedly. "But you couldn't know it. You couldn't possibly know it." She began to recite: "'Strange round bird with three flat wings...'"

"We know that one, don't we, Jasper?" said Lucy, pulling at her brother's arm. "It's 'The Strange Round Bird'!"

Wallace nodded. Soon, they were all reciting together:

"...Never will it stop when it shivers and sings,
Never to be touched even if you are bold,
Turns the world to dust and lead into gold.

Three are the wings, one is the key,
One is the element that clings to the three.
Turns like a planet as it holds such power,
Clings to itself like the petals of a flower."

"How do you know 'The Strange Round Bird'?" asked Faye.

"How do you?" said Noah.

"I though my father made it up," said Faye.

"I thought my mother had," Wallace said, looking down at his feet and wiping his nose with the back of his hand. "My mother *did* sing to me." His voice was so soft, only Miss Brett could hear him. "She would sing 'The Strange Round Bird' as she rocked me to sleep when I was small."

Miss Brett had never heard this rhyme before. It sounded almost like Lewis Carroll's nonsense, only not quite. It seemed more, well, mechanical in style, and less charming.

"Is it a riddle?" Miss Brett asked.

None of the children had ever thought about it before. "It *does* seem to be very much like a riddle," said Jasper. "A puzzle of sorts." He was quite disappointed in himself. He loved puzzles and had never considered 'The Strange Round Bird' to be one. It had always been, well, just something he knew.

But to Miss Brett's trained ears, ears learned in lullabies and children's poems, "The Strange Round Bird" did not sound like any lullaby she knew. It certainly didn't sound much like something Miss Brett would choose to tell a child. Perhaps it was something scientists taught their children.

"Does it go on from there? Is there more?" she asked.

None of them had ever thought about this, either.

CHAPTER SEVEN

BLACK HUMOR

OR

NONSENSE COMES TO SOLE MANNER FARM

"I've been playing violin since before I could read," said Noah over supper that night, his mouth half-full of roast potatoes.

"We never learned to play instruments," Jasper said.

"Do your parents play anything?" Noah asked, shoveling another spoonful of food into his mouth.

"No, they . . . well, I don't know, actually." Jasper grew quiet, realizing he had never asked his parents. Did they? Had they taken lessons? Did they play music? He thought of how little he knew about them.

"My father plays the sitar," Faye said, passing the buttered peas to Wallace, who helped Lucy with a serving before taking his own. "It's an Indian string instrument, for those of you who don't know." There was a collective shuffle from the other children, who found so few things they didn't know and were not yet used to it, though they had learned so much from Miss Brett that day and enjoyed it immensely.

"Did he play for you?" asked Lucy, excited to hear about the sitar as she nibbled her peas, one by one.

"Yes, he did," said Faye, "and he was going to teach me how

to pluck the strings that morning when . . . you know." Suddenly, Faye did not want to be the first to admit that the lunatics in black had turned her life upside-down.

"You mean . . . *them*?" asked Noah, pointing out the window, but he, too, did not offer more than that.

"The men . . . men in black?" said Wallace, guardedly.

"The men in the funny suits and funny glasses and black things?" asked Lucy. "We had one with a big floppy hat."

Suddenly, the mood was much lighter.

"One of mine had on a woman's hat with frills and flowers," Noah said, laughing.

"One of mine had a turban. I thought he was my new tutor. Another had on a lovely lady's bonnet," Faye said, breaking into a smile that turned into a laugh.

"The one that took my father away in the carriage had a long black elephant's trunk," said Wallace, "and big floppy ears. I thought I was imagining it." He began to chuckle. "Sounds like I wasn't."

"If there ever is a competition for the odd-fellows award, they certainly win," said Noah, reaching for some chicken pot pie. Miss Brett had made three chicken pot pies, buttered peas, roast potatoes, and a tray of little strawberry tarts. She and the children had nearly eaten through the lot.

"Well, the ones I fought when I tried to escape, they were horrid," Faye said. "You've got to be brave to fight against all those lunatics."

"You tried to escape?" asked Wallace.

"Of course. Didn't you?"

"Jasper tried," Lucy said, "but when we came with Mummy

and Daddy, how were we to know they were bad? They're adults. They're supposed to know what's right."

"We don't know they're bad," Miss Brett said, trying to keep from smiling at Lucy's insistence that adults know right from wrong.

"Well, I could tell," Faye said. "I knew from the minute I saw them. I mean, the minute I saw the first one. With his dark spectacles and black turban."

"You said you thought the man in the turban was your tutor," said Noah as he bit into another potato.

Faye opened her mouth to bite back, but didn't. It was true.

"We had a group of them, all alike, in dark coats and glasses," said Jasper.

"At first, I only saw them from behind," said Wallace. "I was out by the lily pond, collecting samples of algae, and I noticed three strangers standing by the front door. Two were rather short fat men. The other was a tall thin man. All three were dressed in black. Completely in black."

He described identical black overcoats made of some shiny material, and the very tall hats on the two very short men, black as well, with some kind of tassels running around the edge of their brims.

"Were you frightened?" asked Lucy.

"No, not really. It was different, surely." Wallace thought about it. "I suppose I might have been a bit shocked, but not frightened."

It seemed to Miss Brett there was more she needed to know about Wallace. He had clearly experienced more, real, tangible sorrow in his life than his friends. It seemed not to be mere disappointment or loneliness. As a consequence, things did not frighten him in the same way.

"My odd fellows were different—totally different," Noah said. "The morning after my mother left for a tour, which she does all the time, so I'm used to it, really. No big thing. Only … only this time was harder because for that whole week before we … because—" Noah's voice got stuck in his throat. It was hard because that was the best week of his life. And it had come to an end.

Recovering, Noah spoke of how he'd busied himself after the coach had come to take his mother away. Working on an experiment in his attic laboratory, Noah had gone to the window for better light. He was having a problem with one of his batteries, and he was testing the sulfuric acid's corrosive potential when diluted with red lead at a higher ratio. While he was at the window, he heard a noisy, mechanical rumble from outside. He saw a large black motorcar coming up the driveway, stopping at the front door. Out stepped two incredibly odd-looking men.

Now, Noah was accustomed to odd visitors at the Canto-Sagas home. "But I know who comes to visit," he said, "and those blokes were like no one who comes to visit either of my parents."

Noah's mother had visiting admirers who were of the high social, well-dressed set. They were almost always elegant and fancy and colorful and bejeweled. They came with gifts and sweets and flowers. They were either dandies or duchesses or otherwise well-groomed patrons of the arts, followed by servants, and sometimes even adoring fans of their own.

"Father's visitors could not be more different than Mother's," Noah explained.

Without exception, his father's visitors had neither feathers nor baubles adorning their clothes. They wore dour faces and an air of brittle seriousness. His father's visitors dressed either in serious gray or brown attire, and simple gray or brown derbies, and often wore monocles dangling from their pockets. Some of his father's visitors wore white lab coats and thick glasses and always carried notepads full of computations.

That morning's visitors were neither dressed in feathers nor finery, nor were they in lab coats or prim suits. "They were both dressed totally in black—what a surprise, eh?" Noah said. "I do believe that those two might still be the strangest I have yet to see. Their very shapes were like something from one of Miss Brett's nonsense poems. One man had arms that reached almost down to his knees. He had huge shoulders, but very short legs. If it hadn't been for his enormous moustache, I could have easily mistaken him for an ape. In one oversized hand, he carried a black walking stick, like a prop in a circus show. His eyes were hidden behind thick glasses with lenses so dark they appeared black. His head was covered by a wide-brimmed hat pulled down so low it seemed to sit upon his glasses.

"The other man was very, very thin, but only to his middle. His bottom half seemed to spread out like a Bartlett pear. His arms came just to his hips and sort of hung there at a forty-five-degree angle. He wore a very, very tall stovepipe hat, like they wore in Grandfather's time. He had a standing collar and an oversized black cravat made into a prominent bowtie that fluttered whenever he let out a breath. On his nose was perched an extremely large pair of pince-nez spectacles with dark, almost reflective lenses hiding his eyes. His sideburns were so enormous they completely obscured the small bit of cheek above his cravat. They looked like two bushy gophers clinging to the sides of his face."

Noah remembered watching these strange creatures as they looked around, surveying the area before walking up to the door and raising the knocker.

"I quickly put the volatile chemicals away and hurried to the top of the stairs. My best friend Ralph was with me, and Ralph followed quietly.

"I thought Father would look out the window and send for the police. You can imagine my shock when he opened the door and greeted them, well, not as if they were old friends. But he greeted them as if he had expected them.

"I was pretty well stunned. I really didn't know what to think. But Ralph didn't like them right away, and showed it. And Ralph usually likes everyone."

"So each of you had a very different visitor, it seems," said Miss Brett, standing to clear the table. The children followed her lead and began to help. "Not a single one seems to have been in more than one place."

"How many of these blackguards could there be?" asked Faye, balancing all the plates atop one another. Helping around the farmhouse was a very exciting thing to do, she had found, and something she'd never done before. She walked over to the stove to warm the milk. Miss Brett brought in a tray of miniature tarts.

"Oh, Miss Brett! How scrumptious!" exclaimed Lucy.

"Don't let the Knave of Hearts in here," said Noah.

"Exactly," said Miss Brett.

The tarts were delicious. They were strawberry jam tarts Miss Brett had made. She also brought out whipped cream that smelled of vanilla. Full though they were, all managed to devour two tarts each.

"When did you first meet those blackguards?" Faye asked Miss Brett.

All faces were suddenly upon their teacher. No one had asked before now, but obviously Miss Brett must have come across those fellows before arriving at Sole Manner Farm.

"It was dear old Mr. Bell from the teaching college who had told me, in his strange accent, of this 'special opportunity,'" she said. "Mr. Bell had, more or less, taken me under his wing when I came to study, and with that funny cape he always wore, 'under his wing' is the right way to put it. He had said there was a unique position available for which I would be perfect. Mr. Bell simply told me that I would be contacted."

That evening, when she had arrived home to the lady's boarding house and opened her satchel, Miss Brett found that someone had secretly left her a note. She had clearly been contacted. A meeting had been scheduled.

"My story is much like yours," she continued, "except I had to go to an office. It was there that I met my first man in black, although I wouldn't exactly call him a blackguard, Faye." From there, Miss Brett told them of her meeting. At least, most of it.

On the note Miss Brett was given, there was written a precise hour when a carriage would arrive to collect her. "And at that hour exactly, the carriage came to the boarding house. It drove a most circuitous route, all over town, round and about, until it finally stopped in front of a building. The driver told me to go to the seventh floor.

"I climbed out of the carriage and entered the building. There was no one around, so I simply stepped into the elevator. As it began to ascend, I realized I had not been told what office number to go, but when I stepped out of the elevator, I learned it didn't matter—there was only one door on the entire floor. I walked down the hall and stood in front of the door.

"A high-pitched nasal voice from within told me to come in, just as I raised my hand to knock.

"I entered the room. It was empty except for two chairs on either side of a small desk, upon which sat a small lamp. In the chair behind the desk sat a very small, very thin man who looked as if he might have a twist in his back." He wore a black French-style hat, she added, that pulled down right to the top of his nose. He had on a black shirt with an Elizabethan ruff that came right up to his chin, and short trousers made of black velvet that ballooned out over his chair, almost floating above his knobby knees that stuck out on either side of the desk. Black stockings were pulled up and over those knees. "I would have liked a better look at those stockings," Miss Brett said, "but I could have sworn they were made of the finest, most delicate, most intricate lace."

According to Miss Brett, the man also wore a pair of fine black leather gloves on his very thin hands whose bony fingers threatened to push through the thin tight leather. His spectacles featured dark, almost black, lenses. The hat and the lenses so hid his face that she could hardly see his features, except for the crooked nose upon which the spectacles sat.

Miss Brett observed the man and wondered, briefly, if he was related to her own Mr. Bell. But the unusual choice of clothing, and perhaps the accent, seemed to be the only things the two men had in common. There was no gentle kindness emanating from the opposite side of the desk in that room. Perhaps, she reconsidered, it was just the accent. Perhaps they simply came from the same country.

"The odd man placed a stack of papers in front of me," Miss Brett said. "His gloved hand rested on the stack. I was not sure if he was keeping them from me or keeping them from falling off the desk."

"Your job is to teach," she was told by the man with dark glasses. "But—and take heed, for this is at least as important as your teaching responsibilities—you are to keep those children from distracting their parents. These are brilliant people, Miss Brett, understand?"

"The children?" she asked, grinning inwardly.

"The parents, Miss Brett, the parents. They are vital and brilliant and must be removed from distraction. All distraction. Our work is very important, but you don't need to know that. You don't need to know anything."

"Not know anything?" Miss Brett asked, both amused and incredulous. "But, sir—I'm a teacher."

"I know that," he said with a snort. "Let's just keep it that way."

Somewhat baffled, and certainly not enamored of this featureless man, Miss Brett decided to leave bad enough alone. "I agreed to take the job," she now told the children, "and I signed all of the papers—under this odd cloak of secrecy—and made the commitment to tutor you."

She kept her concerns and questions to herself and did not share them with her charges as she told her story. But she had wondered then, as she continued to wonder, if the parents were doing work for some important government agency. Were they, in fact, some sort of secret agents? Or might they be an international team of scientists working on the world's most top-secret projects? She had learned only that the parents were brilliant. And that they were important. But to whom?

She was handed an envelope containing a train ticket and instructions. She was to leave in the morning for Dayton, Ohio. She was to tell no one where she was going.

"So it was just the one?" asked Noah. "Just one funny blackbird, not a whole mob of them?"

"Just the one," she said.

"But there were more to come, surely," Noah said, as much of a statement as a question.

"The man at the desk was the first," Miss Brett said, offering mystery in her voice. It was then that the seed of the question entered her mind: *Was* that man the first? He most certainly was not the last.

On the carriage ride from the train to the schoolhouse, she decided there was no point in asking the strange driver what was going on. The driver, it should be said, wore a black knit hat, wide black trousers, a loose black shirt, and odd square glasses with very dark lenses. He was silent for the whole of the two-hour ride.

Miss Brett had been told nothing of her students, and she now felt that nothing could have prepared her for what she was to find. Would she have believed that there could be five such children in the world? Her students were perhaps the most brilliant people Miss Brett had ever known. Still, remarkable as her students were, they were, after all, children. No matter how big their brains, no matter how brave they seemed to be—whatever they knew about the steam engine or how incandescent lamps worked, and no matter what they were able to invent during their free time—they were all so young. They needed care and love and attention, Miss Brett believed, even more than they did test tubes and periodic tables. Their worlds had been shaken beneath their feet. She, too, had endured sudden change, but she at least had chosen to come.

"Where are my parents?" asked Faye.

"Oh, yes, Miss Brett, if you know," said Jasper. "We'd like to know where our parents are, as well. Have you heard? Are they, perhaps, with Faye's parents?"

"And my father?" Noah and Wallace said together.

"Where?" Miss Brett was at a loss. "I...I'm sorry, children, I don't know—"

"Are they together?" asked Jasper.

"I...I think they must be." Miss Brett thought back to that day, that interview.

"Are you sure you didn't hear anything?" Faye insisted. "Are you sure you don't know where they're being kept?"

"Kept? I don't think they're—"

"Didn't anyone tell you?" Faye was almost standing now.

"I'm just as much in the dark as you, I'm sorry to say."

"But it doesn't make sense," Faye said, falling back into her seat. "Someone must know."

"I am very sorry, but I do not," Miss Brett said, speaking with the deepest sincerity.

There was a thick silence as one more disappointing answer led the children nowhere. She hoped they believed her, that she simply did not know any more than they did. She hoped that they knew she cared and that she was there solely to support them. She did not want them to see her as part of the machine that had separated them from their parents.

Again, she thought to herself how children, all children, needed guidance and care and nurturing—especially from their parents. She could not imagine what kind of parents would simply abandon their children, even temporarily, without explanation. It was not her place to judge, she supposed, and things could well be out of the parents' control, but no word had been sent and no message received.

With absent parents involved in their own world of invention, Miss Brett could see that she had a larger role to play than merely teacher, no matter what the man with the dark glasses had said.

———

That night, after everything was put away in the kitchen, Miss Brett helped the children get settled into their rooms. The boys were happy in the yellow room with their three beds. They each chose the one they wanted, with, to Miss Brett's relief, no fighting. But Faye was not happy about sharing the big bed with Lucy.

"I want my own room," Faye demanded. "I've always had my own room."

"Well, now is your chance to share a room with someone else," said Miss Brett. "It will be a new experience."

"I've had enough new experiences, thank you," Faye said, "and now I'll have to share a bed with a baby?"

"I'm not a baby," Lucy said. "I don't wee in the bed and I'm very cozy to sleep with. Everyone says so."

"Really?" said Faye. "Who's everyone?"

"Mummy and Jasper and my dolly and—"

"Your dolly doesn't think you're cozy because your dolly doesn't think."

"Faye," Miss Brett said. "This is your room and your room to share with Lucy. It is her room, too. That is that."

"I ..." but Faye could not argue. There really was no choice. The farmhouse could offer only the rooms it had. Faye groaned and went into the white room, throwing herself on the bed. Lucy came in and jumped up beside her.

"This will be fun," she said. "Just us in our own bed."

Faye rolled over and groaned again.

After everyone had gotten into their nightclothes, washed for bedtime, and climbed into their beds, Miss Brett sat down in her rocking chair to read to the children. That night, she read the second chapter of *Alice's Adventures in Wonderland.*

The girls settled in their bed and drifted toward sleep. Faye closed her eyes, and only the thought of the evening's conversation about the men in black kept her from slumber. Lucy, already asleep, rolled over and cuddled up to Faye.

At first, Faye didn't know what to do. No one had ever cuddled with her before. Her parents had kissed her and held her hand. She had embraced them, too, but never this cuddling thing.

"Lucy?" she said softly. Lucy simply snored back. The little girl was deeply asleep. Her little body was warm and soft and, as if by instinct, Faye snuggled closer. Then Lucy burrowed into Faye's embrace.

Faye had a moment of worry, thinking it made her weak, somehow, to want to cuddle and snuggle like this. Knowing that Lucy was asleep, Faye felt safe to hold her, to feel glad to have someone near. Tears filled Faye's eyes and she didn't know why.

Faye put her arm more tightly around the little girl. She let out a long, hard breath and found that sleep came easier than she'd thought.

The boys each had a harder time getting to sleep. Wallace lay in bed, wanting to ask Miss Brett to come in, but not wanting the others to hear him. Jasper, on the other hand, was worried about Lucy sharing a room with Faye. He again thought about Faye— so beautiful it was almost difficult to look at her, yet not a kind person. In fact, Jasper thought the girl could even be cruel. Lucy would need him to cuddle and hold her.

Both he and Wallace managed to fall asleep before Noah. He was the only one awake when Miss Brett came in to make one final check.

"I'm normally a very good sleeper," Noah said. He thought to himself that he was probably more accustomed than the others to having at least one parent gone most of the time. "Do you mind if I play, Miss Brett?" he asked.

"Play?" she asked, imagining building blocks or a ball and jacks. She was about to tell him it was late and he should try to sleep when he reached under his bed and brought out his violin.

"Oh," she said. "Of course, if it helps you relax."

"Well, I won't know until I try," said Noah, giving her half a smile. He tightened and rosined his bow, then tuned the strings on his instrument. He smiled again as he lifted the violin to his chin.

And then, he took her breath away. The sound that came from his violin was like the music of angels. She was sure that the dreams of the sleeping children were being embellished by the beauty and pleasure of his music. Miss Brett closed her eyes—

the tune was both sad and joyous. As it came to an end, she felt the tears coming down her face. She opened her eyes to see Noah crying, too.

"Sweet angel," she said, putting her arms around him. "My sweet, sweet angel, you are amazing. Such beauty, such pleasure, such—"

"I can't play it anymore," said Noah, trying to rub away the tears that had betrayed him. "I . . . I can't play it. Not for a while, anyway." He placed his violin back in the case. "It makes me think of her. She's not, you know, one of them, one of the other parents. Music is what we share, my mother and me. It makes me think: What if she's looking for me and I'm gone, or what if she doesn't know where my dad is or where I am, or . . . I guess it's not making me very relaxed, is it?"

"I understand," Miss Brett said gently. "But I want to thank you for playing tonight. It will make us all dream better dreams. Any time you want to play, let me know so I can be there to listen. I never want to miss a note."

Noah smiled and sheepishly pushed the violin case back under his bed. Soon, he thought—soon they'd know where his father was. They'd know why they'd all been moved so far. They'd know who was behind all this and how to make things right. And soon, somehow, he'd hear from his mother. He'd get one of her postcards—any day now.

CHAPTER EIGHT

THE SOPRANO'S SON

OR

NOAH SHARES SOMEONE FIT FOR A KING

Before that first day at Sole Manner Farm, Noah Canto-Sagas had exactly three friends. One was Marie, the little girl who lived in the flat below in Place d'léna in Paris, France. Noah had lived there for four months when he was about six. The little girl had spoken no English, and Noah had spoken little French. Still, they became friends, and would play at the Trocadéro together. By the end of their time in Paris, Noah's French was excellent, and Marie spoke English rather well.

Noah had given one of her broken dolls new life. Opening it up, he'd inserted a simple mechanism that allowed its head to turn and its legs to move. Using the battery he built, even the tiny spring-loaded eyelids opened and closed, and the left eye winked independently.

Noah and the little girl had exchanged letters for about a year, but when Marie moved to Belgium and Noah moved about twenty times, they lost touch.

Noah's second friend was Zeke, the man who sold newspapers outside their flat in New York City. Whenever they went back to New York, Noah would visit the newspaper vendor. Zeke was about ninety years old, and almost blind. He told Noah funny stories about New York in the old days. He would always let Noah have free chocolate when Noah was sad about his mother being away. Noah would sometimes sit with Zeke on warm afternoons and hand out magazines and newspapers to the people who came to buy them.

Noah's third friend was Ralph. Ralph was really his best friend. They were inseparable.

"People are going to get us mixed up for one another," he once told Ralph. "That's what happens when guys spend a lot of time together."

But, in truth, Noah and Ralph didn't look much alike at all. Ralph had rather wiry mottled hair instead of fair hair like Noah's. And one of his ears was longer than the other. He also had a funny little beard that made him look a bit like one of the three musketeers. And Ralph had wide-set ears, a very long tail, and four very stubby legs.

Ralph was a dog. And, to be polite, he was a dog of mixed heritage.

Ralph was quite a small dog, like Fifi, the poodle who belonged to Noah's mother. Unlike Fifi, Ralph never snapped at ankles, growled at people, or urinated on the upholstery. Fifi had always been very unfriendly to Ralph. When Noah's mother was in town, Noah had to keep Ralph in the kitchen.

———⋙●⋘———

At twelve years old, Noah Canto-Sagas had probably lived in more places than everyone else he knew put together. He once counted. He had lived in fourteen different places before he was seven years old, and probably at least that many since. In cities where his mother often performed, like London, Paris, and New York City, they kept small houses or flats. With his father, a prominent scientist, often on the lecture circuit, Noah was also familiar with hotels throughout Europe and North America. And in some cities, they had still other accommodations. Before his father had given up full-time research and taken a permanent position at the University of Toronto, and while his mother was on a regular touring circuit, Noah was dragged all around the world, living here and there, but always returning to Toronto in the fall to their beautiful bay-and-gable home in Hoggs Hollow.

Like Jasper and Lucy, and unlike Faye, Noah had gone to school. In fact, he had gone to lots of schools. He had been to schools in every city where they had moved, with two exceptions. One was when they lived in Vienna the winter he was five. It was there that he learned how to play the violin. The other time was a year later when they lived in Tokyo for seven months. In both places, he was tutored at home.

Noah's mother was Ariana Canto-Sagas. The famous, glamorous, glorious Ariana Canto-Sagas. The incomparable, regal, Italian-Scottish-French-Albanian diva Ariana Canto-Sagas, whose great-grandmother had been an Egyptian queen. Everyone in the world of opera knew her name. She was strikingly beautiful—tall and shapely, with cascades of thick, deep red hair falling over her shoulders and down her back. Her voice was compared to "the heavenly sound that could only come from the throats of celestial angels" by a reviewer from *The London Times*. She was the world's greatest living soprano, he wrote.

Rodin had sculpted her. Tchaikovsky had been inspired by her. Even Gustav Klimt, it was rumored, had designed and created the simple but utterly elegant platinum necklace she wore day and night. When she toured, the newspapers almost always mentioned her "platinum throat." The necklace that adorned it was never removed.

Because she was so famous, she was constantly in demand. This meant that she was almost never at home. She traveled the world with an entourage of assistants, coaches, and Fifi. When at home, she was there sometimes for hours, sometimes for days, but rarely longer. Noah was not sure he had ever seen his mother for more than seven days in a row.

"Nonsense," she once insisted. "Why, not long ago, I was home with you for almost a month."

"Are you sure I was there? When was it? I don't remember," said Noah.

"Why, of course you don't, silly," she had said. "It was when you were born."

———⊰●⊱———

Noah had seen his mother perform, on stage, bathed in light, in front of her audience, exactly once. Noah was seven. His father had to be in London and his mother had to perform at Toronto's Grand Opera House. Glenda, the woman who cooked and took care of the house and garden when the family was abroad, was unavailable that one night until after eleven o'clock. Because there had been no other choice, Noah got to go to his mother's performance.

"It should be fine, Clarence," Ariana told her husband. "It's Verdi's *Aida*, which can be a bit emotional, and it would be better if it was something silly like *Falstaff*, although there would certainly be no role for me, but never you mind, gentlemen, it will be fine." She turned to Noah and brushed his forehead with her lips. "After all, Noah has already been to a performance of *Roméo et Juliette*."

"I don't remember," said Noah, who tried to recall the event but could not.

"Well, you could not have been more than a couple months old," said Ariana. "Perhaps you weren't there and we left you home. Ah, but I was there and it was marvelous. And I was about your age when I first saw Célestine Galli-Marié play Carmen in Vienna. Utterly moving," she said. "And it was fabulous. Simply fabulous."

Ariana was herself fabulous. The whole performance was fabulous. Noah's mother was radiant, as much a princess in her own right as the princess she portrayed onstage. It was as if she was born to do this, as if her very essence consisted of the music she sang, and everyone in the audience, a full house of thirteen hundred, was mesmerized. Noah knew that, had the Grand Opera House been the size it was before the great fire in 1879, she would have filled that, too. She could have filled five houses and left standing room only.

Opera-goers showered her with flowers and she blew kisses to the audience. Then, looking right up to Noah, she blew a kiss especially for him. He had wished that night would never end.

But it did. A beautiful carriage took Noah home. It belonged to the visiting British minister of culture, who had planned to join the ambassador from France for a champagne-fest backstage in honor of Ariana. Noah had been hustled into the carriage. He thought his mother had waved to him from the middle of the crowd, but he could not be sure.

Glenda had arrived at the house not long before Noah. She greeted Noah as he emerged from the beautiful gold carriage. Noah's mother, meanwhile, had left the opera house with the governor general, the Earl of Minto, to attend a fabulous gala event hosted by Prime Minister Laurier. He had been desperate for Ariana to sing at the Olympics in Paris, because it would be the first year the Canadians would compete.

After making Noah a cup of hot cocoa, Glenda went to bed herself. Noah said goodnight and went to his room to dress for bed, but instead of going to sleep, he took out his violin. He was much too excited for sleep. He tiptoed into the salon and searched among the pages inside the piano bench. He found the sheet music to Verdi's *Aida* and began to teach himself one of the arias so he could play it for his mother as a surprise. He practiced until he fell asleep, only just before dawn. When he awoke, Noah ran into his mother's room to play for her, but she wasn't there. She had left straight from the show for an engagement in Milan.

By the time Ariana returned from Italy, Noah had not only taught himself the entire opera, but perfected the arias. The morning she arrived at Hoggs Hollow, Noah met her at the door, violin in hand. Before she could unpack, he played her "Ritorna vincitor" from the first act, and she immediately fell into voice. The two of them played together for hours until the carriage came to take her away again that afternoon. It had been bliss. Then, and for the rest of his life, Noah could hear no Verdi compositions without visions of Ariana bathed in light, applauded by her beloved fans.

Playing together at home was magic in its own right, but it was different. Sometimes, Noah accompanied his mother on the violin, and they would perform for his father, Ralph, and Glenda, but it was not like seeing her in lights, larger than life. At home, his time with her was always colored by the knowledge that she belonged to the world and not to him. The world could snatch her away at any moment. He would always have to share her, and often get the smallest part. But when he was in the audience, when he was one of those for whom she glowed, she was his as much as she belonged to anyone else.

———

For Noah, the week before the morning when his whole world changed had been one of the best of his life. Not only was it the longest he could remember ever having been with his mother in one solid block of time, but it was the only time he could remember, the only time in his life, perhaps, that his whole family—his mother, his father, Noah, and Ralph—were together in their own home for so many days in a row.

Noah could not help himself—he was overcome with joy when he heard the news.

"Your mother has a very sore throat. She is not able to sing," his father explained. As it turned out, Ariana had to cancel all of her performances and stay in bed, drinking black cherry cider and puree of plum with brandy. She spent that whole week in her coziest nightdresses, with silk scarves wrapped around her neck to keep it warm. Not once in all those days did she put on normal day clothes. Instead, she surrounded herself with pillows and flowers and chocolate bonbons. Because it was Noah's school holiday, he, too, spent the week in his nightclothes, surrounded by pillows and flowers, and munching on bonbons with his mother. Fifi, at the beauty salon for dogs, was nowhere to be seen. Ariana even let Ralph sleep on Fifi's pillow at the bottom of the bed, but only after Noah and Glenda gave him a serious scrub. Ralph seemed quite pleased with himself. Smelling of rosewater and lavender, he was shockingly fluffy.

Glenda baked all of their favorite treats and served the two bonbon-eaters as if they were royalty. They feasted on savory pies, roast sweet potatoes, and iced lemon cakes right there on Ariana's bed. Noah's father was not teaching that week, and though he was holed up in his laboratory most of the time, he would come up and join them for treats when he needed a break. They were all together, but most of all, Noah had his mother, and no one would take her away.

Because Ariana's throat hurt, and sealed lips were required for her recovery, Noah read to her from books he selected from his father's library. The books Noah had chosen, however, were not at all to his mother's liking.

"*The History of the Steam Engine? Discovering the Inner Ear? The Life of the Banana Slug? Ambrose Paré: The Father of French Surgery?*" Ariana croaked. "Honestly, what kind of muck are you reading these days, Noah? You are a boy, not a laboratory rat. Here," she said, pulling a quill from her drawer and writing out a list of books. "Give this list to Father. Tell him to have someone return these other books to their musty old shelves and fetch those on my list." She handed Noah the stack of unacceptable books and the list of those she wanted.

Before lunch, his father's lab assistant returned from the library with a stack of new books and publications.

"*The Three Musketeers? Tom Jones? Dracula? Tristram Shandy?*" Noah read down the list, incredulous.

"These, my dear boy, are fun to read," insisted his mother, whispering in a raspy voice. "Now, shut me up and start with this one." She handed him a thin booklet, a story titled *A Study in Scarlet* by Sir Arthur Conan Doyle, and Noah began to read.

The story was mysterious and exciting. Noah was thrilled as he read. He loved the fact that the detective, Sherlock Holmes, played the violin, and he loved being surprised at the end. He loved the bonbons and the nightclothes, and enjoyed cuddling with the suddenly sweet-smelling Ralph. What he loved most was having his mother's attention focused on him, the only distractions coming from the delivery of delicious treats.

They spent the next several days reading and laughing, eating chocolate and sipping sweet hot tea.

"If the musketeers were dogs, you'd be d'Artagnan," Noah told Ralph, who showed little interest in this pronouncement. Ralph did, however, seem to really listen when Noah read the story of *The Three Musketeers*, the dog curling up on Fifi's pillow, his chin resting on Noah's knee.

Noah and his mother read all the books, some to themselves and some with Noah reading aloud. Noah played violin for his mother, and even sang "The Strange Round Bird" to a tune he had composed on the spot. When he was a toddler, Noah had always found the rhyme odd and a bit scary, but he'd been determined to learn it, memorizing the poem during playtime in the garden and singing it to himself every morning when he woke up so he wouldn't forget.

His father had always been impressed that Noah could recite it with such ease. "It took me ages to learn it when I was a boy," he had said, beaming at his son.

On the seventh day of the best week of his life, Noah woke to the sound of his mother gargling and singing her scales. His heart sank.

"Are you sure you're well?" Noah said, hoping she still needed time to recover. "I mean, really, really well? You never can tell with these things. One minute you're up and the next…" Noah performed a faux faint, crumpling to the floor.

"You silly!" Ariana laughed. "Yes, dear, I'm fine," she said. "Thank you for taking such wonderful care of me. I'm well because of you."

"Then I am to blame. Egads!" Noah jumped up from the floor.

"Such nonsense," said Ariana with a smile. Then she gargled again.

"But maybe it's too soon," said Noah, more seriously. "Maybe you need more rest. Maybe three or four more weeks?"

"Why don't you help me pack?" his mother said.

"Pack? When do you leave?" he asked.

"Not until tomorrow morning. But your father and I will be going to the theater tonight. You'll finally have a night off from your invalid mother."

Noah tried to smile, but it must have looked more like a grimace.

"Don't look so melancholy," Ariana said. "Most likely, I'll be gone just a few weeks or so, and before I head off to Rome, I'll try to stay here with you for two whole days."

"Rome?" Noah asked. *So very far so very soon,* he thought with a shiver. She was going to be gone a long time again. He could feel it. "I suppose all roads lead to Rome, huh? How about a stowaway? I promise to be helpful and courteous," he said. "You can just stuff me in an extra sack. How hard could that be?"

Ariana Canto-Sagas smiled, kissed her son, and shook her head. "It's not that it's hard, darling," she said in her softest, smoothest voice, the voice she always used to let him down easy. "It's just the time. When will I have the time? I'll be here and there and everywhere. It really is impossible, you see. Now, no sad faces on my funny man. There, there. You'll understand, my sweet. I know you will."

Of course, Noah always understood. He understood he would not be going with her.

"Don't worry, my sweet. I will write."

Noah knew this was true. She always wrote. Noah had a collection of hundreds of postcards from all over the world. The postcards would say how she went fox-hunting with the Windsors or saw the bulls run in Spain, and Noah would treasure every word, imagining her voice telling him all about it. He could always pick out his mother's postcards in a pile of letters on the front table. She would tell him about the mad adventures she was having or the magnificent performances she gave for whatever kings and queens were attending. It had never been more than a week before a card came for Noah.

"Looks like you don't have to take care of your mother anymore," Noah's father said with a smile as Noah helped his mother pack. When Noah couldn't bring himself to smile back, his father said, "Hey, want to help me rework that experiment? You're my number one assistant."

Noah and his father often performed experiments together. Noah was dubbed his father's "number one assistant" right after his third birthday. "Father tells me you are his number one assistant," his mother had written. "Today I had tea with the prince of Denmark…"

CHAPTER NINE

THE BIG BLACK BARRIER
OR
 HOW THE CHILDREN FOUND THE FENCE

In the morning of the second day at Sole Manner Farm, there was a bit of misty confusion when the children tried to remember why they found themselves in unfamiliar beds. The boys woke first, each coaxing the other out of sleep, and they were the first to remember where they were. It didn't take long to fall back into snoozing, the comfort of the bed winning over enthusiasm for what was to come.

The girls, however, entwined and in dreams, remained sound asleep nearly an hour longer. Lucy had dreamt she was held in the arms of a large creature that was half horse and half rabbit. It sang to her about pigs and the market and told her that her toes were nimble and soon she would need a candlestick. But she wasn't afraid, she thought to herself. She was safe, here in his arms.

Faye's dreams were less vivid—more a feeling of warmth and safety. Until they woke, both girls clung to one another.

"Get off me!" Faye cried as Lucy pulled herself closer.

"I'm only cuddling," said Lucy, trying to get warm again, moving back out of the cold part of the bed where Faye had sent her.

"Well, it's time to get up, anyway," said Faye, climbing down from the bed. "And put your slippers on, or you'll get splinters."

Miss Brett had been up since the rooster crowed. She had lit the stove and pumped and fetched the water. She had collected the eggs and milked the cow, and then gone about mixing the eggs, milk, and flour batter for the pancakes. She added a heaping spoonful of sugar and a pinch of vanilla she shaved from the bean pods in the pantry. She also added some cinnamon, which she'd also found there.

Hearing voices that before had been snores, she put the first pancake on the buttered griddle and thought, *Funny how nothing will call to children like the smell of breakfast cooking.*

Lucy ran to Miss Brett, hugging her around the middle.

"And good morning to you, Lucy," Miss Brett said.

"Good morning, Miss Brett," the other children said, wrapped in various stages of sleepiness and yawns. Within minutes of the first pancake hitting the griddle, all the children were sitting at the table.

"Are you all going to eat off the wood, or are you going to put some plates on the table?" said Miss Brett. "Come now, I know you're tired, but we are starting a new day. Lucy, get the cups. They're on the lower shelf next to the pantry door. Noah, get the plates. They're higher up. Wallace, the napkins, in the hamper by the plates. Faye, you and Jasper get the milk. It's in those jugs by the sink."

Soon, they were all eating pancakes smothered in sweet butter and sprinkled with cinnamon sugar. They munched on raisins and dried apricots, too.

"We eat these with golden syrup or treacle back home," Jasper said, taking a third helping of pancakes. "Hortensia makes them for us on weekends. These are better, though, aren't they, Lucy?"

"They jolly well are," she said, taking another bite. "They're lovely, Miss Brett. Mummy said she always had crepes when she was small, back in France. They're not fluffy at all. The ones Hortensia makes are a bit fluffy but mostly chewy. Yours are much fluffier than the ones back in England."

"Must you eat like a horse?" Faye said to Noah, who was shoveling in what looked to be two bites at a time. "You, too," she scolded Jasper, who stopped mid-bite and swallowed an uncomfortably large piece, slicing his next very small.

Faye took an elegant bite. "In India, we have *pooda*. And ..." She looked at Lucy. "These are much fluffier than ours, as well."

"It must be Miss Brett's secret ingredients," said Lucy, beaming at Miss Brett. "Miss Brett makes everything so deliciously that she must have a secret ingredient for everything. It's the secret ingredient that makes it work. Isn't that right, Miss Brett?"

Miss Brett smiled at Lucy. "It's always the secret ingredient that makes a thing work best."

Later, as they worked together cleaning up after breakfast, Miss Brett headed for the henhouse. Today's lesson would cover a little nature.

———◆———

"It's hatching!" cried Lucy, halfway through a discussion on caring for chickens. Sure enough, the egg Miss Brett had brought in from the henhouse was cracking open. That morning, Miss

Brett had noticed the crack on the one egg she had left the day before, but supposed it still had some time to go. Now, they all gathered around the warming tray upon which the little egg, nestled in a soft cloth, was perched.

"Once the little thing has dried itself off, we'll bring it back to its mummy," said Lucy.

"Otherwise, it's going to think I'm its mummy," said Noah.

"You look like its mummy," Faye said, but even she had to laugh when Noah clucked and strutted. Jasper and Lucy shared a secret grin, for Noah reminded them, just the teeniest bit, of Rosie.

"Yes, now, we really had better get the little thing back to its nest before it follows Noah everywhere," said Miss Brett, placing a kerchief gently over the tiny chick.

"But I want to see my new friend," said Lucy.

"He needs the warmth and the protection," Miss Brett said.

"Protection from imprinting on one of us," said Noah. "That's what it's called—imprinting. That's when a baby chick decides who its mother is and stays with that mother, even if it's a dog or a giraffe or a girl named Lucy."

After the lesson, while Miss Brett prepared a picnic lunch, the children took the little chick to the henhouse.

"I can feel its little heart beating," said Lucy, who carried it gently.

"Keep it covered or you'll be in trouble," said Jasper, keeping his eye on Lucy, who was inclined to let the cover slip so she could adopt the tiny chick.

"Oh, do we have to put it back?" Lucy said. "I'll be the mummy. Do we have to give him back?"

"Of course we do," Faye said, taking the chick from Lucy and letting it topple gently into the hen's roost. It wiggled up next to its mother and nestled in with the other two newborns. "How do you think the mother would feel if someone else had its baby?"

Lucy looked at her for a moment, then turned to Jasper. "Do you think the mummy hen is like our mummy? Would she be worried if someone else took us?"

"Someone else did take us," Faye said, studying the chickens together. They all watched as the little feathery families pecked, cheeped, and clucked as one.

———⊰•⊱———

"If you look at the clouds," Lucy said, pointing at the sky with her carrot, "you can see an elephant. You do know what an elephant is, don't you?"

"I own elephants," Faye said, selecting another cheese sandwich from the hamper and looking out at the empty road. "We have to do something."

"We are doing something," Noah said, his feet crossed and perched upon the trunk of the willow tree under which they picnicked.

"I don't mean sitting around gorging ourselves," Faye said, knocking Noah's feet to the ground.

"What do you mean, Faye?" asked Miss Brett.

"I mean, we're all captives. We're all here against our will."

"I'm not," Miss Brett said firmly. "I came because I wanted to. I wanted to teach and help."

"Help keep us here?" Faye said.

"Help keep you out of harm's way," Miss Brett answered

calmly, taking another sandwich. She wanted to show she was not hurt, and that she did not feel somehow guilty. But she was their keeper, was she not? Did she not work for the same mysterious forces that had placed them all here? "Does anyone want more milk?" she asked.

"Yes, please," said Faye.

Miss Brett stood and walked back to the farmhouse, glad to be able to wipe her tears without the children seeing.

Once Miss Brett was out of earshot, Faye said, "We need a plan."

"A plan for what?" asked Jasper.

"A plan of rescue, you dimwit," Faye said. "We've got to get out of here and rescue our parents."

"No." Sitting up, Lucy crossed her arms. "I want to stay."

"Don't be an idiot, Faye," Noah said, putting his feet back up. "We're safe with Miss Brett. Our parents are fine, and we'll see them when they're done doing whatever it is they're doing."

"And what do you think that is?" asked Wallace.

"Something for the government?" Jasper said.

"What government?" said Faye. "The Indian? The British? The American? The Canadian? The French? That sounds a bit unlikely to me."

"She's right, you know," said Jasper.

"Well, then ... they ..." Noah stalled, struggling for something to say. "They are plotting to overthrow the world with a secret invention that requires the greatest scientific minds from the world's greatest countries."

"You're an idiot," said Faye.

"But they must be needed for something," Wallace said. "Our

parents are all scientists, are they not?"

"My mother's an opera singer," said Noah.

"Well, she's not been kidnapped, has she?" countered Faye.

"Who said anything about kidnapping?" Noah sat back up.

"I'm breaking out of here tonight," Faye said in a near whisper.

"You're what?" Jasper was aghast. "Are you mad?"

"Are you?" Faye said. "I think it's mad to sit here and wait for doom."

"Doom?" Noah laughed. "Doom? What, you mean if we run out of clover honey or if Miss Brett burns the biscuits?"

"Miss Brett would never burn the biscuits," Lucy said, crossly.

"Fine," Faye said with finality. "If you want to sit here while your parents are . . . are, who knows what, you can do just that. I, for one, am going to try to save mine."

Miss Brett returned with the milk to a very quiet group of children.

"Shall we return to our lesson?" she asked.

In silence, they all carried the picnic's remains into the kitchen and returned to the classroom.

—————

"I'm right here, Wallace," grumbled Faye.

"No you're not. You're here," said Noah, wincing, "and that's my foot."

Miss Brett's five wards bumbled and bumped into one another, walking through the pitch-black dark.

"You're shoving me into my desk, Faye," said Jasper.

"Oh, sorry," said Noah, stepping back into Wallace. "That was me."

"I want to go back to sleep," cried Lucy. "I want Miss Brett."

"Don't be a baby," said Faye.

"I'm not a baby!" Lucy said.

"Shhhhh," they all said.

"You're not a baby," Jasper said, reassuringly.

"If you're not a baby," whispered Faye, "then don't act like one."

"But Miss Brett—"

"Look, we'll come back and save her, too. Right now, we have to figure out a way out of here." Faye found the candle she had hidden in her desk before bedtime.

Noah yawned loudly.

"Will you be quiet?" Faye said. "Do you want to wake the whole farm?"

"I'm tired," Noah said. "It's half past one in the morning."

Faye lit the candle with the tinderbox she'd hidden alongside it. Everyone took a step off of one another.

Very quietly, they opened the door to the classroom. They had chosen the classroom door instead of the door to the farmhouse so they would not wake Miss Brett.

"I've lost one of my slippers," said Lucy.

"Well, get it!" Faye said.

"It's back in the classroom," said Lucy.

Faye opened up her mouth to shout, but bit her tongue. "Get it," she mumbled—mumbling was the best she could do with her tongue bitten.

Lucy scampered back to the classroom and emerged moments later. Although it was late summer, there was an autumn-like chill in the night air. The five of them huddled close.

"Now, as I figure it, we should go for the road. We'll head back in the direction we came—"

"Which is ..?" Noah hadn't a clue and hoped someone else had.

They all looked both ways. Several times.

"Right, I say we go that way," said Jasper.

"Are you sure?" Faye asked.

"No, but I'm pretty certain," he said.

"Why doesn't Lucy know?"

"I only know things I know," Lucy explained. "I don't know things I don't know yet. But I'll know tomorrow if we figure it out tonight."

"Well, glad we cleared that up," Noah said.

"Just walk," Faye said. "Go the way Jasper suggested."

"What are we going to do when we walk down the road?" asked Lucy with a shiver. She was cold.

"We get to that when we get to that," said Faye.

"She has a point, Faye," said Noah. "You've convinced us we need to do something, but what is the next thing we're supposed to do? Wander around in our nightshirts in hopes that some farmer comes by on his horse and picks us all up? Even if that happened, where would we go?"

"To the police," said Faye.

"The police?"

"The police," Faye said with certainty.

After a few moments of contemplation, Noah said, "Well, okay.

But what do we tell them?"

"We say that . . . these men in black . . . that . . ." Faye faltered. "Actually, I think we should just concern ourselves with getting away so we can find our parents. We don't need to involve the police right now."

The five of them trundled in the dark with nothing but the light of the candle to guide them. They tiptoed through the fields of greens and through the apple orchard. At one point, they saw a shadow standing at the edge of the field. They all stopped, thinking, for a moment, that someone was standing there.

"It must be a signpost or something," Faye said.

"There are more of them," Jasper said, pointing to the shadows in the moonlight.

"Fine, then there are lots of signposts. It doesn't matter. Keep walking."

"The signposts are moving!" cried Lucy.

"It's just a trick of the moonlight," said Faye, although she thought she saw the same thing.

Soon, they came to the dirt road.

"All right, everyone ready?" asked Faye. There were nods all around, although the quiet did not mask their fear and apprehension. Faye took a deep breath. "This is it. We're all together. We'll start off and—"

At that moment, a rumbling noise sent them all hiding behind the mound of the irrigation ditch. It was getting louder and louder. Lucy grabbed Jasper by the arm and he held her close. Faye leaned against him, too. Jasper did not have the courage to put his arm around her, but he would protect them both if there was danger.

During the thrill of terror, Faye was the first to realize what it was.

"It's *them!*" she cried over the rumble of the motorcar.

And it was. The huge black motorcar drove past them, and in the light of the moon, the children could see the shape of the big furry cap and funny bow that sat upon the head of what was clearly one of the men in black. Not only that, but the signposts were not signposts at all—and they were moving. Some wore caps or hats or feather boas. Some wore long trousers or jodhpurs or frilly pinafores. But not one of them was a signpost. They were all men in black.

"We're surrounded," said Faye, slumping back into the ditch.

"We're trapped," said Wallace, realizing for the first time that she was right.

"They have us captive," said Jasper.

"I need to wee," said Lucy, her legs crossed beneath her.

Feeling defeated and disheartened, the five children ambled towards the schoolhouse, stopping briefly to let Lucy wee on the far side of the ditch. It felt like a slow march—a march of prisoners headed back to their prison.

Up half the night, they returned unnoticed to their beds, but did not sleep well, and Miss Brett, after readying her jam doughnuts for breakfast, had to go in and wake the children. She did not receive a friendly welcome for her efforts.

The breakfast table proved a solemn venue. The children did not eat very much.

"Is everything all right?" asked Miss Brett.

As Lucy opened her mouth, Faye kicked her under the table.

"Just . . . just tired, Miss Brett," said Lucy, her fingers heading into her mouth.

"The lot of you?" Miss Brett asked. "Were you up in the night experimenting?"

Lucy opened her mouth, but Faye cut her off.

"Yes, Miss Brett. We're terribly sorry. We were all excited to, well, you probably wouldn't understand. Mmmm, these cakes are lovely." Faye indulged in a doughnut. "Delicious. I'm feeling more awake already, aren't you, Wallace?"

"Yes, ma'am," Wallace said, "I mean, Faye. Yes, Faye." But he only looked at his doughnut.

"All right, you five. Listen to me. I do not care whose idea it was, and I do not care what it was you were doing, but we have a new rule on Sole Manner Farm: no midnight experiments. Now, I want you all to go back to bed and come back to the table when you can eat with your eyes open."

The grateful children marched back into their rooms and fairly collapsed onto their beds. Lucy and Noah were asleep before their heads hit the pillows. The other three found they were restless again, and sleep did not come for them.

When Lucy and Noah both woke about an hour later, they were ready for the day. Jasper, Wallace, and Faye limped through the delayed breakfast and managed to get through the morning lessons. Nobody mentioned the failed escape attempt, and no one discussed whether or not they would try again.

CHAPTER TEN

WEEKENDS IN THE MEADOW
OR
 WHEN A SECOND ISN'T ENOUGH

The rest of the week was easier, but now they knew the truth: It was going to be impossible to just sneak away from Sole Manner Farm to rescue their parents. It became the unspoken secret among them and, as they did not speak of it, it became easier to ignore as the days went by.

Lessons became quite interesting. The children found that they enjoyed teaching Miss Brett about all facets of science, explaining chemical reactions and physics. Miss Brett, meanwhile, loved to find things the children didn't know, and they were so pleased that she cared enough to do that. They learned about animals and about trees. They learned about planting and caring for the things they planted. They walked in the meadow, and Lucy picked the last of the apple blossoms as tiny apples began to form on the trees. They read stories about pirates and ogres and princesses and frogs. Mostly, they learned that, however unsure they were about the rest of the world, and however much they didn't fit in with most teachers and students, they were sure Miss Brett cared, they had each other, and they were all in this together.

Even Miss Brett. She might have come to the farm with a minimum of information about her students, hired to teach five children whose parents had simply gone away, but now she knew these were not children like any other. She had come to care deeply for them, to love them. She was there for them, however they might need her. They knew this and loved her for it.

Still, this did not keep them from knowing that everything else was some horrid mystery, some terrible unknown story in which they played some strange role as captives. And the role their parents played? This question could keep them awake at night and sour even the sweetest things Miss Brett did to please them.

———⟶●⟵———

When the men came for the children on Friday afternoon, Miss Brett had a big hamper of treats for them to take on the ride home.

"Home?" said Faye with disdain. "I've never been to the bloody place. In what way is it my home?"

"It will be," said Lucy. "Rosie is lovely. Not lovely like Miss Brett, but she makes delightful cakes and things and she clucks and—"

"Is she a chicken?" asked Noah.

Lucy giggled. "Sometimes," she said.

"I think it will be a very nice weekend. It will give you a chance to get away," said Miss Brett, not realizing the look of alarm she caused in her students. "You are here all week, trapped on this farm."

"And now we can be trapped in a house in Dayton," said Noah.

"You'll have a chance to get away, to take a well-deserved break from school—"

"I think I'd rather stay here with you, Miss Brett," said Wallace.

He looked so small today, Miss Brett thought. She knelt down and held his shoulders. "Let me tell you something, Mr. Wallace," she said. "You are going to enjoy the weekend. You will have fun and spend a little time relaxing, and on Sunday, a mere two days from now, you will be back here and you won't be able to get rid of me."

Lucy threw her arms around Miss Brett. "I'd never, ever, ever want to get rid of you, Miss Brett!" she said.

The driver of the first carriage to pull up was a very round man who wore what appeared to be black duck feet and a rubber suit that went all the way to his chin. His nose stuck out like some crazed duckbill, upon which sat very dark glasses. He had a rubber hat upon his head.

The second carriage was driven by a very small man with an enormous black hat. His black fuzzy slippers came up to his knees, becoming fuzzy boots. He had something like snakeskin leggings and a feathery vest over a furry-sleeved pullover.

The children separated to climb into both carriages, but the man in the fuzzy slippers stopped them.

"The duckman it is, then," said Noah.

Faye leaned up toward the duckman and said, in a soft voice full of venom, "Don't think we don't know, Mister Duckman. We've got your ticket and the game's almost up. We're not the simple mindless fools you think we are." She then climbed into the cabin. The duckman appeared not to have understood a word she'd said.

"It will be all right," Miss Brett whispered into Wallace's ear. He held her hand tightly.

Slowly, Wallace looked up at Miss Brett. She smiled back at him, nodding. He seemed to either relax or succumb to the inevitable, letting go of her hand and climbing into the cabin. Jasper handed the hamper up to Noah, who had climbed in while Faye was threatening the coachman.

Jasper turned to Miss Brett, to whom Lucy now clung.

"Come on, Lucy," Jasper said. To Miss Brett, he said, "Thank you."

When they were all in the carriage, they found it most comfortable to sit across the back of the extra-large, soft seat. With the first jerk of the reins and the movement of the carriage, Lucy climbed up and waved, and Miss Brett waved back, but every time Miss Brett was about to put her hand down, Lucy did not, so Miss Brett waved and waved and Lucy waved and waved and Miss Brett waved back until the carriage was out of sight.

———————

It wasn't long before they were hungry. They opened the hamper to find butter biscuits like they'd had that first day. There were jam tarts and cheese sandwiches and an icy cold bottle of juice for each of them. Lucy reached for a jam tart and gobbled it in a flash. She reached for a butter biscuit and a cheese sandwich and ate them together, one in each hand. Completely covered in cheese, jam, and crumbs, she received a napkin from a thoroughly disgusted Faye. Now tidied but thirsty, Lucy took about three sips of juice before Jasper caught the falling bottle.

"Be careful, Lucy," said Faye.

"Never mind. She's asleep," said Jasper. "She does this sometimes. She'll be starving and eat so fast it knocks her out."

"Takedown by strawberry tart," said Noah.

It wasn't long before there were five sleeping children in the back of a carriage driven by a black-billed duckman.

⟫◆⟪

"And there's the yellow carriage house!" Lucy announced. The others were in various states of stirring, except for Noah, who leaned heavily on Faye's shoulder.

Faye jerked away from Noah. "You had better not be drooling on me," she said.

Noah looked as if he didn't know where he was.

"See, there's the firehouse and the lovely park," said Lucy. "And look, we're passing the green grocer again, and there's that statue of the thing."

"What do you mean again?" asked Noah, rubbing the sleep from his eyes.

"Well, I've been awake for hours and hours," said Lucy, "and this is the third time we've passed that statue."

"You're wrong," said Faye, trying to orient herself to her surroundings.

"No she isn't," countered Jasper. "Lucy's almost never wrong. She can remember things."

"I know," said Faye, "but this time she's wrong. Why would we pass that statue more than once? There must be more than one of them."

"Not another one on the street where the little barbershop sits next to the lovely lady with the flowers. And we've passed the same bicycle shop twice."

Wallace pulled out the last butter biscuit. He divided it equally into five pieces and handed them out.

"Well, we sure seem to be mighty far from Sole Manner Farm. And it seems to be a long way from wherever we're going," Noah said, tossing the piece of biscuit into his mouth.

"Obviously," said Faye.

Even as they spoke, though, Faye could see that they were once again coming around the corner and passing the green grocer and the statue.

"The idiot must be lost." Faye reached forward to climb over the rear-facing seats and to knock on the driver's window, but Lucy clapped her hands.

"Look, we're almost there!" shouted Lucy. "There's the duck pond and—"

"Our coachman is headed home," said Noah.

"And here's Hickory," said Lucy, "and next will be Hawthorn and then—"

"Look," said Faye, "that's Hawthorn Street there! My mother spent her summers with her cousin Katharine around here somewhere."

"Your cousin? How lovely," said Lucy. "Perhaps we can visit her."

"Well, perhaps," Faye said, doubtfully, as the carriage turned again.

"Oak!" cried Wallace, and in a sudden panic, he rummaged in his pocket.

"What's wrong?" asked Noah.

"It's just this," Wallace said, struggling to pull from his pocket a folded piece of paper. He unfolded it, his hands almost shaking with excitement.

"What is it?" Faye asked.

"Now I understand," Wallace said quietly, as if speaking to the paper.

Faye took the paper from Wallace's hand. "'One Oak'? That's all it says?" she said.

"It's my street. Address. It's my house. Now I understand."

"Understand what?" asked Faye, handing him back the paper.

"I understand the note my father left me. He gave it to me as the carriage he was in pulled away, but he never explained what it meant. It was my only clue." Wallace looked again at the crumpled piece of paper. He read it and looked up.

He looked out the window as they passed a house, the only one on the block. And there was One Oak.

And there went One Oak.

"We've passed it, sir," Wallace said. But the duckman ignored them and immediately turned the corner onto Maple. There was precisely one house on this block as well—One Maple—and again the driver went around the block, making a right onto Chestnut and passing by its one house. One Chestnut.

"Our street is next," said Lucy, sitting on the edge of her seat. "I wonder if he'll stop there."

But he did not. Again he went around the corner, this time finally stopping at One Oak. As the duckman jumped from the carriage and threw down Wallace's satchel, a very tall, thin woman came out of the door of One Oak, waving her long arms. Wallace stayed in his seat. The woman came right up to the carriage, without a glance at the coachman.

"Wallace?" She looked around.

"I'm Wallace," Wallace said meekly.

"Well, you are, aren't you? Look at you. I bet you're starving. I'm your Daisy, and I'll be taking care of you while you're home for the weekend."

"Is my father here?" Wallace asked hopefully.

"Well, no," said Daisy. "Not yet."

"We told you about that 'not yet' bit," said Jasper quietly. "Don't hold your breath."

But Wallace stepped down and allowed Daisy to take his hand. With the other hand, she picked up his bag as if it weighed nothing, and Wallace followed her into the house.

For a moment, the others just stared. They had not been separated for a week.

"I miss Wallace," said Lucy.

"You can't miss him," said Faye. "He's been gone for all of thirty seconds." But Faye, too, watched the door to One Oak close as the coachman jerked the reins.

The coach turned right and right again.

"That's our house!" cried Jasper, pointing at One Elm, but the driver passed it. All these turns, Jasper decided, must have been some kind of security precaution. They were making sure no one was following.

The carriage drove around the block twice again, then stopped at One Maple. A plump, dark-haired woman with freckles all over her nose and cheeks came waddling down the walk to the carriage, all smiles and belly.

"Let me see my boy," she said in a gruff but jolly tone. "Noah?"

"I'm Noah," Noah said, raising a hand.

"Well, there you are. I'm Myrtle, and I'll be doing the feeding and watering around here, me laddie. Come on," she said as Noah climbed down. "Hmm, let's see if we can't fatten you up." With a brisk wave back, Noah followed her into the house at One Maple.

Faye, Jasper, and Lucy sat in silence as the carriage drove thrice around the block.

"I suppose we're neighbors, then," Jasper finally offered as Faye stared out of the window. *She looks so alone*, thought Jasper. *I hope she's let out before us so she doesn't have to be the last.*

But Jasper's wish was not granted. The carriage pulled up and stopped at One Elm, and there was Rosie, clucking and waddling down the path.

"Um, want me to wait with you? I mean, on the ride around the block?" Jasper said to Faye. "I mean, it's no bother, no bother at all. It's only just around the block. I can walk home in a jiff."

"No," said Faye, "it's just around the block as you say, and ..." She faltered as Jasper stepped down from the carriage.

He paused, waiting for what would follow the "and."

"Thanks," said Faye. "Thanks for asking, I ... I suppose."

"Anytime," Jasper said as he closed the door behind him. He could feel the flush rising in his cheeks. He could feel the warmth in his belly, and in his feet of all places.

"Come on, Jasper!" shouted Lucy. "We've got crumpets and

custard and blackberry jam."

Jasper followed the call of food and the clucking of Rosie into the house they called home.

———————

After they'd been filled with the most delicious treats, Wallace, Faye, and Noah discovered their homes for the first time. They each had a laboratory in their nursery. Faye had a drafting table and Wallace had burners and a large selection of chemicals for his experiments. To his immense pleasure, Noah found tools and gears and pistons to use in his own motor and engine experiments. He was less enthusiastic about the music room, complete with a music stand, sheet music, and rosin, all set up by the window.

Meanwhile, Jasper and Lucy wandered into their meadow—only now, they realized, the meadow was theirs to share with the others. Standing right in the center between all four houses, Jasper and Lucy concluded that it was still their private place—but private for all five of them.

"Will you look what the neighborhood dragged in?" shouted Noah from his back porch. As he ran down to meet Jasper and Lucy, Wallace emerged from his house as well. Soon, Faye had joined them.

"This is quite lovely," Faye said. "I suppose."

"Amazing," said Noah. "Did old crotchety grumbletrousers just say something was lovely?"

"Oh, shut up, you idiot boy," Faye said.

"Ah," said Noah, "that's the girl I know and loathe."

Faye gave him a rude hand gesture, but could not completely hide the smile on her face. Noah was very funny. And the meadow was, after all, quite lovely.

———⊷⊶———

That first weekend brought Faye an interesting mixture of comfort and concern. She was glad to have a room and a home of her own. She had her own laboratory and her own space, and she had her fellow scientists nearby. But she seemed haunted by fear for her parents.

Noah and Wallace understood Faye's concern, but unlike Faye, both boys were rather sure their fathers voluntarily went wherever it was they had gone. Like Jasper and Lucy, who had the note from their parents, they wanted to believe that all would soon be revealed.

Faye could not, or would not, bring herself to believe that her parents had left her of their own free will. This had never been done to her, and therefore had not been done to her this time. She was resolute in her conclusion that her parents had been kidnapped, and she had to rescue them.

Still, even Faye enjoyed the weekend in what the children, referring to the neighborhood street names, dubbed their "tree houses." They ran around the meadow during the day and explored each others' houses at night. Daisy taught them to play draughts, explaining that she was always the best when she was a child back in Ireland, and Camelia, Faye's nanny, taught them halma, which she said was much like a game called Hoppity that she, too, played as a child. Rosie taught them hopscotch, or Scotchhoppers.

"I'm quite fond of hopscotch," said Lucy on Saturday, tracing the court with a piece of chalk on the stone patio out back. "It's jolly fun."

"Well, it is fun," said Wallace, "and it is amusing. There's no logic required—simply skill at tossing and hopping. Daisy showed me yesterday."

"Well, sometimes cleverness doesn't help us have fun." Lucy handed Wallace a stone to toss and suggested he go first.

They even had an enormous picnic on Saturday afternoon, with Daisy, Myrtle, Camelia, and Rosie each bringing their specialties. There was a lot of laughing and playing and Lucy collecting wildflowers. With a coconut from Faye's house, the children and their nannies played a makeshift form of bowling, knocking over a line of sticks balanced against one another. They played until it got dark. Jasper smiled to himself more than once when he caught Faye laughing as she tossed her stone in hopscotch or when she won at draughts. He got that tingle when she smiled, like the first time he met her, before she told him he was an idiot. Her beauty shined through her smile.

<hr />

Their Sunday departure for Sole Manner Farm came more quickly than they had expected. Like Jasper and Lucy, Noah and Wallace felt they had homes of their own, and were no longer fearful of weekends away from Miss Brett. Faye had warm feelings, too, although she did not admit it. The weekend's easy fun helped dispel some of her fears and distrust. The nannies were so lovely and kind. The games were unforgettable, especially for Lucy.

With a hamper filled with onion tarts and caramel custards, Jasper and Lucy were the first in the carriage. The coachman wore an oddly square hat that seemed to come down below his chin so that his whole head looked like a living pillow, along with something like a black sheet over his entire body. He took their bags and tossed them in the trunk. Jasper and Lucy waved to Rosie until they turned the corner onto Chestnut, where Faye stood with a loaf of Camelia's cinnamon raisin bread. Noah was next, with a very big hamper filled with sandwiches and five small pecan pies.

When they pulled up to One Oak, Wallace was sitting next to Daisy on the porch swing. His head leaned on her arm, because he was not tall enough to reach her shoulder. Daisy gently caressed his head and pointed to the carriage. Wallace sat up and walked with Daisy, who kissed him on the forehead before he climbed aboard.

———

The next two weeks consisted of lessons with Miss Brett, weekends at the tree houses, and a series of impossible rescue ideas that seemed to grow ever more ridiculous.

"Tunneling?" said Noah after one suggestion. "Do I look like a gopher?"

"Disguised as what?" Jasper said about another idea.

"Maybe we can dress like giant black bunny rabbits," Noah said. "Then, at least, we'd blend right in."

"Are you trying to make this into some absurdity parade?"

Faye said. "Are you making fun of the fact that our parents are suffering somewhere without us?"

"We don't know anything of the sort," Jasper said. "Suffering? Where did that come from? You're just trying to make us feel bad for something that is just not likely so."

"Not likely so? We know we're being held captive by these men in black!" said Faye, who was growing livid.

"How do we know they aren't trying to protect us?" Jasper said.

"How do we know they aren't keeping us for ransom?" Faye responded. "How do we know we aren't victims of some horrid plot?"

"Faye, think about it," Noah said. "And for the hundredth time—"

"For the hundredth time, we don't know! We don't know that they are safe. We don't know that they are not suffering. We don't know anything."

"And we don't know that they haven't been turned into daffodils, either," said Noah.

The children felt less and less like following Faye into misery. Although it was true they wanted to know why they were surrounded by men in black and what was happening to their parents, they didn't feel as if they were in immediate danger. Besides, tunneling, wearing disguises, or simply dashing away in broad daylight all held with them the certainty of failure.

It was the third weekend, and the children sat among the detritus of their afternoon snacks on the way back to Sole Manner, sleepily emerging from naps. Had they been more awake, they would have noticed the countryside around them.

"I'm thirsty," said Lucy with a yawn.

"Why do we always fall asleep?" Jasper asked himself, trying to shake off the sleepiness.

"Look at these delicious treats, and the long, bumpy ride in the cozy, comfy carriage," said Noah. "How could we not fall asleep on the way back? There's just no escape from—"

"You're right," said Faye, sitting bolt upright, suddenly not sleepy at all.

"I'm what?" Noah said. "I'm right about what? You're scaring me, Faye. You never think I'm right."

But Faye leaned back and thought about her idea. Now wasn't the time to present it—not when they were all so happy to see Miss Brett again. It would have to wait until tomorrow.

———✦———

"That is absolutely crazy," Noah said.

They had been back at the school for two days, and Faye had asked for everyone to join her outside after lunch.

"Look," Faye said, "it was foolish to try to escape from here. I'll admit it. We're out in the middle of nowhere, and it would take us a month to walk to civilization. But if we sneak away from the houses, we can just run to the first big street we find and ask for a policeman. We'll be right in the city. We can get away. We can find our parents."

"The city is not a children's nursery, Faye," Jasper said. "We may find ourselves in worse danger than—"

"So that's it? You're afraid of a little risk? You're willing to have your cakes and custards in exchange for your captivity and that of your parents? Well, *I am not!*"

Faye walked away, leaving her classmates in stunned silence. She didn't speak a word to them for the rest of the day, and not a word at breakfast the next morning. It was hardest on Lucy, who shared a bed with her and most felt the coldness of rejection.

"We have to talk to her," Lucy said to Jasper and the others when Faye was out of earshot.

At lunch, Faye sat alone on the far side of the front garden while the others sat beneath the tree. Jasper went over to sit with her.

"Faye, listen, we all feel what you're feeling," he said.

"Clearly, that is not the case, Jasper," Faye responded coldly.

"We do, but we just … it just behaves differently inside us."

"Well, I want to be sure." Faye's voice cracked. She began to wrap her uneaten lunch in the kerchief. "I want to know. I don't want to wait to find out that something horrible has happened and I could have done something. I am not willing to sit here and do nothing at all." She stood up and ran back to the schoolhouse.

For the rest of the week, Faye was willing to talk more about it, though she kept quiet. Everyone felt they had let her down, and her dark feelings were contagious. The effect was just as she had hoped—as the days passed, the other children wondered if they were indeed being weak, letting their parents down by choosing the comfort of the cage over the risk of freedom.

After supper on Thursday, the children came to speak with Faye. They told her what she loved to hear—that she (and this was qualified by the fact that no one had absolute faith in this, but they all did entertain the possibility) was right. As a team, the children decided that something should indeed be done, and sitting here in comfort was not going to get them anywhere.

Friday morning's first incident, however, drove everything from their minds.

Not that the arrival of the odd fellows in black was anything new. What was new was that there were three dressed in beekeeper suits.

"A beehive?" Miss Brett was utterly surprised. She hadn't seen a beehive.

"Six. We must collect it," the tallest one said as he stood in the doorway to the farmhouse. He held three large buckets in his hand.

"There are six beehives here?" Miss Brett realized she had not even noticed one.

"It must be done," said the fattest, who held a small pail of coal and something in his hand that looked much like a can.

"We will give it here," said the shortest, who held a bellows in his hand.

"Children," Miss Brett said, seeing an excellent opportunity for a lesson, "these men are here to collect the honey from the hives at the edge of the green field. They're wearing beekeeper suits to protect themselves from the bees."

"Oh, I thought they were just wearing their normal silly, silly suits," said Lucy.

"Well, we read about how bees make honey and why," Miss Brett said.

"And I knew much about such things back in India," said

Faye, "although our hives were more elegant."

The others, however, had not learned about bees until Miss Brett read to them about their behavior in hives.

"The queen babies get the royal treatment," Lucy said. "They're the only babies who are given jelly and they get special cuddles and then, also, the honey comes from the pollen the little worker bees collect on their legs and fly all over and find good pollen flowers and blossoms and—"

"We jolly well know you remember, Lucy," Jasper said. "I think Miss Brett just wanted to let us know that we've got the real thing now."

"I don't want to be eaten alive by a swarm of bees, thank you very much," said Noah.

"They do not eat," said the fattest man.

"They will buzz," said the tallest man.

"Do not attack them," said the shortest man.

"Attack them? Lunacy. Madness," mumbled Faye.

"Actually, he's right to say this," said Miss Brett. "A bee will die when it stings."

With five very wary students following her, Miss Brett trailed the three beekeepers to the edge of the field of greens.

"I didn't think any of them would be beekeepers," Wallace quietly said as they lagged behind Miss Brett.

"I thought they were just keepers," said Noah.

"Well, yes," Wallace said, "I did think they were just guardians, here to—"

"Keep us captive, perhaps?" Faye said.

"Well, it is odd, isn't it?" said Jasper. "They do more than behave like coachmen or strongmen or captors."

"Are you saying you don't think they're preventing us from leaving?" said Faye. "Does anyone remember the motorcar keeping guard? The guards who patrol the perimeter of the farm at night to prevent our escape?"

Of course, they remembered. Even as they watched the men in black beekeeper suits retrieve the honey, they remembered.

"Oh, may we taste it?" asked Lucy, jumping up and down as the men finished.

"You may have two buckets," said the shortest man.

"We care," said the tallest.

"You what?" asked Jasper.

"For the bees," said the fattest man, as they all returned to the farmhouse. They left two buckets at the farmhouse door and walked back to the road where a black truck was waiting.

―――――――――

"Lucy, we are not being cruel to Miss Brett."

As the children packed their things for the weekend, Faye was not pleased. They had been through this three times already since lunch.

"Yes, we are too!" cried Lucy. "We're not telling, and not telling is pretending that there isn't something to tell when there really is, so we're lying, and lying is cruel, and I don't want to be cruel."

Faye was as worried about being heard as she was about Lucy backing out on the plan. She sat beside the little girl on the bed. Lucy's feet were miles above the floor, her fingers firmly planted in her mouth.

"This is the way it has to be," Faye said softly.

Lucy looked up, took her fingers from her mouth, and said, "It hurts. It's too heavy. It weighs like bricks all over me. I don't want to lie to Miss Brett." Lucy put her hand back into her mouth.

"Listen, Lucy," Faye said, speaking gently now, and taking the little girl's hand from her mouth as she had seen Jasper do so many times before, "this is not a lie. It's dangerous, and we don't want to put Miss Brett in danger. We want to make sure we can break free. Then we can come back and make sure she's safe as well. We must make sure she is safe, right?"

Lucy looked into Faye's eyes to see whether there was truth in them.

But Faye did believe this. This was not a lie.

It was then they heard Noah call, "They're here!"

———————

"Hello!" shouted Lucy to the driver as she climbed into the carriage. The driver wore great fluffy earmuffs over nearly half of either side of his head. "Do you know who invented the earmuff?" The driver did not answer or react in any way.

A loud caw, like the sound of a giant vulture, came from Noah's corner of the carriage. "Well, seems safe to me," Noah said. They all realized they could speak freely.

From there, the whole ride back to Dayton was one greatly animated conversation about the "rescue" plan. At that point, it was more of an escape plan, as they had no idea how they would rescue their parents once they were free. That was "step two," as Faye put it.

"Why don't we just leave, like we're going for an evening walk or something?" said Noah.

"Because they'll see us and bring us back. I think those buggers are everywhere, watching . . . waiting in the dark of night," said Faye.

"What about during the day?" Wallace suggested.

"We don't know if they have spies waiting for us," said Faye. "During the day, we are most vulnerable since we can be seen."

"But it might be worth a try," Noah said. "But only after one of Myrtle's fabulous roast beef and onion sandwiches. I need her lunch to give me the strength to attempt it."

"And that's another thing," Faye said. "Our nannies—"

"Not Rosie. She loves us," Lucy quickly countered.

"I'm not saying they aren't lovely ladies who care for us and want to feed us delicious things..."

"I'd agree there," Noah said, his stomach growling loudly.

"But they are employed by the same men who keep us captive. The nannies would never let us go, and they'd be after us as soon as we left."

The thought of spies everywhere gave Jasper chills, but it wasn't enough to break his resolve.

"I think—and this is for the best—that Lucy and I will excuse ourselves from this," said Jasper gingerly. "Our parents left us a note when we first arrived—they made it clear we must not bring attention to ourselves, and we must stay put. We're not going through with the plan."

Faye fumed. "Then you're a fool, Jasper Modest," she said, and she said no more.

After several minutes of the silent treatment, Jasper said, "And that's all you're going to say?"

"What can I say? If you choose to put your head in the sand, what am I to do about it?" Faye turned away again.

"But Mummy left us the note," Lucy said. "She said 'Remember Lewes Castle.' We didn't know exactly what that meant, but maybe it means we should trust people who don't seem very nice and don't get cross when we poke them in the bum."

"How do you know she wasn't forced to write it?" asked Faye.

"I don't know," said Jasper. "But it's all we have. We've not heard from anyone else. And it doesn't seem as if we know enough about all of this to go running around blindly searching."

"So you like being held captive?" Faye asked.

"What kind of a question is that? I want to be sure Lucy is safe. And our parents said—"

"You trust those lunatics in black?" Faye crossed her arms aggressively.

"We trust our parents," Jasper said, wishing his voice hadn't cracked as he said it.

"And Rosie doesn't dress in black," said Lucy, shaking her head. "Rosie is so kind and always makes the most lovely—"

"Of course she is," said Faye, pointedly. "They would select someone who is kind and comfortable and bakes you delicious puddings and sings to you and is like the granny you wish you had. All those things make you want to stay, don't they? They've set us up to think we're in loving hands. I can't believe I took so long to think of it."

"But you always think of it!" said Lucy. "You always think of naughty things people might do."

"I do not," insisted Faye. "I . . . I trust people." But she knew this was simply not true.

More softly, but with as much passion, Lucy said, "I trust Miss Brett and I trust Rosie."

"Rosie? The very one who lied to you about your parents?"

"She didn't lie," Jasper said. "She was forced to—I mean, they made her…she didn't—"

"See, you're admitting she was under their control," said Faye.

"But Rosie cares about us," said Lucy.

"Cares about you?" Faye said. "Cares about you? She doesn't care about you! She's been hired to act like she cares."

"We can't be sure of that," Jasper said. But not being sure was exactly the problem. Was he putting Lucy in more danger by being so trusting? His mother's letter seemed to say they should be more aware of who they trust. But what exactly did that mean?

Faye, he feared, made sense in some way that little else seemed to.

———⊷⊶———

Jasper had not been able to sleep, so when 11:45 p.m. came around, he was ready to go.

By the time they'd made their fourth trip around the block that afternoon, they'd decided to meet at midnight in the meadow and head to the nearest police station they could find. There, they would explain their situation and enlist someone to help them find their parents. Having lost his confidence that everything, however odd, was really all right, Jasper, and then Lucy, changed their minds and agreed to take part in the plan.

Jasper took a candle into his sister's room.

"Lucy, wake up," he said.

Lucy stirred, her eyes focusing on the candlelight until everything came back to her and she tried to sink back into her pillow.

"Lucy, they're waiting for us. We have to go through with it. It. . . it's the only way." Jasper swallowed hard "Come on, Luce."

Slowly, Lucy climbed out of bed. She was dressed, as Jasper had been when he got into bed that night. She slipped on her shoes and buckled them, wishing the whole time she didn't have to go.

As they tiptoed out of their room and down the hall, they could hear Rosie's clucking snores from the room on the other side of the nursery. They walked past their parents' room, which now sat perfectly tidy—all pretense at having parents sleeping there was gone. They tiptoed down the stairs and into the kitchen, then carefully opened the kitchen door and closed it behind them. Jasper looked back, thinking he might never see the inside of the house again. A lump stuck in his throat.

But then, he turned back to the task at hand.

By the time Jasper and Lucy arrived, everyone was already there. The moon was so full and bright they could see easily without flashlights.

"It's almost like daytime out here," said Lucy.

"Then keep low and keep quiet," said Faye. Everyone lowered themselves so they were more hidden in the shrubbery.

"Right, now," said Faye, determined and unshaken, "I suggest we sneak out between my house and yours, Jasper. That hedge there would be an excellent place to hide if any of the nannies wake before we make a run for it."

Like thieves in the night, the five children stole through the bushes, shrubs and tall trees to the hedge between Faye's and the Modests' houses. They waited for a few seconds. A carriage passed. From the outline of the outsized hat worn by the driver, they assumed it was one of the men in black, but it was hard to tell.

Then they heard someone walking along the sidewalk. They waited until the footsteps were no longer audible. After that, it was quiet.

It was time.

And then it wasn't. Just like the time before, on the farm, a motorcar came around the corner, driving slowly down the block. They all froze where they were, waiting for the car to pass.

"When it turns the corner," said Faye, "then we'll—"

"We know," Noah said. "We'll make a run for—"

A horse whinnied and Noah stopped mid-sentence. Following the motorcar was a horse carrying a dark figure. It was the black bird wings and feathery cap that gave the man away.

"It's one of them," Noah said, although they all knew.

Coming the other way around the block was another. Altogether, the children counted four horses, one carriage, two motorcars, and what looked like a clown on a unicycle. They knew then that they would never get out unseen.

Faye motioned and they all turned back toward the meadow, but then they stopped in their tracks. Rosie was running down the front path to the street.

"Jasper! Lucy!" she called. Her clucking was loud enough to hear from where they sat.

Lucy made a noise and hid her face in Jasper's chest. Jasper looked right at Faye and mouthed, "What do we do?" Faye motioned to stay still.

Rosie was now frantic.

"Children! Where are you?" she called, standing at the street and looking around. It was then that the feathery rider pulled up in front of the house.

"What missing?" he asked.

"The children, I . . . I . . ." Rosie blew her nose.

"Must keep them," he said. "No run away."

"Oh, my dear me." Rosie looked around, up and down the streets. "My darlings? I . . . I just don't know where they've gone. They've been through so much, the darlings and, oh, don't let anything happen to them! I love those sweet souls. Dear dear me. Dear dear me."

"If they start searching for us, they'll find the lot of us. Then we'll all be in trouble." Jasper was firm and clear, determination in his voice. "Stay here until we're done, and then head back to your houses—all of you."

Without a look behind him, Jasper grabbed Lucy and ran into the meadow, into the kitchen, and through the house. The others stayed in the shrub, anxious to see what would happen next.

Suddenly, Jasper and Lucy walked out the front door in their nightshirts, swaying just a bit as if stumbling out of sleep.

"Rosie?" Jasper called.

Rosie turned. "Oh, saints preserve me!" she cried, waddling quickly to embrace them. "Where were you? I went to tuck you in just around midnight and you were gone. Not in your beds. I . . . I got so worried, my darlings."

"Well, Lucy sometimes sleepwalks, and I went after her, and we both fell asleep in the . . . study."

"Oh, my babies," said Rosie. With her arms around them, she walked them back into the house. Turning very slightly, Jasper motioned to the others. As soon as the door closed behind Rosie and the Modests, Faye, Noah, and Wallace ran back to their houses.

———⋘•⋙———

The next morning after breakfast, Jasper and Lucy wandered out to the meadow. They could see Wallace through his kitchen window, and he could see them. He waved, and out he came moments later. The three of them walked over to Noah's, just as Faye came out her back door. They all sat on the grass in a circle, under the willow tree at the very center of the meadow. Lucy picked some wildflowers and put them in her apron pocket.

"Why are you always picking flowers, Lucy?" asked Wallace.

"I'm pressing them," she said, twirling another flower between her fingers.

"Where are you pressing them?" asked Jasper.

"Does that really matter right now?" asked Faye. "Last night was—"

"Horrid," said Lucy with a little shiver.

"I think we made a mistake," said Wallace. "I don't think our nannies are working to fool us. They care. They . . . they really do."

"Don't argue, Faye," Noah said.

"I agree," said Faye.

"You . . . you do?" Noah was taken aback.

"I agree. I agree that the nannies care about us. Camelia comes in at night when she thinks I'm asleep and ... and she kisses my forehead. She makes all my favorite foods and she sings to herself. It's ... it's sweet. It's kindness. I ... I realize that now."

"Rosie sings, too," said Lucy. "Old Irish songs we don't know."

"But I still say the men in black are evil," said Faye. "You heard that one last night. 'They cannot escape, must be captured.'"

"He didn't say that," Lucy said. "He said, 'Must keep them. No run away.'"

"That's the same thing, isn't it?"

"No, it isn't," Wallace said. "You can regard what he said as concern, and not the words of a prison guard."

"Well, you can't be sure, can you?" said Faye.

"I want to have a real afternoon," said Noah. "I want to bowl and play and not worry about what miserable crazy thing we may or may not be facing. I don't want to have to think that I can't trust anyone in the whole world. I want to be able to trust and believe that some folks are really okay. Can we just have a little break from being terrified? Can we just enjoy the beautiful afternoon? In the houses we call home right now, with the nannies who care for us, with the friends we are?"

Faye opened her mouth but found she couldn't say anything. *Friends?* Was it true?

"Want to look at an idea I have?" Noah finally said after a moment of awkward silence.

"For what?" asked Jasper.

"Well, I'd been toying with the idea of using a petrol mixture for combustion in this new engine. In theory, it can generate over ten horsepower."

"What about the pump problem you said you were having?" asked Wallace.

"Well, I'm not using a fuel pump with this design," said Noah, and that was enough to send them all to Noah's house to see what he was doing in his laboratory.

CHAPTER ELEVEN

SOMETHING RINGS A BELL FOR JASPER

OR

FAYE FLIES OFF THE HANDLE

That Saturday evening, all the children were served shepherd's pie for supper outside. Rosie smothered the top with butter so the potatoes she placed there were crisp. On the side were roasted parsnips with leek soup and bread she had made that morning.

Noah had gotten his wish for a real weekend, or at least a real Saturday. They spent some time looking through his engine designs, then discussed Faye's problem with her glider's loft, and they spent several hours playing in the meadow. Somehow, the games, the inventions, and the play felt more real, more authentic, than before. (Wallace was the winner at bowling.)

Later, Myrtle brought out a phonograph and Rosie put on a recording of some very festive Irish songs. The lot of them followed her lead and learned a few steps to the jigs she showed them. The four nannies seemed to know some jigs in common.

"Every true Celtic lass learns to jig," said Rosie, catching her breath from laughter and dance. By the end of supper, everyone was ready for bed.

"See you in the morning, then," Jasper said as they headed to their homes.

"See you in the morning, Jasper," said Faye, a smile touching the corners of her mouth.

Jasper again felt that hot flush in his cheeks. He turned and quickly headed home, Lucy racing to catch up.

As Jasper and Lucy lay in their beds that night, they listened to Rosie humming and clucking as she turned off the lights in the house and pattered to bed. Though Jasper was tired, he found sleep slow in coming. He thought about how much this day had changed the way he felt about their captivity. Faye was still furious at her parents, whether they were to blame or not, and Faye wanted them all to rise to her passion, to feel her fears and her anger. But Jasper felt calmer and more settled than he had in all the weeks he and Lucy had been in Ohio. Jasper took a deep breath and sighed as sleep finally came upon him.

And then it happened. It happened out of nowhere. Jasper sat up in his bed, his heart pounding. What was it? The ringing, the noise—and then he knew.

It was the bell. The bell he and Lucy had set weeks before when they wanted to know if their parents had come home. The bell was ringing!

Jasper looked at his watch. It was 3:07 in the morning and the bell was ringing. Fumbling, Jasper unhooked the wire. He sat there for a moment, his senses sharpening, the ringing still echoing in his ears.

He listened, straining to hear anything. He slipped out of bed and went to Lucy's room. She was sleeping. He decided not to wake her. Could it simply be Rosie in his parents' room? Might she have closed the door? At 3:07 in the morning? Jasper could hear Rosie's snores from the nursery and knew that she, too, was asleep.

Jasper tiptoed into the hall. He could definitely hear something, and it was coming from his parents' room. Quickly, he slipped back into the nursery and went to Lucy's room. Very carefully and quietly, he reached under her bed. First, he found the green book. Lucy had tied a ribbon around it. Reaching further back, he found what he had been looking for—the mirror contraption Lucy had created.

Taking it, Jasper tiptoed back down the hall and listened for a moment at the door. He then bent down and pushed the mirror into the space between the door and the floor. From there, he could see that there were two men in the room. One was the man with the top hat and velvet waistcoat. The other seemed to be wearing long black robes and a pointed cap. They spoke very softly in a mixture of English and something else.

Jasper could hear some words, but they made no sense. They sounded like "gurnal," "periklu," "romak," "gadim," and "verit," but the men were facing away from the door, so the sounds were indistinct. Still, Jasper heard bits and pieces that he could understand.

"Must make fear … capture …"

"Hunt down … keep hidden …"

"Truth … terror … kidnap …"

And then, as the top-hatted man moved aside, he saw that the men were looking into his mother's drawer—the drawer from which the green book had been taken.

Scrambling to his feet, Jasper pulled back the mirror and ran to his bed. Covering his head with his blanket, he tried to catch his breath. Were those men plotting something? With every thump of his pounding heart, Jasper felt less and less certain that everything was going to be all right. These men had said "kidnap" and "hunt down"—words undoubtedly meant for them. Or for their parents.

Jasper sat in terror, clutching the mirror, begging for the sun to come up faster than it was willing.

⟶❖⟵

"I'm telling you, I know what I saw and I know what I heard." Jasper could not keep the fear from his voice, but glancing at Lucy gave him strength. It was for her that he had to be strong. No one was going to hurt her.

It was Sunday afternoon, and the five children were on their way back to Miss Brett in a big, single, black motorcar. Jasper had waited until they were moving along to tell them—until the noise of the road kept their voices from the driver. Jasper filled them in on what he saw the night before, but also on what he and Lucy had seen the night the man in the velvet top hat had bounced on their parents' bed and found the book among their mother's nightclothes.

"Why didn't you tell me, Jasper?!" cried Lucy. "Why did you let me sleep through the danger?"

"It wasn't danger then," said Jasper. "It's just ... I think Faye's right. She's been right all along."

"Jasper, come on. This is not how you felt before," Noah said.

"Well, it is now."

"It's been almost a month and no one's been attacked or hurt," said Noah. "Are you sure Mistress Faye's fears aren't catching up to you?"

"What is this book you said the other fellow took out and kissed?" asked Faye.

"It's just an old shell of a book—an old book binding, actually," said Jasper. "It was used to press flowers, as far as we can tell."

"Maybe it belonged to a queen or a prince?" said Wallace.

"It would have if it had been in my mother's drawer," Noah said. "Now, if Faye can find something evil in that—"

"Noah, you are a fool in so many ways," Faye said. "Have you not noticed that we haven't heard from our parents at all? And hunted? Kidnapped? Doesn't that sound familiar? If our parents were really fine, why haven't they contacted us? They could have sent a letter."

Leaning forward, Lucy slid open the driver's window and shouted to the driver, "Why don't our parents write us?"

The driver turned around as Jasper pulled Lucy back and shut the window. "What are you doing?!" Jasper said gruffly, hiding his fear behind a scolding.

Lucy looked up into her brother's eyes. "I . . . I . . . you shouted at me."

"I didn't shout, Lucy, but I don't want them knowing we know something's amiss," said Jasper.

"But I always ask," Lucy said in her defense. "I keep asking where our parents are in case someone has an answer."

Jasper opened his mouth to argue, but felt the sting of truth in the power and innocent wisdom in Lucy's approach. Ask until someone has an answer. Jasper hugged Lucy.

"What do you suggest?" asked Faye, uncomfortable watching the embrace.

"I don't know, but we've got to think of a way to get to our parents," said Jasper. "We absolutely must."

They could see the orchard across the green field as they arrived at Sole Manner Farm.

"Promise me we'll work on a plan," said Jasper as the carriage came to a stop in front of the schoolhouse.

"Of course we will," said Faye. "I've been telling you all along that we've been prisoners. I'm the one who said it from the beginning."

Just then, a loud thump hit the carriage window. Lucy, her nose pushed against the glass, looked down and cried.

"Oh, sweet wee little thing!" she said, climbing out of the carriage. She bent down and scooped up a tiny little bird in her hands. The children climbed out of the carriage to see. It was ruffled and scruffy and very, very small.

Miss Brett came out of the schoolhouse door.

"Welcome home, my sweet angels," she said, beaming. "I have just put some—"

"Miss Brett, it's a baby!" cried Lucy, bringing the bird to Miss Brett.

Miss Brett took it from Lucy and they all went inside. Miss Brett brought the tiny thing over to her desk.

It was not a baby bird, but it was very young. Fortunately, it was not strong enough to have been going very fast. It didn't look terribly injured. It was mostly just stunned.

"That may have been his very first flight," Miss Brett said. "I think he will be all right."

"It could have broken its neck," Faye said. "It happens because they see a reflection of the outside and don't know they're flying into glass."

"Well, it doesn't look like anything is broken," said Miss Brett.

"Oh, can we keep him?" asked Lucy. "He can sleep with us, can't he, Faye?"

"I'm sorry, Lucy," Miss Brett said gently, "but he needs to be free. He's a wild creature and needs to be in the wild."

"But he doesn't look like he can fly," said Lucy.

"I think he's just a bit dazed," Miss Brett said. She looked at Lucy, who seemed so very determined to play nursemaid. "I do think he needs a little care, however. Lucy, why don't you make a soft bed for him—a place where he can rest and regain his strength?"

"I will, Miss Brett," said Lucy, "I will, I will." Turning to the bird, she said, "Don't worry, Samson. We'll take good care of you." Lucy ran around collecting soft cloth, making a little bed for the bird.

"Wonderful," said Miss Brett. "Then we'll put the little fellow in Lucy's hospital bed and let him rest. We'll open a window and place the bed in the frame. That way, as soon as he is able, he can take to the skies and escape."

Faye gasped.

"Are you all right, Faye?" asked Miss Brett.

"I...I...Yes, I'm quite all right, sorry, thank you." But Faye was clearly distracted, and the others watched her carefully.

"Oh, Samson will be fine. He jolly well will. I know it," said Lucy.

"Oh, um, yes, lovely," said Faye, grabbing Jasper's arm and pulling him aside as the others looked at the bird. "We've got to talk."

"Miss Brett is right, Faye," said Jasper, putting his hand on Faye's shoulder. "The bird will be fine, really. Don't—"

"I'm not worried about the bird, you idiot," growled Faye. "We've got to talk with the others."

———⇒●⇐———

"Barking mad," was all Noah had to say.

"I'm telling you, it's our only hope," Faye said as she and Noah turned the jump rope for Lucy. Miss Brett had become more and more insistent that the children take exercise. She was a firm believer in walks and play as an important part of keeping the person healthy. She had taught them about cricket and baseball and tennis. She had shown them how to play kings corners, which she had learned from her mother, and she'd shown them how to jump rope and play kick the can. But now, while Miss Bret prepared supper, Faye used the afternoon exercise to tell the others her idea.

"It's madness! We have no wings," said Noah. "Now, if we could tie a note to little Samson's toe—"

"Oh, shut up." Faye tossed the rope down and Lucy stopped jumping. Then the little girl picked up the shorter rope and jumped on her own, singing the elements of the periodic table.

"I think we need to listen to Faye," said Jasper, cautiously. "I know what I saw the other night and it was real. Those men are blackguards in every sense of the word."

"Fine," Noah said, sitting down and leaning against the tree. "What's the plan for our flight to the moon?"

"You can be such a dreadful bore, Noah," growled Faye. "Only you're a fool if you don't think we can do it."

"Do what, exactly?" asked Wallace.

"Rescue our parents by using our invention—the invention we've all been dreaming of, the invention we've all been working on, piece by piece. Now it has an immediate purpose."

She met a sea of faces whose expressions ranged from disbelief to total lack of comprehension.

"The aeroplane! The flying ship! My wings, Jasper's propeller, Lucy's tail... Noah's engine!"

"An aeroplane?" Noah laughed. "What makes you think we can build something that flies when generations of men before us haven't managed to do it? What makes you think that five children in the middle of America can do what has never been done anywhere before?"

"Because we are always doing what has never been done before," Faye said simply.

Noah put his hand to his chin to think for a moment. "Fair enough," he said. "I'm in."

"Oh, me ... too!" said Lucy, still jumping rope. "I've been ... thinking... about... the tail."

"Yes," said Jasper, "Lucy thought about it back when we were making the flying whirligigs. She said with a proper tail, we'd be able to fly forward and not just propel up."

Wallace looked down. He couldn't look them in the eyes. "I'm sorry, I ... It looks like I'm the one who hasn't given you anything."

"Well, you're a chemist, and we don't need a—"

"We need more than your chemical expertise, Wallace," Jasper said, throwing Faye a dangerous look. "You're the most organized and critical-minded. We'll *all* do it."

Suddenly, it felt real. Suddenly, it felt possible. Their invention could be both an achievement as incredible as any in history, and the most outrageous, and possibly the only workable, plan of rescue. Both goals seemed real and within their grasp.

"All right, colleagues," Noah said with a bow. "Let's get to it."

CHAPTER TWELVE

ALL PLANS UP IN THE AIR

OR

FAYE FINDS A SOFT SPOT

The glider Faye had was most aerodynamic, even before she combined forces with the other children to create a powered flight. Jasper's propeller work was stellar and better than anything Wallace had ever seen in that field. Even Lucy, six-year-old Lucy, had developed a tail design that rivaled that of the eagle.

Wallace, meanwhile, was spending more and more time alone at the classroom's chemistry table. One day, Jasper, who had been studying the problem of overheated engines and was sure of a cooling method that would work with very few adjustments to Noah's overall design, found Wallace there and asked for his advice.

"There are certainly excellent combinations of chemicals you could use," Wallace said, "but the simplest thing to do is to use water."

Jasper looked his classmate in the eyes. "You think that's the best idea? It's not just the best way to get back to your individual work?"

Wallace tried to hide his hurt. Jasper had been his confidante since the first day at Sole Manner, but the more the others worked on the flying machine, the more Wallace made himself into an outsider. He spent more hours on his polymer than ever before. At times, he found himself slipping so deep into his work, he could not even think of anything else. Only Jasper understood why— Jasper alone. But Jasper also never let him get too far away, always bringing Wallace back for advice or opinions.

Wallace removed his glasses, wiped nonexistent specks of dust from them, and replaced them on his nose.

"Water really is the best thing in this case, Jasper," he said calmly, looking up. "I'm not trying to get out of working on a coolant or trying to do anything except help when asked. I ... I know I'm not really a part of what you four are—"

"You jolly well are," Jasper countered. "There's loads of things we'd never have gotten right without your help."

"It's not the same as what you're doing," said Wallace. "No, don't deny it, Jasper, Please. I know. It's just that this polymer and ...I'm running out of time, and...well...

"I know, Wallace," Jasper said, placing a hand on Wallace's arm. "I know how important this is."

Wallace handed Jasper a sheet of paper on which he had drawn a diagram for the engine modification that allowed the water coolant system to work most efficiently. Jasper smiled. He knew Wallace was walking a fine line between two vital projects.

———⟶◆⟵———

The classroom was busier and quieter than usual as the children all focused on the work at hand. And there was something to the fact that they all were truly working as a team—even Wallace, Jasper reminded everyone. There was a proximity to their work that began to change the way they felt about one another. They had really begun to see themselves as a team.

As they used their free time in the classroom that week, it did not go unnoticed that Faye used the word "we" more often than ever before. Faye had shared all the research she had collected on her favorite figures in flight (or attempted flight), sketching the details of their own calculations (or miscalculations) for her fellow classmates.

"Imagine," Faye said. "Any day now, man will fly over the land."

"And you're going to be that man, Faye?" asked Noah with a grin.

"Balloons fly," said Lucy. "Hot air balloons have been around since the 1700s."

"Well, man will fly like a bird," Faye said.

"That Brazilian Frenchman, Alberto Santos-Dumont, has been flying around Paris," Noah said. "He can steer and guide his balloons. Some say he can fly like a—"

"Well, I mean, without hot air. Even Santos-Dumont admitted he may have solved the lighter-than-air problem, but not the heavier-than-air problem. I want to really fly."

"Leonardo da Vinci was working on this in the fifteenth century," Jasper said. While developing his propeller, he had loved reading about da Vinci's helicopter. "We're in good company if we fail."

"But he was trying to create a hanging and gliding type of craft, and a sort of whirly-bird contraption," said Faye, "not a motorized air vehicle. I already invented a better glider than that."

Faye had loads of information on the experiments of Sir George Cayley, William Henson and John Stringfellow, Otto Lilienthal, Octave Chanute, and Samuel Langley. She knew that Wallace, with his uncanny attention to detail, would be able to review the notes and the data from the would-be flyers and discover where they went wrong.

"Now, Cayley, Chanute, and Lilienthal were brilliant with their gliders," Faye said, "but Henson and Stringfellow had theories about using steam engines. I don't think they ever got off the ground, but they believed an engine would work. Samuel Langley—"

"He's the secretary of the Smithsonian Institution in Washington, D.C.," said Wallace. "I wanted to meet him, but Father and I had no time."

"Well, his unmanned aerodrome flew over four thousand feet," Faye said. "His engined craft flew for ninety seconds before the engine fell out."

"Well, that doesn't sound promising," said Jasper. "Let's not follow his lead."

"But it's proof that it can be done," said Faye. "Look at these sketches. I believe that the shape of the wings is one of the most important things to consider. They need to be cambered—"

"What?" said Wallace.

"Cambered. Curved like a bird's wing. Then the air currents will be able to lift the craft. Think about how the wind can carry things much heavier than air. The wind gets beneath the thing and it planes on the air. It would be an aeroplane. We have to make it so the wind will get beneath the wings and the motor will propel—"

"Wait," said Wallace. "Did you say propel?"

Faye nodded, a gleam in her eye. "I did indeed. Jasper has created the best darned propeller this world has ever seen." She looked at Jasper. He looked back and, as he held her gaze, a moment passed between them—a moment that passed so very quickly and silently that no one else even noticed. But Jasper would remember it in times to come. He had seen something there, and Faye had let him see it. In a subtle but profound way, that changed everything.

⟶⊷⊶⟵

Thursday night, after supper, Miss Brett began to read aloud the last chapter of *Alice's Adventures in Wonderland*. It had been ages since they had last heard the story—Miss Brett had put Alice aside some time back, holding off on the final chapter. It was something she had done in childhood, too. She had not wanted the story to come to an end.

All the children were on the edge of their seats, listening with every ounce of their bodies, looking forward to the conclusion. Miss Brett took her time, savoring the book, reading only small sections, leaving the children time to think.

"Remember," she said, "there is often much sense in the nonsense we find."

The sounds of sleeping children filled the house, and Miss Brett, sleepy herself, took her candle and, as she did every night, walked over to each child and placed a kiss upon each forehead.

"Goodnight, sweet angels," she said to Lucy and Faye, who,

sleepy as they were, were still slightly awake.

"I remember when Miss Brett first told us about Alice," Lucy whispered as Miss Brett's candlelight faded from the room. She squirmed with pleasure at the memory.

"You remember everything, Lucy," said Faye, feeling the weight of sleep bearing down upon her.

"Oh, I'd so love to have a friend who was mad," said Lucy.

"No, you wouldn't," Faye said. She was getting a bit grumpy. "And the story isn't real."

"Oh, come now, Faye," Lucy said, curling up right next to her. "You loved it as much as me."

Faye felt the warmth of Lucy's breath on her arm and the little girl's hand in her own, and she didn't know why this made her cry. But she was glad the lights were out so Lucy couldn't see her tears. Crying in silence until her mind began to work again, Faye thought to herself how much like Alice she felt. Falling down the rabbit hole could not have been loonier than her life was now.

Alice, when asked by the Caterpillar to explain herself, had said she couldn't because she wasn't herself anymore. This had struck home with Faye. She found she still cared so very much for the other children, who said they were her friends, though at times she had been terrible to them. And now, they were planning some crazy escape—by flying over the farm? With a new invention? In search of their parents? Who were kidnapped by men dressed like bunnies and ducks and ladies in bonnets? Could anyone believe such nonsense?

But, strange as it was, there was sense in the plan.

Faye softened. "So . . . right, well, yes," she whispered. "I did. And all the rhymes and poems and lullabies, too. Remember piggy toes?"

But Lucy was long asleep. Faye kissed Lucy's head and felt the heaviness of sleep come down.

CHAPTER THIRTEEN

TELEPHONIC REASONING

OR

WALLACE'S SPECIAL SECRET

After the kitchen was clean and everyone was asleep, Miss Brett relaxed in her rocking chair. The children certainly saw themselves in the stories she read them. They were, in so many ways, on some crazy adventure with nonsensical characters who offered no answer to the mysteries at hand.

And Miss Brett was not much different from them. She had always expected to live out her teaching years in a small, single-room schoolhouse somewhere out in the country, or perhaps at a small neighborhood school where she would teach many children, and then their children, and then theirs. She had expected to settle down in a small house or apartment with window boxes full of geraniums and at least three cats, to start. But she'd been intrigued when Mr. Bell had suggested she call at a downtown office about that "special opportunity." She could never have imagined just how "special" the situation actually was.

Miss Brett had said that, yes, she would be interested. Mr. Bell took her hand and held it tight, a subtle spark of excitement in his voice. She adored him, and she considered him, as much as anyone had ever been, her mentor.

"I think you are the one, my dear Astraea Brett," he had said in his odd accent. She had wondered at times if he was Welsh, but there was something of an eastern European roll to some of his words. At times, the accent almost seemed to come from Arabia.

Mr. Bell's wizened face had broken into a grin, and then he nodded, mumbling to himself. He had always been a bit unusual. Mr. Bell seemed to be age itself, crooked and shrunken, but energetic beyond compare, flitting around the campus of the teaching college, gliding down its halls. His black cloak and scarf, along with his almost silent movement, sometimes made him appear to be a giant bat as he rushed from classroom to classroom. Miss Brett thought he had an unusual grace, like a man who had once been a dancer. He always wore a black felt cap that seemed to have been made in the early part of the last century. It seemed to slip right down to the bridge of his nose, sitting upon his great black spectacles. In the years she knew him, she could not remember clearly whether or not she had ever actually seen his eyes, but she supposed she must have, at one time or another.

While Mr. Bell's ways were odd, and many of the other students found him queer, Miss Brett had had few champions in her life, and she knew in her heart that she had one in Mr. Bell. She believed in him as he believed in her. During her two years at the teaching college, they had become quite close. Miss Brett remembered telling him how she had lost her parents to pneumonia when she was fourteen and that she had been alone in the world since then. He had been so kind to her. And he had asked if she truly had no family—no family at all. He had showed such understanding, nodding and thoughtful, when she had answered, "Yes."

Miss Brett had unpacked her things that morning before the children came. In her sunny room was lovely floral wallpaper, a single medium-sized bed, a desk and bureau, and a big comfy chair covered in soft red velvet. If it were to rain, or if the chores were done early, she would invite all the children into her room and read to them from this chair. She quite liked the room—it was cheery, and she saw it as something of a sanctuary.

She thought about being there, and Mr. Bell, and why she was chosen. A shiver ran down her spine and she shook it off. Mr. Bell would never lead her into something he didn't feel she could handle.

She placed her handbag on the bed and walked down the hall to look around.

With the driver looking over her shoulder, she took a peek into every room. The two other bedrooms were set for the children. She found there was also a tiny room on the other side by the back door. That room contained only one thing: a telephone, which was, to Miss Brett's astonishment, an almost glowing shade of red—the only telephones she had previously seen were black. In fact, Miss Brett had only used a telephone three or four times in her life. She found them fascinating and very modern.

"The telephone is not for use," the muscular driver had told her. "If you pick it up, we will know."

"Well, I won't use it, then," she said. "I hadn't planned to, so I won't."

"Unless," the man said.

"Unless what?" she asked.

"Unless," the man repeated. He then walked out of the house, leaving Miss Brett to answer the question for herself.

Miss Brett closed the door to the telephone room and left it closed, turning the small key already in the lock. What "unless" would ever require a telephone call?

⋙●⋘

Now, sitting in the rocking chair, Miss Brett opened *Alice's Adventures in Wonderland* and began rereading the last chapter. As she read, she could hear rhythmic breathing coming from the bedrooms.

Poring over the last paragraph, when Alice's sister contemplates Alice's adventure and how she will one day grow up, her breath caught as she thought of these children who would also grow up one day. She closed the book. She smiled. Miss Brett knew that the children were asleep.

All, that is, but one. But that was expected.

"Miss Brett . . ." Wallace stood tentatively in the doorway to the boys' room.

"Of course, Wallace," she said gently. She patted her lap and opened her arms.

Wallace climbed up onto the chair, into her arms, and curled up onto her lap. She rocked the chair, humming softly and caressing his head until he was asleep.

It had been their special secret ever since his arrival. Wallace had been so fearful. He hated himself for needing to be held like a baby. He was desperate for the others not to know. He wanted to be strong and fearless and powerful like his dad, but he wasn't.

But Miss Brett understood. The little boy's feeling of loss had made him especially fragile. A warm lap and loving arms was something she could provide. He needed a mother's love.

Looking down at the sleeping boy in her lap, she thought of that baby bird Lucy had held in her hands. Miss Brett looked at this sweet, sad little boy, and she wanted, more than anything, enough time to add joy to the story of Wallace Banneker.

CHAPTER FOURTEEN

A Brain For Dr. Banneker

OR

WALLACE FINDS HIS FEET

Wallace Banneker knew about the past. He came from a long line of American inventors, scientists, and mathematicians. It was said that if past and present Bannekers stood in a line of their own, hand in hand, they would represent some of the world's greatest scientific minds in history. His parents would both have stood in that line. Both were been brilliant scientists, and both had exposed their young son to the magic of science from the day he was born.

Wallace's earliest memory was seeing a human brain in a vat. That was when he was three years old. The brain belonged to his great-great-great-grandfather, Benjamin Banneker I. Wallace's father, Ben Banneker IV, kept it on a shelf.

"That brain changed America," Dr. Banneker would say. "In fact, it changed the world."

Wallace knew all about his great-great-great-grandfather, the first famous Benjamin Banneker. He knew the man had been born in America, in Maryland, in November of the year 1731. He knew that Benjamin Banneker I's own grandfather had been a slave. That grandfather (Wallace's great-great-great-great-great grandfather) was named Banneka, and he had married Molly Welsh, a brilliant, brave, and beautiful European lady who freed him from slavery. Their daughter, Mary, was Benjamin's mother. Wallace knew, too, that Banneka had come originally from a tribe of astronomers in Africa before he was sold into slavery.

Like Wallace, Benjamin I didn't go to school. Instead, he was taught at home by Molly, or at the home of their Quaker neighbors. Wallace also knew something about the Quakers: They were believers in racial equality and abolition of slavery, and were pleased to help such a clever young man, no matter the color of his skin.

Wallace knew lots of stories about his great-great-great grandfather. He knew that everyone who ever met Benjamin Banneker believed the man to be brilliant. Wallace's favorite story was the one about the clock. When Benjamin Banneker was twenty-one, he took apart a neighbor's clock, drew sketches of all the parts, and put the clock back together perfectly. He then built a clock of his own out of wood, following the sketches of his neighbor's clock. This wooden clock worked perfectly, and it ran perfectly for more than fifty years. It probably ran longer than the neighbor's original.

Benjamin Banneker I did all sorts of amazing things, and so did every other Banneker descendant, all the way to Wallace. In fact, the line stretched back to before Benjamin I, to before Banneka and Molly, and into the distant past, when Wallace's ancestors, including great astronomers from the African tribe of Dogon and European scientists (in France, for example, with the *Société Scientifique*) originated some fabulous discoveries and inventions. The only thing Wallace knew about these, though, was that, if they really existed, they were so important they were all kept secret.

Wallace had heard bits and pieces about the secret inventions and magical creations. The stories supposedly went back to ancient lands and mystic leaders. They told of legendary mysteries, and the stories always seemed rather jumbled and confusing. When he was small, Wallace, wanting to document all of these bits and pieces, asked his father to tell him more, but his father didn't know, either.

Truthfully, Wallace found the mysterious magic and legends a tad mystical for his taste. He liked the tangible. Magic was not anything one could ever really do. It wasn't real—it had no order to it. For Wallace, it was so much less interesting than science, which one could do if one knew how. Wallace knew enough about the Bannekers, and he was proud to be a part of such a family. With documentation bestowed upon his great-great-great-grandfather, he was no longer compelled to dig any deeper into legends.

And that was just his father's side. On his mother's side, Wallace was the great-nephew of Lewis Latimer. Latimer was himself an inventor, among other things. He was most famous for being a master draftsman, and he was the person responsible for getting Alexander Graham Bell the patent for his telephone. If Lewis Latimer hadn't been such a fine draftsman, and hadn't worked so fast and hard to get the draft of the invention done, the patent would have gone to someone else who had also invented a telephone, and was applying for a patent that very same day. Wallace heard it had only been a matter of hours between the two inventors getting their patents into the office.

"You've got some shoes to fill, son," Wallace's father would say.

In fact, he said this a lot.

Wallace didn't have to try to fill someone else's shoes, though, because he had some pretty impressive shoes of his own. From an early age, he showed great talent for organic chemistry and molecular physics. It was lucky for Wallace that both of his parents could help him hone his skills. Until Wallace was six, his mother would stay home three days a week and teach her son all about geometry and algebra. The other two days a week, Wallace's dad stayed home and tutored him in chemistry and physics.

"We don't want to waste your mind in school," his father would say.

When Wallace was eight, he invented a device for measuring tiny particles. They contacted Uncle Lewis, who helped them draft a patent for the invention.

"Your mother would have been so proud," Wallace's father had said. He said this a lot, too.

Wallace's mother had died when Wallace was six years old. He missed her every single day afterward. He would close his eyes and he could hear her, smell her, feel her—her smile, her touch, the way she laughed. He thought about her every night before he fell asleep. He imagined her caressing his cheek and telling him she loved him. Sometimes it helped. Sometimes it just made him feel the empty space where his mother once stood. Wallace had always had a hard time falling asleep. At least, he had had a hard time since he was six years old.

After Wallace's mother died, Wallace's father did not come out of his bedroom for three weeks. Then, one morning, he stepped out and began his new life without his wife. He changed his schedule so he could tutor Wallace in everything—everything important, that is. Benjamin Banneker IV believed that science and math were important. He would stay home every morning and teach Wallace until noon. They would usually have lunch together, and then do some stretches or races or some kind of exercise.

"The body is the home of the brain," Dr. Banneker would say as he performed these exercises with ease and grace. He had always been a tall, strapping man, broad-shouldered and well-chiseled. Wallace, who had always been a bit pudgy and awkward, hoped that he would grow to be like his father. So far, the exercises had not made him strong or strapping.

After lessons and exercise, Wallace's father would go off to his lab, leaving Wallace to his own devices. It was on his own time that Wallace had created his minute particle-measuring invention. It was because of this invention that he was invited to travel with his father from their home on Long Island, New York to Washington, D.C. to meet President McKinley.

"You are surely the youngest boy in history to get a patent," Wallace's father had said.

The trip to Washington, D.C. was the only time Wallace had ever gone on a trip with his dad. At least, it was their only trip before setting off for Dayton. When they got to Dayton, Wallace's father had simply abandoned him on the side of the road. On the trip to Washington, D.C., Wallace had been left sitting on benches outside of closed doors. He had been hoping to have some fun on that trip. He didn't have much fun at all. Wallace had wanted to go to museums and walk around the National Mall, but they were only able to stay in the capital city for one day after meeting the president. And Wallace's father spent most of the time talking to scientists and politicians, but not to Wallace. Wallace spent most of his time waiting and thinking. It made him feel even lonelier. At least at home, he had his own room, his lab, and his greenhouse. Here, he just sat on a bench while his father busied himself doing other things.

Mostly, it gave him time to sit alone and miss his mother. He knew his father believed in him, but not the same as the way his mother believed in him. Wallace's father never held Wallace in his arms and told him how special he was.

"By your tenth birthday, you will create something that will save the world," Wallace's mother had told him when Wallace felt he could never live up to his legendary ancestors, and especially his father, who had been offered a place at Oxford when he was only fifteen. "You are your own man, Wallace. You are your own Banneker." And Wallace promised not to disappoint her.

Wallace thought about that as he sat alone in Washington. He kept his hand in his pocket and held his lucky coin so tightly in his hand, it left a mark in his palm. His mother had given him that coin. She told him that if he always keep it near, it would always bring him good fortune.

"It's very, very old, sweetums," she said. "For generations, it has been in the hands of an inventor—an inventor from your own family." He had looked at it for hours before placing it deep in his pocket. It was old, for sure, and it had a good weight to it. But it was unlike any coin he had ever seen. It felt good in his hand. The best part was that whenever he put his hand in that pocket, there it had been—for him, for his mother, and for all those who came before them. It was like carrying a little piece of her, a piece of her he could touch, in his pocket, always.

It was Wallace's mother who had named him Wallace, instead of naming him Benjamin Banneker V, which is what was expected.

"We've had enough Benjamin Bannekers," Wallace had heard his mother say in defense, time and again. "Let there now be a Wallace Banneker, the first." She had never told Wallace he had any shoes to fill but his own.

Though Wallace's mother had been a very busy person, too, she'd never been too busy for Wallace. She had meetings and laboratory work and late nights at her desk, but she would come home every night and climb into Wallace's bed and cuddle close, caress his cheek, and rub his head with the bottom of her chin. The thought of it made him feel warm inside.

Sometimes, Wallace's mother would scoop him up in her arms and sit with him in the rocking chair, telling him about her day and listening to him about his. Wallace tried to remember, and thought she might have sung to him, too, but he wasn't sure. Thinking about it had been keeping him up nights, angry with himself for forgetting.

Wallace's mother would never leave the house in the morning without getting a kiss from Wallace, even if she was just going out to collect the morning paper. When she left for work at the laboratory, she made it clear how important those kisses were.

"It's hard for me to go an hour without a kiss from my number one boy," she would say. "Can you imagine? Me going through an entire day without one? I just would not survive."

Wallace would give her the biggest kiss he could muster to get her through what was usually a very long day. She would close her eyes and soak it in.

Wallace knew now that his kisses—even his biggest kiss—had not been big enough. Wallace had never heard of brain fever before. He knew all about it now.

Miss Brett knew some of Wallace's story. She never asked him to tell her things, but she was always there to listen. He had told her about his lucky coin.

"I always kept it in my pocket," Wallace had told Miss Brett. "But Father said he needed the luck and took it while we were on the train to Dayton. He never said why. He just took it." And then Wallace's father had just driven away, leaving the little boy standing there, alone, at the door of a hotel, with nothing but a paper that said "One Oak" and no explanation as to what that meant.

Miss Brett could hear the pain in Wallace's voice and see the confusion and hurt in his eyes when he told her about that day. She could imagine the little boy, standing there in a cloud of dust, the piece of paper in his hand, watching his father leave. She could imagine that little boy feeling utterly alone as the carriage disappeared.

As Wallace followed the doorman to Room 258, his hand had gone instinctively to his empty pocket.

That night, alone in the hotel, Wallace didn't go down to supper. Instead, he lay in bed, wondering what life had thrown at him. He had never been totally alone before, although there were times when he felt he was. He had taken off his glasses and closed his eyes. He imagined his mother tickling his head with her chin. It was hours of lying there, fighting tears, fighting fear, fighting to understand the reason he was alone in a strange city with no one to tell him why. He had tried rocking himself to sleep. He rolled himself into a ball and tried to imagine being held by someone. He tried, but failed.

In the morning, he realized he had actually fallen asleep at some point in the night. For a moment, he forgot where he was and why he was lying, fully dressed, on a strange bed in a strange room. But quickly, the lack of understanding flooded back, and he lay there for a long while, staring at the tall arched ceiling. There were carvings of little angels and something that, at first, Wallace thought was a moose. He reached for his glasses. The moose turned out to be a unicorn.

Wallace had told Miss Brett about much of this on that first night. He had also told her how his mother used to rock him to sleep every night, no matter what else was going on. After his mother had died, Wallace had found sleeping the hardest thing to do. He would climb into bed with his father, but it was not the same. And Wallace could never imagine asking his father to rock him. That kind of weakness would never have been tolerated.

Miss Brett thought about the little boy alone in the hotel. She thought about the little boy, scared and lonely, lying awake in his bed, afraid to tell his father he couldn't sleep. The poor little boy, Miss Brett thought to herself as she rocked him to sleep. Poor, sweet little boy. At least she could give him this.

CHAPTER FIFTEEN

THE GREEN BOOK SHARES A SECRET

OR

LUCY'S FLOWERS

"The thing I still don't understand is what those devils were doing in your mother's nightdress drawer," said Faye. Miss Brett was in the kitchen making supper and all the children were in Faye and Lucy's room, discussing the same thing they always discussed—until Faye brought up something new.

Three weeks had passed since deciding to pursue their flying machine as both a fabulous invention and the means to rescue their parents. Every day, they worked and worked, and they came close to finishing several times, but there was always something not quite right.

And there were a few moments when things were very wrong indeed. As they tested the speed of Jasper's propeller, they accidentally launched a cornhusk they were using to balance it, creating a rocket that shot through the orchard into a grazing pasture—they could hear the angry retorts of a sheep in the distance. They then sent a propeller over the trees and startled a passing birdwatcher, who most likely thought it was some kind of never-before-seen bird. Wallace had to be revived after his nose got a bit too close to the diethyl ether he was using to power up the engine. (Luckily, Miss Brett had been making supper at the time.)

Through the weeks, they fell victims to some of the same pitfalls that had prevented would-be flyers from getting off the ground for centuries. The thing just wouldn't fly.

But in some ways, they were getting closer. With Noah's engine adjustments, Faye's change in wing angle, Jasper's propeller enlargements, and Lucy's tail designs, they were getting closer every day.

All the while, Wallace felt heavy guilt because he was mostly working toward perfecting his polymer. He avoided Faye's glare, but he felt it. And his guilt was not only about his contributions to the aeroplane. It was double guilt.

He knew he had helped—some. His suggestions had made the engine powerful and efficient, even though the original idea to use diethyl ether was Jasper's. But more than anything, Wallace knew he had a promise to keep, and he was not sure he'd be able to do it. He could not help feel the importance of what he was doing on his own, and balance that against the importance of what his classmates were doing.

And Wallace knew he was not in the only one who felt his absence.

"Where's Wallace?" Faye asked when they were trying to move the cockseat, which was attached to the engine, from the wooden gardening table to a more stable workspace. They could have used the extra hands and, because he was near an open window, Wallace had heard her ask. But he couldn't put down his burette at that moment.

"He's never around when we need him, is he?" Faye had groaned in frustration.

Wallace had flinched from the comment, dropping the beaker and wasting the fluid inside. He could have gone to help them then, he thought, because he had failed to finish this stage of his experiment. It had only made him feel worse when Faye walked by and saw him there, burette still poised in the air. She looked at him, daggers in her eyes, then shook her head and walked away.

The children kept their notes and drawings in Lucy's desk, all proof of their singular focus. Though they felt they might very well be headed for a successful mission, they spoke very little about how they would escape from the farm, and what they would do once they did. Where would they go? How would they find their parents?

"We are surrounded," said Noah. "Whether by love or greed or nefarious men wearing bear suits, we are certainly surrounded."

"I can't help but think there's more to this than simply keeping us from harm," Jasper said. "We've been invaded, not just surrounded. Those men were in my mother's room, in her things."

That's when Faye asked the question. "I just don't understand it," she continued. "What was that book, when it was a book? Why do they want it? Why is it important?"

Jasper jolted up from the girls' bed where he had been lazily reclining. Was he a fool? An idiot? A dimwit? Had he never questioned what the men were doing or why that green book was important?

"Lucy, where is that book?" he asked.

"It's pressing my flowers," she said without concern.

"Where is it pressing your flowers?" Jasper asked.

"Why?" asked Lucy.

"We want to see it," said Wallace. He, too, was at full attention.

"Why?" asked Lucy, concern rising. The book was hers now, she felt. It was her flower-pressing book.

"Because it might have something to do with all of this," Faye said, trying to keep her anger in check. Did they have the answer in their possession? Did they actually have a clue that they'd ignored? Had Jasper been so stupid as not to have looked at the thing?

"We looked at it," Jasper said to Faye's silent accusation. "It was just an old green leather book with no pages." But he felt something nagging at him. Had he really looked at it?

"We did not *all* look at it, Jasper," Faye said. "You told us about it. I want to see it for myself."

"It's my flower book!" Lucy said.

"Get it, Lucy," demanded Faye, crossly. "Get it now."

"Don't shout at her," Jasper said, rising to his feet as he turned to Lucy. "But it would be good if we could see it, Luce."

"But I want it back," she said.

Faye rolled her eyes. "It isn't yours, Lucy."

"Yes, you can have it back," Jasper said, throwing an angry look at Faye. It was none of her business, and the book certainly wasn't hers to command.

"Well, if that's a promise, then I'll let you see it." Lucy reached under the bed and pulled out her weekend satchel. She opened it and took out the green book. It was tied with a ribbon, as it had been when Jasper had seen it under her bed at the house. She held it close to her chest.

"Give it over," growled Faye, which only made Lucy cling to it all the tighter.

"Lucy, I promise," said Jasper. "No matter what, you will be in charge of it."

Faye shook her head, "You can't—"

"I promise, Lucy. I am your brother and I've never lied to you or broken a promise."

Lucy looked at Faye and, almost imperceptibly, stuck out just the very tiniest bit of her tongue in Faye's general direction. But Faye, focused on the green book, did not see this. Lucy handed the book to Jasper.

"It doesn't have any pages," said Lucy, now swinging her legs off the bed, "except the one and that's the one everyone has always been using to press flowers."

"What do you mean, Lucy?" asked Wallace, who, like the others, leaned over the book Jasper was trying to open.

"Careful!" shouted Lucy. "All of our flowers are going to fall."

But Jasper found it hard to open. The covers were stuck together.

"What did you put in here?" asked Jasper.

"Just flowers, like everyone else. Except I did put that clover I found by the beehives. It was a bit sticky."

"Who is everyone, Lucy?" asked Noah. "Do you have a bunch of imaginary friends?"

"No," Lucy said, "everyone who had the book before. There were loads of pressed flowers and broken petals and bits and pieces of flowers from long ago."

"I can't get it open." Jasper had been trying to gently pry open the leather covers, but that only made a few old and brittle petals fall out of the book.

Faye picked up a few. "Well, these are flower petals, and they are old." She rubbed a few petals between her fingers. "But these other ones are pages, linen pages, from a book. This was once a book of some kind."

"Don't break them," whined Lucy. "They might have been in there for a hundred years."

"She's right," said Wallace, sniffing the petals and bits of linen pages Faye had dropped onto the bed.

"Oh, give the thing to me, will you?" said Faye, grabbing the book out of Jasper's hands and pulling the leather covers apart.

There was a collective gasp as a shower of pressed flowers fell upon the children.

"You've broken it!" cried Lucy, grabbing the book back from Faye.

"No I haven't," Faye said, taking it back from Lucy. "I just got the thing apart."

But Lucy pointed to the single linen page upon which she, and what seemed like generations before her, had pressed flowers. There were impressions of flowers, and stains from flowers, and bits of flowers all over the page. However, the corner of the page had been pulled away from the inside of the leather cover where it had been stuck. It was just the corner, but it was enough to see that there was writing under there.

"Be careful," Jasper said, taking it gently from Faye's hands. He began pulling the page slowly and carefully away from the cover, so it would not tear.

Flakes of yellowed paper caught in the leather straps looped through the spine of the binding. The cover was blank, except for some slight indentations.

"It looks like it might once have said something—yes, it did. And from all of the flakes here, this book clearly had pages once," said Wallace, running his finger along the inside of the spine.

"Look at this," Jasper said, his voice hushed as he pointed to the words on the page that had stuck to the cover. He turned it over and placed it face-up on the green book so all could look.

On it was a written list of dates and names, handwritten in various inks, spanning many years.

The earliest dates were almost totally illegible, with the exception of "Breda, November, 1618," and a few other partial entries that seemed to go back to the mid-sixteenth century. But dates such as "Muktsar, Spring, 1705," "Edinburgh, Late Autumn, 1738," "Amsterdam, Mid-Summer, 1740," and "Vienna, Early Spring (but too late), 1827" were clear to the eye. There was an entry for "Naples, Spring, 1872," although the ink was slightly smudged. The date was not obscured, but the word "spring" was hard to make out.

"That's the year Mt. Vesuvius erupted," said Lucy.

"My mother has been to Naples," said Noah, "once about two years ago, and once when she was a girl."

"My mum, too," Jasper said, "when she was a schoolgirl. I think even my dad went when he was small."

"What was it doing in the nightdress drawer?" asked Wallace, caressing the smooth leather. "It's ancient."

"When did you take it?" asked Faye.

Lucy blushed slightly. "After the man was jumping on the bed and stole into Mummy's night things, I went and took it and put it under my pillow so it would be safe. Then I saw all the flowers everyone had been pressing and I started pressing flowers, too."

"It must have been there when we arrived," said Jasper. "And it must be Mummy's, even though we'd never seen it before."

"What does that say on the front?" asked Noah. "There are words, or there *were* words."

"I know what to do," said Wallace.

———⟫●⟪———

Wallace handled the book as if it were a treasure. Careful not to place it near anything that might harm it, he brought it over to the classroom's laboratory table.

"Are you using chemicals on it?" asked Lucy, fearfully.

"No," he said, "only some ash, and not on the leather itself."

He placed a very thin piece of tissue on the cover of the book. Then, most carefully, he rubbed the ash on the tissue, and used a stick ruler to rub evenly. Words came out as if written by ghosts from the past. Just four words. "The Young Inventors Guild."

"What does that mean?" asked Noah.

"Who were they?" asked Lucy. "All I know is one thing they did."

"What's that?" asked Wallace.

"They pressed flowers," said Lucy. "Whatever else they did, they pressed flowers."

"My guess is they invented things," said Noah.

"But who *were* they?" Faye asked, running her finger across the cover.

"*When* were they?" asked Noah.

"Well, it's ours now," said Faye. "Whoever the Young Inventors

Guild was, we have their book and it's ours." Faye looked at it again. "It is awfully strange, isn't it?"

"What?" asked Jasper, still looking at the book.

"Well, here we are," Faye said, "and we're inventors, and whoever they were, these people considered themselves inventors. I wonder just how young they were. As young as us?"

"And you know what?" asked Lucy, jumping from her perch on the table, scurrying to her desk, and pulling out all of their notes on the flying machine. "Now *we're* the Young Inventors Guild."

The children were silent for a moment, reflecting on the book that lay in their hands and the inventions that lay in their brains. Who was this Young Inventors Guild? Why was the book hidden in the nightie drawer? Why did the Modest family have it anyway?

"But what does this have to do with our parents?" Noah asked.

"Well, it might not have...I don't know," said Jasper, staring at the book.

Faye took the old page with the list of places. "Naples, 1872. Your mum was there, Jasper? When she was a girl?"

"My mother, too," said Noah. "She was there around then."

"Yes, but your mother is an opera singer, not a scientist or an inventor. Jasper, your mum was there when she was young?"

"I think she was, but I don't know the year," said Jasper. "Do you, Lucy?"

"She never told us," said Lucy.

"What about you?" asked Jasper, looking from Faye to Wallace. "Were your parents ever in Naples when they were young?"

"I don't know ... I don't think so," Wallace said. "Maybe."

Suddenly, they all felt very far from their parents—as if they didn't know them very well at all.

———

That night, when Miss Brett returned from checking on the cow, which had a mouth infection from trying to eat the bottom of something that looked like a rocket, she chose to read to the children from a new book by a woman who had been a friend of her mother in England, where her mother lived until she was nineteen.

"Edith Nesbit and my mother went to school together as girls, in Kent. Ms. Nesbit moved around quite a bit when she was young, but the two of them kept in touch until Ms. Nesbit moved back to London. But then my mother moved to America, and after a while, they lost touch. This book by Edith Nesbit was published last year, and I was so thrilled to find it. It's called *Five Children and It*. Somehow, I thought you might enjoy it."

"Because it's about five children?" asked Lucy.

"Well, yes, but it's not just about five children. It's about five children who are made to leave the city and live out in the country, where they discover the most incredible thing."

"But they're away from their mummy and daddy?" asked Lucy.

"Yes, dear, they are," Miss Brett said gently.

The children let the rest of the world fall away as Miss Brett read them the book's first chapter.

When the children were all quiet, Miss Brett closed the

book and blew out the candle. But the children were not asleep. The story made them think about how far away they really were from their parents. They might as well be on another planet or in another century. And what did they even know about the people they loved most?

Out of habit, Faye reached for her necklace, Jasper and Lucy for their bracelets, and Wallace for his lucky coin in his empty pocket. Noah thought of Ralph.

Tokens of comfort, all out of reach.

CHAPTER SIXTEEN

Lucy Tells A Tail

OR

 PIECES BEGIN TO FALL

The children were up before Miss Brett the next morning. This had been happening more often than not recently, as sleep was elusive, coming late and leaving early. All their dreams were peppered with failed flights, fallen birds, and wayward rockets, and the children often woke one another with new and exciting ideas. The boys bounced ideas around their room until well after midnight, and even little Lucy was prone to waking Faye, talking in her twilight sleep about tails and wings.

"Faye? Do you think we need an extra thingie on the wing?" she'd say—or "Faye, your canard elevators might need to be adjusted." Faye would groan into awareness as Lucy would drift back to sleep.

Lucy and Wallace were the perfect team for keeping the designs, blueprints, equations, and drawings in order. Wallace had the best handwriting and was the most focused on organization, while Lucy was so clever with sketching, her drawings could be used as actual blueprints. As promised, Lucy was the keeper of the Young Inventors Guild journal, which is where they now kept everything. She slept with it under her pillow, in order to protect it from any more of those men in black, and she kept it tied tightly with a ribbon to maintain her fragile flowers.

"If Lucy's memory is perfect," Wallace had asked at one point, "why are we keeping everything in the book? Writing things down might be dangerous."

Faye rolled her eyes. "Yes, she can remember everything, Wallace," she said, "but she's six, and her explanations are not always, well, explanatory."

Faye was right. No matter how brilliant Lucy was, the explanations she had to offer could sometimes be a bit cumbersome. Wallace, on the other hand, had a knack for precision. He kept beautiful notes. Everything was clear and precise, and it made progress easy, because they could detect miscalculations and adjust with each attempt. The green book of the Young Inventors Guild was now a real book.

"I don't know if Wallace should get to keep the notes," Faye had said to Jasper.

"Why on earth not?" he asked.

"Because he never is around when we need him," she said, a frightening amount of sincerity in her voice.

Jasper wanted to argue, but he couldn't. With a look, they both seemed to agree to leave things be and let it remain a silent truth between them.

They still had much to overcome—like the fact that, to hold an engine as heavy as Noah's, Faye would have to design her wings to span two hundred feet. But in order for Faye's wings to be moved by Jasper's propeller, they would have to be no longer than six feet each. And Lucy's tail, on paper—actually, made of paper—worked to balance the wings, but the flight pattern was erratic and the wings flip-flopped through the air. They had run out of material from the classroom, so they used the old tractor, the siding for the old barn, and the tin roof for parts.

But today, as the children sat under the willow, snacking on the first apples of the season and looking at the birdwatcher as he untangled himself from his binoculars, Wallace thought that a truly good birdwatcher could not be so clumsy. A good birdwatcher needed to become a part of the tree—invisible, so the birds would not be frightened away.

Wallace suddenly felt as if he was not a part of the tree. Only he had done nothing to contribute to the aeroplane.

"I know what you say, Jasper, and it is kind, but the truth is I'm mostly a chemist," he said, biting into an apple. The apples were definitely not ripe yet—they were small and tart and hard as a rock. "My work doesn't include wings and tails."

"Wallace, you're doing something very important," said Jasper, who had noticed how downcast Wallace sounded. "Besides, you *have* helped. It was you who pointed out the adjustments that got more than five horsepower out of that last engine."

"But that was only after Noah said there needed to be an adjustment. I simply suggested that—"

"It was you who pointed out that a weight balance needed to be attained in the space between the glider wings."

"Only because Faye knew there was a ratio issue and asked me to calculate her estimation." Wallace looked pleadingly into Jasper's eyes.

"Well, it was you who found 'The Young Inventors Guild' written on the cover of the journal." Jasper put his hand on Wallace's shoulder.

"Jasper, it was only because I opened it."

"But we might never have—"

"You know that isn't true," said Wallace. "I've done nothing vital. You have your propeller and—"

"And without you, I'd never have considered the angle-shift improvements you suggested."

"That isn't true. You know that. And Faye has the wings and Lucy has the tail and Noah has the engine."

"But Wallace—"

"Is Wallace feeling insignificant?" Faye said, walking over.

Jasper shot her a look that she understood. "Jasper's right, Wallace. You have been helpful. Truly. Every step of the way," said Faye, looking back to Jasper as if to prove she understood what was needed. She did not, however, totally believe what she said. What could be more important than the wings? And what a waste of time Wallace's little experiment was. Faye resented Wallace, but the wilting look Jasper gave her kept her quiet.

"Look at that bird!" she said suddenly, pointing to a bright red bird perched on the fence at the edge of the field.

"It's a cardinal," said Wallace. "They're not so uncommon."

"Well, the birdwatcher seems excited about this one," said Faye. "That's probably why he's come back again."

"Maybe there's a nest around here somewhere," said Lucy.

"Maybe," said Faye, absentmindedly.

"Samson has a nest," said Lucy.

"I said I—what?" Faye said.

"Our little bird. I can hear him tweeting," said Lucy, who proceeded to tweet. "See? He answers me."

"You're mad, Lucy Modest," Faye said. "You really are."

"Well, when he flew out of my hand—"

"Flew out of your hand?" Noah's ears perked up. "When was he in your hand?"

"Oh, I visit him sometimes," said Lucy. "When you're all arguing about the aeroplane and being silly, I go and visit Samson. I call him down and he comes. He's thinking of starting a family."

"He's what?" Faye looked at the little girl. "You are barking, howling mad."

"Anyway," Lucy continued, dignified and upright, "Samson is able to use his tail to cut the air when he takes off and lands. Maybe we can make the tail less flat, as I had it, and more angled."

"Angled?" Faye was about to argue when she realized Lucy was correct.

"I don't know what it needs exactly," said Lucy. "I don't think I know the word for it. But we can try."

⟶⟫●⟪⟵

After weeks of designing and redesigning, Lucy's comment on the positioning of the tail made everyone reconsider its importance.

"I don't know what it's called," Lucy said at least three times a day.

"It doesn't matter," said Faye, standing on her desk with a paperboard copy of the wing-and-tail design, with Lucy's adjustments. "It probably doesn't have a name. It's just the position of the tail."

"Or not always," said Lucy. "Sometimes not the tail."

"Lucy, you're starting to make as much sense as those men in black," said Noah.

Faye shushed him.

Then she launched the model.

With the wound miniature propeller, the plane, for the first time, maintained height in the air and flew across the classroom.

"Yes!" said Faye. "Yes! We've done it!"

Everyone cheered. Getting the tail right had changed everything. They would have to try it again, this time with a properly weighted center.

No one but Wallace noticed Lucy's thoughtful pout.

Lucy looked at Wallace. "There are more bits," she said, tugging at his sleeve.

"Yes, but the pieces are coming together," he said.

And putting the model into action, in the meadow, was the next thing to do.

———————⟫●⟪———————

During the carriage ride home for the weekend, Lucy, having dozed since she stopped waving, sat up.

"I'm famished," she said, rubbing her eyes, then her belly.

"Amazing, after having nearly eaten your entire fingers," grumbled Jasper, trying to get comfortable again after just beginning to sleep.

"Jasper!" Lucy said, holding out her hands like a little waif begging for alms. Jasper sighed and reached down to the basket on the floor between his legs. Pulling back the napkin, Jasper released the smell of the butter cakes. He took one out and handed it to Lucy. She took it in both hands, deeply breathed in the scent, then took the biggest bite possible for such a small girl.

"You're going to get it everywhere," he said, but Lucy seemed determined to catch every crumb.

"Anyone else hungry?" he asked. There was enough for everyone to have two.

When they passed Willow Street and Magnolia Street, Lucy clapped her hands in excitement. "We live near here," Lucy said.

"How do you always know?" Jasper asked. The neighborhood *did* look somewhat familiar, but so did the several other neighborhoods they had passed.

"Look at the names of the streets, silly. In our neighborhood, I remember seeing Willow and Magnolia. And that elm tree there," she said, pointing. "It has a birdhouse on that second-lowest branch. I remember that. Also—"

"Sorry for asking," Jasper said, rolling his eyes.

The driver turned right, passing the Modests' One Elm Street, but the carriage didn't stop. Instead he turned right onto Oak.

"Okay, here we go," said Noah. "Bets, anyone? I call seven. It was six last week. Maybe they're stepping up security!"

"Five," said Jasper.

"Three," said Lucy, hopefully.

"Four," said Wallace.

"Seventy-two," said Faye, slumping in her seat.

The children had been making bets to see who guessed correctly the number of times the carriage went around the block.

This time, Jasper was right. After five rounds, the carriage stopped in front of One Maple, and Noah took his bag—his small, but heavy, package—into the house.

Wallace was eager to get inside. He knew it was fanciful, but even after months of disappointment, he still hoped, every weekend, that his father would be home to greet him. His hand darted to his pocket, for what he knew would not be there.

But it was not until Jasper, Lucy, and Faye had already left that the carriage, after making one more tour around the block, that the carriage finally stopped in front of One Oak. The driver took Wallace's bags and walked them to the door, handing them to Daisy, who greeted him with a giant smile on her face. Wallace clung tightly to his bundle.

"Well, my darling boy, you must be hungry, mustn't you?" said Daisy, smiling a smile almost like Miss Brett's.

"Hello, Daisy," Wallace said.

Before he could ask, she said, "I'm sorry, darling. He's not here today."

"I didn't think so, but, well, you know, I had hoped." Wallace looked down at his feet.

"But there is a letter…"

CHAPTER SEVENTEEN

LETTERS FROM NO ONE
OR
 WHAT HAPPENED IN THE MEADOW

Each child had received a similar note. All said, basically, the same thing:

Dearest Wonderful Child(ren),

We (I) miss you so very much and we were (I was) so excited thinking we (I) would see you this weekend. Unfortunately, things require that we (I) stay here a bit longer. We (I) hope to get home by Saturday afternoon. Or possibly Sunday morning. Perhaps late morning. Or evening. Or perhaps the following weekend.

In any case, we (I) will do our (my) best to see you.

Our (my) everlasting love,

Father (and Mother)

Wallace, upon reading the letter from his father, again reached his hand into his empty pocket and, in that giant oyster of despair, felt a tiny grain of relief that his father had the lucky coin and, therefore, something that belonged to Wallace. He felt a surge of joy to know that his father had taken the time to write, and that he would be home soon. Or probably soon. Or, at least, home sometime.

However, once Wallace had settled in, eaten, and really scrutinized the letter, he realized that, unless his father had gone to a finishing school these many weeks, he had not, in fact, written this letter with his own hand. Wallace's father was left-handed, and wrote in a kind of chicken scratch, on a slight angle to the page. This letter was written in perfect script—no scratch, no slant. Could his father have dictated the letter? Did Wallace believe that?

Wallace's face burned with embarrassment for having felt so excited.

Faye did not have to read much of her letter to throw it onto the floor in disgust. Then she picked it up again and threw it down with even more force. Once was not enough. She wanted to keep throwing it as hard as she could.

Noah, too, tossed his aside. He was not furious like Faye or hopeful like Wallace—he just saw it as some silly way to make him believe his father planned a return. But his father had never before used the phrase "everlasting love." This was not his father's writing.

Lucy and Jasper were no different. They knew their mother's voice, her writing, and her language, and they knew instantly and without a doubt that this letter was not from her. And their father simply did not write letters at all.

"Do they think we're idiots?" Faye asked soon after, standing with the others in the meadow. "Leaving us generic notes clearly mass-produced for our benefit?" She took her crumpled letter and threw it at a tree. "What a load of hogwash. If my father wrote this, he would have called me his little *marmelo*. This is not from him. It proves they have him captive. If he was able to write, why didn't he just write to me? If our parents were not held hostage, they'd have the freedom to write, to visit, to take us with them. My father is in trouble, and we've got to find him. We've got to find all of them. If you can't see that these notes aren't even in our parents' handwriting, they aren't even—"

"We know that, Faye," Jasper said. "We all know that. You think we can't tell these notes didn't come from our parents or that—"

"Not right away. Wallace didn't even—"

"Leave him alone," Jasper said.

"But you don't understand—"

"What? Don't understand? What does that mean, 'You don't understand'?" Jasper's voice cracked. "No matter how different we are from each other—no matter if we even like each other—there are things we certainly share. Things that no one else shares but us. How dare you put yourself on a pedestal of understanding! Of course we bleeding understand." Jasper's face was red. How could she accuse them of not understanding?

Faye opened her mouth. Then shut it. Then opened it again.

"I . . . I didn't mean . . . I mean, I know . . . well, you know." Faye couldn't say it. For the first time, Jasper seemed truly to be angry with her. He hadn't let her rant and rave—he had told her off. She didn't know how she felt about it, but she did know he was right. Of course, they bleeding understood.

Wallace stood back as Jasper and Noah attached the wings to the cockseat. Noah's engine weighed more than they had hoped, but calculations confirmed it was still within the desired weight, and with twelve horsepower, there was no question this was the engine they needed. Once they found that the balance was right with the engineless model, powered by a twisted rubber band and Jasper's propeller, Noah would work on the placement of the engine for the real prototype—the child-size, but not doll-size, version of their flying machine.

All the while, Faye could feel the chill coming from Jasper. Somehow, she was aware of his detachment. She could feel something and she didn't like it. She didn't like him being cross with her. Her emotions flipped back and forth from being furious with him for his anger to being hurt that, after all the times she had been awful to him, he'd suddenly decided to shut her out. She had always trusted he'd never turn his back on her.

"Look, Jasper," she said, "the way I feel is—"

"I don't care how you feel, Faye," Jasper said coolly. "It doesn't matter."

"What does that mean?" Faye felt herself flush, her cheeks burning.

"For you, it only matters what you feel. You don't care what anyone else feels." Jasper looked right into those frosty green eyes and, with all the strength he could muster, said, "You don't need anyone else to care, Faye, because you spend so much time caring for no one but you. I've got other people's feelings that concern me now." And he turned away.

She didn't want it to happen, but tears threatened to fall like tiny wet soldiers ready for battle. She feared the worst, turning away so no one would see her soldiers march down her cheeks.

CHAPTER EIGHTEEN

Faye Takes Her Seat

OR

WALLACE FINDS THE MISSING WORD

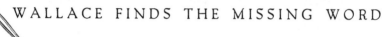

The following weekend, in the meadow, the children were ready to launch a properly weighted, rubber band-and-propeller-powered paperboard aeroplane model. It was about the size of a very large blackbird with a slightly wider wingspan.

To simulate a real pilot, they used one of Lucy's porcelain dolls, balanced with a sandbag, so that it properly compensated for the weight of a real person and the weight of the engine relative to the weight of the aeroplane. Faye could not help but silently bemoan the fact that she was too big to be the test pilot herself.

"Is it fine with the rest of you if I set it off?" she asked politely. Jasper finally nodded when the others agreed.

"Thank you," Faye said, her eyes coming to rest on Jasper. He offered her a nod and, perhaps, she hoped, the tiniest of smiles.

Faye knew she had to watch what she said and try to be more considerate. In the middle of all the excitement of trying to fly the model aeroplane, it would be quite a challenge. Taking a deep breath, she reminded herself that launching it was the closest thing to actually being on the craft and being the pilot.

Because it needed to be launched from a reasonable height,

Faye climbed the elm tree in the middle of the meadow and stood on a thick, firm branch. She drew back her arm, her finger holding down the rubber band to keep it from unwinding.

Lucy leaned over to Jasper. "She'll have to watch out for *them*," she said.

Then, in a sharp rush, Faye drew in her breath and nearly fell off the branch. There she froze, arm in the air.

"What is it?" said Jasper, worried she was about to fall.

"It's *them*!" she cried.

"Them?" The others looked around the meadow, but no one was there.

"It's them, *them*, patrolling the streets. We can't launch this. What if they see it?"

The children looked, but they couldn't see the street. The trees and the houses blocked the view.

"Patrolling in the daytime? How could we not know?" Jasper asked.

Lucy raised her hand. "I knew."

"We've never left the meadow," Wallace said.

"We never needed to," said Lucy. "We get lovely treats and the meadow is jolly good fun."

"How did you know, Lucy?" asked Jasper.

"Because I saw them and I counted when I was in my bedroom," Lucy explained. "My room is at the front of the house, upstairs, and I can see the street. When we spent the day in our rooms, when we were cross with Rosie for telling us the man in the tall velvet hat was Mummy and Daddy, I saw the black carriages and bicycles and riders riding down the road. It's all right, though," she added quickly. "It's not like at night. It's more like Fridays at the farm when they hardly patrol at all. Or Sundays here. During the day, they only pass every nine and a half minutes."

"Why didn't you tell me?" asked Jasper, surprised by all the information his sister had kept to herself.

"Tell you what?" Lucy asked, equally surprised.

"That there were patrols in the daytime!"

"Why?" she said, eyebrows raised. "Was it important?"

Jasper opened his mouth to answer, but couldn't. So he looked up at Faye and asked, "What do we do?"

Faye was still silent, still poised with her rather tired arm, frozen in the air.

"What is it, Faye?" Jasper watched her up there. She seemed petrified. "Faye?"

Faye looked down and smiled. "It's been ninety seconds and they still haven't passed. I think we need to wait until they pass again. Then we'll know how long between patrols."

"But Lucy said it was every nine and a half minutes," Jasper said.

"Yes, well..." Faye considered her words. "Let's be sure, shall we? It's only a few minutes to be sure it is always nine and a half minutes."

They waited. And waited. And waited.

Nine and a half minutes after the carriage passed, another black carriage driven by what appeared to be a black banana circled the block, then drove off to a wider patrol farther away.

Partially hidden by the trees, Faye looked around and, taking aim with her outstretched arm, launched the aeroplane.

As it flew from her hand, five faces shined in the speckled sunlight twinkling through the trees. They watched for what felt like long, long minutes as the tiny model aeroplane and its porcelain doll pilot soared through the air, flying on its own power.

The craft stayed aloft for twenty-eight seconds before crashing, nose first, into the willow in Wallace's backyard.

"Twenty-eight seconds!" Faye shouted from her perch. "Twenty-eight marvelous seconds! That's wonderful!" She practically danced down, from branch to branch to ground.

"But we'd all be dead if we were on board," said Wallace, pushing his glasses upon the bridge of his nose as he retrieved the model from the willow branches. It was fairly crumpled.

"Perhaps Wallace is right," said Noah, picking up the head of the doll that had rolled away from the wreckage. "'Wonderful' might not be the most appropriate word."

Wallace tossed him the rest of the doll he'd salvaged from the wreck.

"My dolly!" Lucy exclaimed.

"Sorry, Lucy," Noah said, handing her the doll and its severed head, "but it's all in the name of science."

Lucy took the pieces in her arms and hugged them.

"I'll fix your dolly, Lucy," Jasper said. "We've got glue in the nursery. She'll be as good as new, and you can put her in the hospital bed next to the dollhouse." He quickly received a hug from Lucy.

"We need more room to fly, to really fly our prototype," said Faye. "This was fine for a doll, but for our engine-powered aeroplane, we'll need running space. If we only had more room—"

"It wasn't just the room," said Wallace.

"What do you mean?" Faye turned to Wallace.

"We need to have something that allows for—"

"What is it?" said Faye. "What are we missing? We're so close!"

Suddenly, Lucy jumped up, knocking Wallace over, pencil and paper still in his hands, her broken doll falling to the ground.

"I know what went wrong!" Lucy cried with mounting excitement. "I know what it is! I know it, I know it, I know it!" She was skipping around in circles.

"What is it, Lucy?!" shouted Faye. "Will you stop whirling like a dervish and tell us?!"

"It's the tail!" she cried, picking up the folder and waving the papers in the air. "It's the whatsit! It's the thing, the moving thing, the thing that—"

"The tail?" said Jasper, Wallace, Noah, and Faye together.

"It has a tail, Lucy," said Wallace, "or have you—"

"Forgotten?" Noah said, glancing at Wallace.

"I just don't know the word for it," Lucy said. "Funny, that. I know what it is but I don't know what it calls itself."

"The tail? The parts of the tail?" asked Wallace.

"But it's not the right tail, of course," said Lucy. "The tail must be able to wiggle along with the wings."

"I know the word!" cried Wallace. "I know the word, Lucy. I know what she means!" Wallace seemed stunned by his own lack of observation. "It a rudder! We're missing a rudder."

"Like a rudder on a boat," Jasper said, realizing exactly what Wallace meant, "to help it steer."

"A rudder! It's called a rudder!" cried Lucy.

"We have to be able to steer the craft," Noah said.

"Of course, we can't just give it lift," said Faye. "We have to control the lift *and* the loft."

"Lift and loft!" cried Lucy, laughing and clapping her hands. "Lift and loft!" And she whirled again to the chant of "lift and loft."

"I hate it when she acts her age," Faye said, but she smiled just the same.

"Not only that," said Jasper, looking at the drawings, "but we have to control and coordinate the up-and-down movement—you know, the pitch. Also, the roll of the wings—when one wing goes up or down against the other—and the movement of the nose from side to side."

"That's called the yaw," said Noah.

"Yes, the yaw!" shouted Lucy, who whirled some more, chanting, "Yes, the yaw," much to Faye's bemusement. In fact, Faye was in love with Lucy and her brilliant discovery. This would surely make it all happen.

"And then," said Faye, "with propelled air and an engine to drive it, we'd have total control of the driving." She looked up to the sky. "We'd be able to fly."

—————•◦•—————

The children brimmed with plans and secrets and what felt like pure magic. But they also knew that, like their homes, the farm was under constant surveillance. Casually, Faye asked Miss Brett if she knew about patrols.

"Well," Miss Brett said, thinking hard about the question, "on Fridays, I have noticed a patrol, if that's what you call it, but only in the morning, then none until the drivers come to fetch you for the weekend. I always just assumed it was a carriage checking to see that all was well, as when they came for the honey. Or perhaps just a carriage coming from a different direction." She shrugged. "I never really thought about it. As for the weekends, I've never seen anyone patrolling. Come to think of it, I rarely see anyone, and certainly no one when you are away for the weekend."

Miss Brett did most of her gardening and outdoor work over the weekend, so she would have seen the men in black patrolling if they did.

That confirmed it: It was the children, and the children alone, they were guarding. This made launching the aeroplane—a manned, wooden, real aeroplane—right out in the field a dangerous thing to do during the school week.

Back at the schoolhouse, the children spent most of Sunday afternoon and Monday timing the carriages' tours around the farm. During the day, it seemed, they were not as diligent—they passed any given spot once every eleven minutes. If they were careful, the children would be able to launch the plane and hide it again before the men in black could catch them in the act.

The birdwatcher seemed to be on no specific schedule, although by luck he never ran into the patrolling men in black. He appeared to be following some bird that moved around a lot, with no apparent pattern, and he was away whenever the patrol came by the farm. On Fridays, he missed the sporadic patrols entirely. The children wondered what might happen to the poor funny man if the men in black found him there.

"He could be our ticket out of here," Faye said.

"What do you mean?" asked Wallace, nervously.

"With all our packages, how else can we get away from the

farm without being caught? We'll have to move so slowly that we'll be caught red-handed out in the middle of a field."

That's how they came to decide that their only hope for a quick, clean departure from the farm was in the back of the birdwatcher's truck. It was, after all, the only vehicle that did not belong to the men in black.

In the schoolyard, with bramble and blankets they had collected to help hide what they were actually doing, the children had been putting together the flying machine. This one would be large enough for a child, even a large child, or a fair-sized young woman, perhaps, laying face-down in the center. It had wings that spanned twelve feet. Adjustments were made to Faye's calculations when Noah found a problem with the way she had attached the wings and the tail-controlling mechanism. Lucy reminded everyone that several of Lilienthal's gliders had lift problems because of control.

She also suggested that they paint the aeroplane what she considered to be a lovely shade of pink. (This elicited, from Faye, a sound very similar to a cat trying to extricate a hairball from its throat.)

Wallace discovered a ratio problem between the length of the wings and the body of the machine, but Faye said she had already corrected it. The biggest problem of all was that there just wasn't much wind. As the weather grew cooler, the calculations had to be reworked again.

"Maybe we could use a bicycle," Noah suggested. "Maybe Katharine has one—Cousin Katharine who lives in Dayton, right? With a bicycle, we could drag the craft and give it a chance to get going."

"I don't think we'd be able to explain our departure to the nannies," Faye said. "They'd want to come, or else tell the men in black."

"I say we should make a bicycle ourselves," Jasper said.

Wallace shook his head. "But making the wheels and everything would take time."

"We can ask the birdwatcher," Jasper said.

"Before we involve anyone else any more than we have to," Wallace said, "let's see what we can do on our own—something that won't take too much time."

"And remember what your parents said?" Noah said. "I'm sure they were speaking for our parents, too. It's dangerous. For us and for them. They wanted us to be invisible." Noah looked around at his classmates. "Now, who's going to invent *that* serum?"

"Oh, me!" shouted Lucy. "Pick me!"

"We can use the wheels from those rusted old wheelbarrows in the garden shed," said Wallace. "They're small, but if we run down a slope with the machine for speed"—Wallace looked at his notes—"perhaps we can use the air friction to get lift without much wind."

By Wednesday, they had finished construction on not a full-size aeroplane large enough for a pilot and passenger, but rather a child-size, pilot-ready, engine-powered aeroplane. Even at child-size, the pieces were impossibly large and difficult to keep hidden. They used the potting shed to store the parts. The small incline behind the schoolhouse led out into the backfields, mostly unused by anyone other than crows. Out of sight from Miss Brett, who was busy making supper in the kitchen, the children decided to try out their creation.

"The craft will be attached to a rope," said Wallace. "It's not really ready to be piloted."

"I want to be in the pilot's seat," said Faye. Faye immediately wished she had said this differently, but try as she did to believe that they each played an important role in the invention, Faye still felt that, at heart, the aeroplane was hers, and she alone deserved to be in the pilot's seat, sink or swim, crash or fly.

Besides, although she could not admit it to herself, she would never have been able to bear the burden of guilt if anything happened to one of the other four.

———⟶⟨⟨———

Strapped in place with cushions from Miss Brett's chair, with all of the pillows from their beds under her stomach, around her arms and legs and even attached to her head, Faye lay facedown in the craft, looking as if she could float up and fly without it. When she gave the signal, the others ran, pulling her along behind them.

She pulled the lever and engaged the engine.

"You're in the pilot's seat now, Faye!" Jasper said, smiling. Faye could barely hear what he said, but her heart swelled. She smiled and gave him a salute.

"Just remember Sir Isaac Newton and his law of gravity," Noah said.

Faye gave him a wink. She had not heard what he'd said at all.

Their breathing grew heavy as the craft motored along behind them, but just as they felt their legs weakening, they ran down the small hill at the edge of the grove. First, Noah tripped over a stone, and then Wallace fell into Noah. In a jumble, the four runners tumbled and rolled, pulling the rope along with them.

Suddenly, there was a gust of wind. The propeller turned. The wind picked up.

And Faye was in the air! She was only two and a half feet in the air, but she was in the air, and safely back on the ground shortly thereafter, in one piece, her head still firmly attached to her shoulders.

"We did it!" Faye shouted as the others scrambled to their feet and ran to her. "We actually flew!" They all embraced and jumped and shouted and laughed. They made one big bundle, with Faye like a huge marshmallow on the inside.

"We didn't get very high, but we *did* get off the ground," Wallace said, disengaging himself from the bundle and looking at the machine. "We need to do more adjusting. The engine needs to be positioned better. The canard elevators need to be re-secured. We want to be certain it wasn't an accident of nature and we can fly it again."

"Oh, nonsense, Wallace," said Faye, unstrapping herself from her puffy suit. "We flew. And we'll do it again!" She smiled at him. Wallace, unable to contain the pleasure from it, smiled back.

"Well, this brings us into the second phase of our plan, then. Once we improve our elevation, we'll be able to follow one of the carriages," said Wallace. "They'd never think to look up."

"And then we'll find Mummy and Daddy!" Lucy said, jumping with excitement.

"Let's get these cushions back," said Noah, "before Miss Brett decides she'd like to sit down."

The plan would be simple enough—they would take apart their flying machine, hide it, and then, before the nefarious men in black came to take them back to their homes, the five of them would sneak into the back of the birdwatcher's truck. They would go wherever it was he was going and, if he discovered them hiding before they could climb out unnoticed, they would beg the birdman to take them to some nearby field where they could put the pieces together and get into the air—higher, much higher, with the proper adjustments. From there, they would follow those men in black to wherever those lunatics were keeping their parents. Once they got the aeroplane in the air, the pilot would be undetectable, and as soon as the pilot was able to determine where their parents were being held, they'd be able to go, all together, to release them.

They considered contacting Faye's cousin, but it would be almost impossible to get past the watchful eyes of the nannies, let alone the men in black. Besides, one of the last things the Modests' parents had asked was for them to keep quiet and keep from being seen. Their parents wanted them to be invisible.

But what did that mean? Were their parents worried the children might do something to endanger them all? The children did not know. They certainly did not want to bring danger down upon their parents—or themselves. But they had invented a flying machine to find their parents, and they had to be sure it remained hidden and secret.

It was also of the utmost importance that they keep danger

away from Miss Brett. They did not want to cause her problems with the men in black or otherwise put her in harm's way. In their own moments of heightened terror, all had nightmarish visions of Miss Brett being tortured by some maniacal black-hooded devil with dark glasses—and probably black fuzzy slippers and a black bowtie the size of a railroad crossing flag,—amd dropped down some dark well, or something worse. The best way to protect her was by not involving her.

The birdwatcher, too, had to be protected. He was a total innocent and should not be involved any more than necessary. If all went right, he would never know they had hidden in the back of his truck, and he would never know the role he had played in the first-ever flight by a human being.

CHAPTER NINETEEN

THE POWER OF FLIGHT

OR

THE LANGUAGE OF LIGHT

Then Friday came and it was time. They had hidden the aeroplane, and they had kept an eye on the birdwatcher's truck, but Wallace had felt the need to complete his experiment. He had failed—he had needed twenty-seven seconds more—and now, as the carriages kicked up a cloud of dust driving up the road, as Miss Brett helped Wallace clean the blackboard, the children waited for their classmate, despite Faye's thoughtless insistence on leaving him behind.

"Look," said Faye, struggling to defend herself, "with him distracting Miss Brett, we'll have a better chance of—"

"He's coming!" shouted Lucy.

All eyes turned to the schoolhouse. Wallace was running, top speed, toward them. Faye bit her tongue. "He's free. Let's go," she said.

With no time for greetings, they all turned right at the ruins of the old silo and ran around the side of the farmhouse to the potting shed.

Working quickly, they began tossing aside the old broken plant pots and leaves. They removed the old burlap sacks to reveal the tightly-wrapped bundles hidden beneath. Noah carried the engine—or, actually, he rolled it, using the bottom part of an old wheelbarrow and tying the package atop it using the rope they found in the shed. A big, flat, square package wrapped in the spare tablecloth held Jasper's propeller. He carried that. There were three more packages, two wrapped in spare quilts and light for their length. These were Faye's wings, and Wallace and Faye each carried one. The last package, wrapped in the throw blanket that always hung over the back of Miss Brett's chair, was Lucy's tail. It was not very heavy, and Lucy carried that all on her own.

Noah went first, peering from behind the old wooden door of the shed. The shed was not visible from the window of the schoolhouse. But they could still see the birdwatcher. He was lying flat on his back, probably having fallen again from the tree.

"Do you really think it will be safe in that truck with that fellow?" asked Noah, swinging his burden over his shoulder and casually walking out the door. "We might very well be risking our lives more by driving in a motorized vehicle with the birdwatcher over there than, well, you know ... remaining in the hands of our odd friends in black." "They're not my friends," said Lucy, marching behind Noah.

"Well, it is a Knox truck, Noah," Jasper said, "and it's a new model, so it's safe—"

"It's not the truck that makes me nervous." Noah's implication was clear as he and the others observed the birdwatcher trying to disentangle himself from his own binoculars, but falling down once again.

The children all stood staring for a moment. It was a moment too long.

"Children," Miss Brett called from the schoolhouse, "they're going to be here in a few minutes. Are you packed for the weekend?"

They all looked at one another for an answer. The birdwatcher was parked across the field, on the very small dirt road leading away from town.

"I say it's now or never," said Faye. "Let's make a run for it. We'll come back for Miss Brett, unless they—"

"Unless they what?" asked Jasper, not wanting an answer.

"You don't think they'll hurt her?" whined Lucy, her fingers already planted in her mouth.

"There's no time for this!" shouted Faye. "Grab your bundle and let's ..." But the words stopped there. There was nothing left to say and nothing left to do.

When they turned to run to the birdwatcher's Knox truck, to hide themselves and their invention, to hitch a ride into Dayton or wherever they could put their invention together and set off to save their parents ... they found he had gone.

There was nothing they could do. Faye stared as if she might be missing something, as if she could will the truck to reappear by staring hard enough.

But now there was another thing they had to face. Miss Brett was coming to look for them.

"Quick!" Jasper said. "Let's get everything back in the shed!"

"No," hissed Faye. "She's going to clean the ruddy place out. We've got to take it all with us."

"Take it with us?" Jasper's tone was incredulous. "We're supposed to take all of these bundles back home without anyone noticing?"

What Miss Brett found when she got to the children were five of the most falsely innocent faces she had ever addressed. She was a bit confused by both their appearance, which was in no way how she had last seen them, and their collective behavior—not to mention the strangest-shaped packages she had ever seen. A few moments of open-mouthed surprise passed before she could say anything.

"What on earth are you doing, children?" she asked. "What have you been up to?" At this point, they were all more than a little disheveled, with leaves in their hair, dirt on their chins, and bits of dead plants stuck here and there. When she tried to make eye contact, she found each one of them staring off into the distance, at the old oak tree, or somewhere else. She looked at their bundles. "What in the world did you pack in those bundles? Are those your things for the weekend?"

They all nodded emphatically, or otherwise assented. Then each, in his or her own way, once again tried to avoid the ever-penetrating gaze of Miss Brett. By now, she knew them quite well, and knew something was amiss.

"Children? Is there something you'd like to tell me?"

"Oh, yes," cried Lucy, "I would, I would, I truly, truly would."

"But it will have to wait," said Faye, interrupting Lucy. "It's ... it's a surprise."

"Well, I suppose," said Miss Brett, looking in the direction of the dirt road. The cloud of dust carving a line through the fields was now within a minute of the schoolhouse. If they had been driving those big smelly motorcars instead of carriages, they would have arrived already.

Two enormous carriages pulled onto the front field.

"Please, Miss Brett, don't say anything," said Faye. There was fear in her eyes.

"I don't have anything to say, dear," said Miss Brett, "but I want you to know that I trust you children. If I am asked, I will explain that these are part of a class project, and you are bringing it all home for the weekend. Is that an apt reply? And truthful since you are, actually, the class, and this is, actually, your project, is it not?"

"Yes, ma'am," Wallace said. They all nodded.

"That it is," Noah said.

"And I take it that your, whatever it is, cannot remain here?" Miss Brett added with an air of resignation, knowing the answer before she asked.

"You've taken it just right," Noah said.

"Well, then," Miss Brett said, straightening her apron, "let us greet our visitors, shall we?"

<hr />

As they drove down the road from Sole Manner Farm, the driver looked back at his burden in the boot of the carriage.

"Are you growing something?" asked the driver in the giant black sombrero hat.

Answers of "Yes" and "No" came from the cabin.

This did not seem to bother the driver, who took both answers as if they were one and continued, in silence, into town.

The five children remained quiet, too, for some time. Jasper watched as Lucy tilted her head to lean sleepily upon his shoulder.

Everyone else seemed tense, wearing various expressions of worry on their faces.

It was Wallace who caught Jasper's attention. Wallace sat there, silent, his hands shoved deep in his pockets. As Jasper watched, tears welled up in his eyes.

"Wallace," Jasper began, but quickly realized he wasn't sure what to say.

"I've let her down, Jasper," Wallace said, turning to the window. Then he said it again, this time in a whisper.

"You have not," said Jasper.

"My birthday is in two days," Wallace said.

"Right, it's in two days," Jasper said. "You have two days to put it back together and—"

"That's not true," Wallace said with an insistence that made him sound unusually forceful. "Those chemicals take weeks, months even, to formulate. I only got there after working on it for almost a year, and I'm still not finished. And I don't know if I had it right this time, either. I ruined it. I dropped it on the floor."

"You'll do it." Jasper was equally forceful. "You are a brilliant chemist, Wallace, and—"

"What's Wallace on about?" Faye asked. "Is he crying because he didn't get to finish his polymer?"

The carriage was now on its circuitous route around the neighborhood, growing closer and closer to their houses. Wallace had remained silent and Faye only noticed his tears when she leaned forward to see what street they were passing.

"It's not that—well, not what you're thinking," Jasper said.

"Oh, honestly," Faye said dismissively. "We're all trying to save our parents from likely peril and Wallace is crying because he didn't get to finish his chemistry experiment."

With that, Wallace climbed down from the carriage, which had stopped in front of his house. He left without a word, and without the help of the sombrero-wearing driver.

"What?" Faye responded to a look of cold disbelief. "It's true. He was selfish and wanted to mess around with that experiment when we were trying to save our parents. He's the reason we failed. He obviously doesn't—"

But Jasper turned his back on her and followed Lucy out of the carriage, leaving Faye mid-sentence with a slightly confused, semi-awake Noah at her side.

⊷•⊶

Faye came out to the meadow looking for Jasper that evening. She pretended that she was just walking out there, after supper, but she really wanted to talk to Jasper. And she was unhappy about wanting to talk to him, too. She was mad at Jasper for not telling her whatever it was that Wallace had told him about the polymer, but she also knew that Wallace was clearly struggling with something.

As for Jasper, he had gone to the meadow to watch the fireflies and have a moment of quiet while Lucy had her bath. When he saw Faye coming, he almost hid behind the willow before she could see him. He realized, though, that this was a silly thing to do because she had probably come out to talk to him.

"What do you want, Faye?" he asked, not sure whether she really did want anything.

"What do you mean?" Faye said. "I just came out to ... to watch the fireflies."

"Fine," said Jasper, now certain Faye had come for him.

As they watched the fireflies in silence, Jasper steeled himself for the onslaught of accusations or complaints or whatever it was that Faye was pretending not to have brought with her to the meadow.

"I was wondering if you've spoken with Wallace," Faye finally said.

"What do you mean?"

"He was upset—you know, unhappy," Faye said.

"And?"

"And I was hoping he was all right."

"I'm sure he's fine," Jasper said, focusing on a firefly that glowed in pulses. He thought it must be the language of light.

"Oh, well, if you spoke with him, then you know," Faye said. She wanted to know what Jasper knew. But Jasper simply sat there and stared at the dratted fireflies.

"Jasper," Faye said after several seconds of silence, "what is it about Wallace? Is he so obsessed with his experiment that he doesn't care about anything else?"

"Are you trying to be cruel or is it just the way you are naturally?" Jasper asked, turning to look at Faye. Her face was lit by the moonlight. Her green eyes sparkled like glowing fireflies trying to communicate. But her beauty hid the nature that Jasper was sure lay just beneath those eyes. Faye cared for no one but Faye.

She opened her mouth, but no words came out. Jasper was glad for this, because he hadn't finished.

"You don't care how Wallace is feeling," he said. "You don't care about anything. You were ready to leave that boy behind. You don't even know what caring is, do you?"

"I...I...it's just that...well, Wallace didn't do anything—"

"He jolly well did. He helped us all with the—"

"You know perfectly well that none of his help was vital," Faye said, without cruelty, only honesty. "We all could have and would have had equally helpful design ideas. We would not, however, have been able to make the propeller, the tail, the engine, or the wings without the rest of us. Wallace has been on the outside and I want to know why."

Jasper wanted to yell back that she was wrong, and that Wallace had been vital to saving their parents and had been an equal part, but Faye was right. It was what Wallace had been saying all along—that he was a chemist, not an engineer. His contributions were certainly helpful, and he may have seen things before the others, but nothing was particular to his genius. His genius was being spent on his own work—not theirs.

"Wallace has to do this, Faye," Jasper finally said. "I can't say why, but the boy lost his mum, and he has to do this. He has to finish, but...there's only a couple days left to do it."

"Why?" said Faye. "Why? I don't understand, Jasper. It's crazy. What, did his mother tell him he had to finish this before he turned ten?"

Jasper said nothing. Faye had found that grain of truth again and made it sound ugly. But it was the grain of truth from which the whole thing grew.

And suddenly, Faye knew it, too: what only Jasper had known.

Wallace's mother had issued a proclamation before she died,

that Wallace would change the world by the age of ten. She surely meant to show her son how much she loved and believed in his brilliant mind, never expecting it would become something by which Wallace measured himself. The tenth birthday probably had not meant anything at all to her.

But it meant everything to Wallace.

Faye felt the power of a parent's words—a parent who had died and gone and left her child with a promise that now, Faye understood, he would not be able to keep. Wallace had indeed tried to help them, but for him, there was always another challenge—the race to achieve something for a mother who would never see her son grow up and never know how hard he tried.

Faye ran back to her house so Jasper would not see the tears threatening to rain down in the meadow.

CHAPTER TWENTY

THE DISTURBING SUBSTITUTION

OR

WHAT JUST FLEW IN

Sunday, which was Wallace's birthday, came quickly. Faye was unusually quiet, everyone noticed, but no one said anything to her. Truthfully, most were glad to have a break from her bossiness. Jasper felt twinges of guilt for hurting Faye, but in truth, she had done it to herself. It was important for a person to know that other people had feelings, too.

Saturday had been spent working on various modifications. Faye had been especially kind to Wallace, asking his opinion about the wingspan and the weight ratio. By the end of the day, they were ready to test the aeroplane again. Loading the packages onto the carriage the following morning, the flappy-hatted, fuzzy boot-wearing driver simply placed the packages in the boot without question. The other driver must have given some explanation that was sufficient to prevent further inquiry.

Once they were back at school, it was plain that Miss Brett had plans. She'd placed fresh flowers around the classroom and had cut out papers to form letters that said "HAPPY BIRTHDAY WALLACE!"

Wallace was stunned. There was cake and candy apples and

honeyed milk for everyone. "Thank you, Miss Brett," Wallace said while the others indulged.

"You are very, very welcome," she said, kissing the birthday boy on the top of his head. Wallace closed his eyes. Not since his mother would wake him with kisses did he have such a gift. Today, the weight of his promise to her felt heavy in his stomach.

After Miss Brett's birthday treats, the children used their time to reassemble the aeroplane and make some minor adjustments. They successfully flew three more times, although never more than thirty seconds. By the third flight, they were sure it was because they did not want to be seen—not because the aeroplane was incapable of flying longer. They then successfully hid the pieces in the crumbled silo, which they were certain would not be tidied up anytime soon. The gardening shed was now full of seedlings for winter lettuces, cabbage, and kale.

Miss Brett never asked, but they all knew she suspected they were up to something. As for the birdwatcher, they had seen nothing of him since their failed attempt to hitch a ride on the back of his truck. Lucy began to worry that the birdwatcher had not simply driven away.

On Friday morning, the weather was rather rainy. The sun made only a brief appearance, only once or twice peeking from behind the curtain of clouds. A wet chill hung in the air like a hostile audience, unwilling to depart. Miss Brett lit a fire in the kitchen and made thick vegetable potage. She served it with her delicious buttermilk biscuits for lunch. She and the children ate in the farmhouse and, after cleaning up and putting the dishes away, returned to the classroom for afternoon lessons and free time. While they enjoyed discussing new books, like *The*

Wonderful Wizard of Oz and *Five Children and It*, and how the stories were the same and different, thoughts of the aeroplane flew around their heads and distracted them from everything else. If only Miss Brett knew, it would be a fabulous surprise.

But, at that moment, the surprise belonged to them instead. It was neither fabulous nor wondrous. What they saw as they stepped into the classroom stopped them cold.

First, a man was sitting in Miss Brett's chair. Second, this man wore no black at all. He was not wearing a black coat or a black woman's bonnet or a pair of dark-lensed aviator's goggles. He wore neither a black swimming costume nor a black furry coat nor a pair of black bunny rabbit ears. Instead, he wore a light brown tweed suit. He was very thin and had a very pointy, one could even say sharp, little beard at the tip of his chin. He wore spectacles, but they had clear lenses. He sat with his legs crossed twice so that his toes touched at the tips of his brown leather shoes. These toes continuously tapped together, as his fingers twiddled round and round and his hands rested, thumping, on Miss Brett's desk.

Miss Brett was the first to find her voice. "May I ask what you are doing at my desk?" she said. "May I help you?"

The man, having been staring out the window, jumped, surprised. He uncrossed his double-crossed legs and stood.

"I am Reginald Roderick Kattaning," he said, rolling his Rs. "And you are the beloved teacher, I presume."

"Well, I am most certainly not one of the students," she said.

"Ah, yes, but of course," said Reginald Roderick Kattaning. "I am here to observe."

"No one said there would be someone here to observe," Miss

Brett said.

"Well, Miss, there is much you are not privy to. I am here to both observe and to relieve you of your duties."

"No one ever said anything about—" Miss Brett began, but she was cut off by the wave of Reginald Roderick Kattaning's hand.

"That will be enough. I am here in an official capacity."

"Official?" Miss Brett said.

"Very, extremely official," Reginald Roderick Kattaning said, importantly.

Miss Brett said, "I want to see some identification—"

"That will not be necessary."

"Not necessary? Just what is it you plan—"

"Officially, I will observe, and then I will take over."

"This—this is most irregular—"

"Nonsense," said Reginald Roderick Kattaning. "I will simply be taking over in order to . . . be sure that . . . the instruction is adequate. I will be . . . quizzing the children in your absence."

"Quizzing us on what?" asked Jasper.

"None of your business, is it?" sneered Reginald Roderick Kattaning. "If I told you, it wouldn't be a quiz, eh?"

"Well, I cannot allow someone to just arrive and remove me—" said Miss Brett, but again she was cut off by a wave of Reginald Roderick Kattaning's long, bony hand.

"You have no choice. Now, go on as if I was not here. I shall sit in the back of the class and observe." He picked up a paper folder and a pencil from Miss Brett's desk. "And I will be taking notes."

Miss Brett and the children stared at Reginald Roderick Kattaning as he walked to the back of the class, seated himself on the laboratory table, and re-crossed his legs. Twice.

"Well? What are you waiting for? Teach," he said.

Miss Brett sat heavily down in her seat. The children followed into theirs.

"Well, class," she began, quite distractedly. She was trapped. What could she do? She wanted to make contact with someone. And then, suddenly, she was thinking about that tiny room off of the kitchen. It was the room that contained the red telephone. She tried to think of a way to use it. "Well, I think it's time to discuss *The Wonderful Wizard of Oz.* Please take out your—"

"I think it is time for a science lesson," said Reginald Roderick Kattaning.

"Well, I was going to read from—"

"That will be all, Miss. I can take it from here," Reginald Roderick Kattaning said, standing up and walking to Miss Brett's desk.

As Reginald Roderick Kattaning helped her out of her seat, Miss Brett said, "Look, I will need to speak to—"

"I am in charge here, Miss," Reginald Roderick Kattaning said in a fierce voice. "You will do as you are told. Now, go prepare lunch." He walked over to her desk, picked up a stone she had been using to hold down some papers, and crushed it in his fist. He allowed the dust to fall into the wastepaper basket next to the desk, then wiped his hand on his trousers.

Miss Brett opened her mouth to speak, then thought better of it. The children were about to complain, but she subtly shook her head to quiet them.

"All right, sir," Miss Brett said, trying to unclench her teeth. "I will do as you wish." With as much dignity as she could muster,

Miss Brett turned to go into the house.

Right then, Lucy slid from her seat and rushed to Miss Brett's side. When she tugged at Miss Brett's sleeve, Miss Brett leaned over and Lucy whispered in her ear. Miss Brett kissed Lucy on the top of her head, smoothed back her hair, and tried to give her a reassuring smile, urging her back to her seat. Then Miss Brett straightened her skirt, opened the door, and stepped into the kitchen.

"Take your seat, girl!" Reginald Roderick Kattaning shouted at Lucy. Lucy quickly returned to her seat next to Noah. As this was happening, Reginald Roderick Kattaning marched over to the kitchen door and slammed it shut.

"Now, class," said Reginald Roderick Kattaning, putting on a professorial air, "we shall resume our instruction. This lesson, we will be discussing science. Scientific items, to be more precise."

No one moved. They were all too confused to say anything.

"I will pick a student, and that student will discuss one of their experiments," he said. Then, Reginald Roderick Kattaning moved his finger, pointing around the room as if considering who to choose. The entire time, however, his eyes were focused on just one of them.

"Why don't we start wiiiiiiiith . . . you," Reginald Roderick Kattaning said, pointing at Faye. Removing a notebook from his pocket, sitting double-cross-legged at the desk, Reginald Roderick Kattaning began to write.

"Well . . . um . . ." Faye said, looking at her classmates for encouragement. Noah gestured for her to continue, and Faye said, "Well, you see, it's really quite complicated. You see, the level of complexity that the most complicated of complications can provide…"

With Faye uttering a load of nonsense, yet keeping the intruder's attention, Noah got Lucy's with a subtle wave of his hand next to his desk. Lucy looked at Noah, equally as subtle. Her face, Noah could see, was as white as a sheet. "What did you say to Miss Brett?" Noah asked Lucy, trying to speak without moving his lips or making a sound, keeping one eye on the babbling coming from the front of the room.

The effect of his silent and motionless question was that Lucy had no idea what he was trying to say. Noah took his pencil and wrote his question on the piece of paper he had on his desk. He tilted the paper up so Lucy could read it.

"I had to tell her who he is," said Lucy in a loud whisper.

"Who is he?" asked Noah, no longer trying to be silent. Jasper and Wallace turned their heads slightly to better hear what Lucy was saying.

Lucy looked at Noah, fear in her eyes.

"That man," she whispered, pointing at Reginald Roderick Kattaning. "That man is the birdwatcher."

CHAPTER TWENTY-ONE

THE BIG UNLESS

OR

MISS BRETT MAKES THE CALL

It had taken all of Miss Brett's resources to remain calm as she walked out of the classroom. Lucy's words had left a buzz in her ear. She knew there was something strange about that man. If he was official, why didn't he even know her name? And what did it mean that this Reginald Roderick Kattaning fellow was the birdwatcher? Had he been spying on them?

Standing in the kitchen as fear settled in, Miss Brett was overwhelmed with questions. What should she do? Whatever she did, she had to be careful. Mr. Reginald Roderick Kattaning could not know she knew something was amiss. She looked around the room. She decided she had better make it look as if she was cooking lunch. She filled a large pot with water and put it on to boil. There were sacks of potatoes, onions, and rice in the larder. She grabbed a few large onions and threw them into the pot, not bothering to peel or slice them. There was no need. This was only pretend. In case Mr. Reginald Roderick Kattaning came in to check, the steamy kitchen would seem alive with lunch's preparation.

Looking around the room again, her eyes settled on the door

to the tiny room. She knew what was in there. Just behind that door was the shiny red telephone.

In the classroom, as the children pretended to be transfixed by Faye's chatter, Reginald Roderick Kattaning, who had stopped taking notes, sat slightly cross-eyed, staring at Faye.

"And so..." Faye was running out of nonsense. "And so..."

"I'm waiting, missy," said Reginald Roderick Kattaning, tapping one double-crossed foot against the other.

Faye swallowed hard. "Waiting?"

"Waiting for you to get to the point."

"The point? You're waiting to get to the point?"

"I said I am waiting," Reginald Roderick Kattaning said, a bit gruffer.

"Sorry," Faye said, trying to sound innocent. "I must have missed the question."

Noah leaned over to Lucy. "Are you sure?" he asked.

"Yes," said Lucy, her whisper cracked by a swallow that kept her from crying. "Even without his half-moustache. It's him."

But Faye was no longer speaking.

"Perhaps the little whiner in the back row would like to share her whimpering whispers with the rest of us," Reginald Roderick Kattaning said with a nasty sneer.

"My sister has had a bit of a cold," said Jasper quickly. "Surely you knew that from the note sent to the, uh, central office."

"Well, of course I did," Reginald Roderick Kattaning said with a wave of his bony hand. "Someone get her a handkerchief or something. Disgusting little snotty things, these...small..." With a shiver, he turned back to Faye. "Well?"

"Well," she said, "I was born in a lovely city called—"

"I do not give an owl's hoot about where you were born," Reginald Roderick Kattaning growled, uncrossing his double-crossed legs and leaning forward toward Faye. "And no more of your infernal drivel. You will answer my question now."

"Um, what was that question again?" Faye asked, hoping to stall until something better came to mind.

<hr />

As the strong smell of boiling onions wafted through the kitchen and, she hoped, into the classroom, Miss Brett put her ear to the classroom door. She could hear the squeaking, growling voice of Reginald Roderick Kattaning. She then banged a few pots together and made some cooking-type noises before she tiptoed over to the tiny room where the telephone was kept.

<hr />

"Blast you!" shouted Reginald Roderick Kattaning. "I want a report on the *thing*!"

"The thing?" asked Noah, innocently.

"The...blasted...snglrumpfrsss...grmblfrng..." Reginald Roderick Kattaning turned quite red. "The ruddy, the...the bloody thing, the *thing*, the pieces, the...the thing you used...and don't any of you dare deny it...and that blasted machine that you have been so obviously busy working on and obviously successful in getting off the blasted ground! The *thing*!!!"

Trapped in the front row, both Wallace and Jasper suddenly wished they had brought umbrellas to shield them from the spittle that flew from the mouth of Reginald Roderick Kattaning.

"Well, I wouldn't say successful, really," Faye said. "Actually, it was a rather silly thing. You see, when I was in India, I had a little parrot. Well, it wasn't my parrot. Actually, it *was* my parrot. Not exactly *my* parrot, more like—"

"Oh, shut up, shut up, will you?" Reginald Roderick Kattaning screeched. He began rubbing his temples with his long bony thumbs.

"Actually," said Faye, looking reflective, "that brings to mind—"

"I said shut up!" Reginald Roderick Kattaning turned and pointed directly at Wallace. "You! Where is it, boy?!"

"I, sir, I . . . I . . . I'm sure I don't—"

"Don't 'don't' me," Reginald Roderick Kattaning said with a sneer. "Don't you dare 'I don't' me when you know I know you know you do, you know, I do, don't you, hm?"

Wallace opened, then closed his mouth. He then opened it again, then closed it. He did this several times, like a fish.

"Oh, shut up, the lot of you!" Reginald Roderick Kattaning stood up, dropping his paper folder from his lap. In it was a long envelope he snatched up before anyone could see what was written on the front.

Well, not everyone. Lucy saw.

He grabbed Jasper by the throat and pulled the boy's face right up to his own. The rest of the children were about to intervene when Reginald Roderick Kattaning dropped Jasper suddenly. He then brushed off his sleeves and attempted to regain control of himself again. But the cruelty that had come through his eyes when he held Jasper in his grasp had not escaped any of the children.

He spoke in a hissing whisper. "I want you all to pick up your pencils and write one hundred times, 'I will obey Mr. Reginald Roderick Kattaning and tell him what he asks.' Right now, all of you," he said. Grumbling to himself, he muttered, "Think they're so clever ... think I won't get what I came for ... blasted smelly little children ..."

———⋙●⋘———

Meanwhile, on the other side of the door, Miss Brett had concerns of her own. The problem was this: She had no idea how to use a telephone. On three occasions, she had been handed a telephone and spoken into the mouthpiece—twice at the home of a friend of her parents, and once in the lobby of an office building when a call was placed to an upstairs office. In each case, she was able to hear someone respond on the other end. It was very exciting.

On one other occasion, she had seen a call placed and received. In fact, there had been a demonstration in front of a shop near her boarding house. One man stood on one side of the street and another man stood on the other. The first man picked up the earpiece and spoke into the mouthpiece connected to the stand. She hadn't heard what the first man said, because she was on the other side of the street next to the second man. Moments later, however, an alarm bell had sounded on the phone next to her and the man picked it up. She was thrilled to see the whole thing in action. Several people had signed up right then and there to get their own telephones in their own homes. Obviously, the more people who had them, the better. At the time, she had been excited about the idea of these modern devices and would have loved to have one, but she hadn't the money or the proper home. She hadn't known anyone who had a telephone, either. And after her parents died, there really hadn't been anyone to call.

But still, there in the farmhouse of Sole Manner Farm, she had to try. Miss Brett tried the door to the little room. It was locked. She had forgotten. She had placed the small key in a jar above the kitchen sink. She went to get it, hesitating when she heard Reginald Roderick Kattaning shouting at the children. She wanted to run in and demand he leave at once, or remove the imposter by force, or at least dump the great big boiling pot of onion water on his head. She was so angry at herself for not having been forceful from the start, leaving the children alone with that man. But he had crushed a rock with his fist. She had taken that to be a threat. Any overt action on her part could put them all at risk. If she was going to help the children, she would have to make the "unless" call. And she would have to do it now.

She took the little key and opened the door to the tiny room. There sat the glowingly red telephone. She approached it gingerly, looking to one side, then the other. She leaned toward it.

"Hello?" she whispered, looking around to see if anyone but the telephone had heard her. She waited a moment, then cleared her throat.

"Hello?" she said in a strong voice—not too loud, she hoped.

There was still no answer. Of course—how foolish of her. One had to pick up the earpiece and speak into the mouthpiece in order to be heard. She did just that.

"Hello?" she said into the mouthpiece. "Hello? Please, somebody." She listened and waited. Still there was no reply.

She sat on the floor next to the contraption, the earpiece still in her hand. *Think, think,* she thought. What had the man on the other side of the street done before speaking? She looked at the telephone and jiggled the little arm that held the earpiece.

"Hello?" came a voice in her ear.

"Oh, hello, yes, hello, hello," Miss Brett said excitedly, before remembering the mouthpiece. "Hello, hello, hello."

"Enough hello, Miss Brett. What is happening?" The voice sounded gruff but concerned.

"Oh, I'm so sorry," said Miss Brett, at once quite shocked to hear her name and quite glad to be recognized. "You see, there is a man—"

"A man?" The voice went up an octave.

"Yes, he's in the classroom and—"

"In the classroom?" The voice went even higher, now almost shouting into Miss Brett's ear.

"I'm terribly afraid. I didn't think he was one of your people. You see, Lucy thought she saw—"

But now Miss Brett heard a jumble of voices, all talking frantically at once, and quite a bit of confusion on the other end of the receiver.

Then she heard a door slam shut. But the slamming door was not in her earpiece. The slamming door came from the kitchen.

Reginald Roderick Kattaning had been pacing back and forth, mumbling rude things about the children. The children, on their end, were doing their part to foil him. Jasper wrote as slow as humanly possible while still appearing to move his hand. As Faye sat, pretending to contemplate the meaning of the assignment, doodling pictures of Reginald Roderick Kattaning in various states of peril, Lucy and Wallace each tried to write as quietly and neatly as possible. Both of them were terrified that Reginald Roderick Kattaning would again lose his temper and do someone physical harm.

Noah, meanwhile, wrote a note, which he tried to get to Jasper. Jasper was able to grab it subtly. It said, "Patrol will see him! They'll help us!"

Jasper passed this to Faye, who nodded.

The children now found themselves in the strange position of hoping the men in black would come and save them.

But the note came back from Lucy, who shook her head. "Friday," the note said. "No patrol."

As his pacing became stomping, Reginald Roderick Kattaning walked over to the door connecting the house to the classroom. He sniffed the air and muttered something, rubbing his belly. He opened the door to the kitchen and peeked inside. Suddenly, he slammed it shut and ran out of the classroom.

All pencils stopped. Several moments passed before anyone could even move. Of all the things that could have happened, the abrupt departure of Reginald Roderick Kattaning was utterly unexpected.

"What happened?" Jasper said.

"Do you think he's gone?" asked Noah.

"I hope so," said Lucy, looking at her brother with the deepest of doubts.

The children looked out the empty doorway through the field to the quiet road. The Daytonic Birdwatching Society motorcar was nowhere to be seen. And there was no sign of their unwanted visitor. But none of the children believed they had seen the last of Reginald Roderick Kattaning.

"Sorry. What was that?" asked Miss Brett into the mouthpiece.

The voice in the phone said something, but it sounded very strange. They may have been words in another language, she thought.

Then, suddenly, the line went dead.

CHAPTER TWENTY-TWO

FEARS OF FLYING

OR

MISS BRETT DISCOVERS THE YOUNG INVENTORS GUILD

"Hello?" Miss Brett called into the telephone receiver. There was no answer. No sound coming from the telephone receiver. Only silence.

"Hello?" Miss Brett tried again, but it was clear there was no longer anyone at the other end. She replaced the earpiece and ran into the kitchen, then through the door to the classroom.

The children were all in their seats, looking rather shaken.

"Is everyone all right?" she asked, looking into each of their faces. A few nodded, a couple shrugged, but they all seemed to be unhurt. Jasper rubbed his neck and Miss Brett could see red marks from where Reginald Roderick Kattaning had grabbed him.

"Where is that man?" asked Miss Brett, looking around, controlled fury in her throat.

"He was pacing and chattering and rubbing his stomach," Lucy said, "and after he opened the door to the kitchen, he just ran away."

Miss Brett went to the window and looked left toward the gardener's shed and the pile of hay bales. There was nothing moving and nothing apparently amiss. Taking a deep breath, Miss Brett looked around for something to use if she needed to clobber someone. She grabbed the old broom by the door and gingerly stuck her head through the threshold. Carefully, as if stepping on glass, she walked out of the schoolhouse. She looked to her right and to her left, and again. There was no one there.

Broom raised, she walked cautiously to the right, along the wall, and around the corner to see if Reginald Roderick Kattaning was hiding in the bushes. He was not. She walked to the side of the farmhouse and stood below the kitchen window. She looked behind the bundles of hay piled up to the sill. Reginald Roderick Kattaning was not behind the hay bales.

She *did* notice, however, a wire hanging out of the wall of the house. She had not seen it before when she'd been out there bringing potato peelings to the compost pile. She followed the wire to the wall of the building. It went into a little hole that led inside. She stepped back and quickly realized it led directly into the telephone room.

She turned around and saw the other end of the wire. It hung from a pole that ran along the road.

"He's cut the line to the telephone," she said to herself.

———✦———

The children were all huddled at the window, watching Miss Brett and the wire.

"Reginald Roderick Kattaning cut the wire," Wallace said.

"It's a telephone wire. He cut off our telephone," Jasper said.

"I didn't know we had a telephone," Lucy said.

"Do you even know what a telephone is?" asked Faye.

Miss Brett came back into the classroom. "I can't for the life of me imagine what he wanted," she said, almost to herself.

But the children heard her. They looked to one another, knowingly. This exchange did not escape Miss Brett.

"What?" Miss Brett said. "You know something? What is it? What did he want?"

Faye raised her hand.

"You do not need to raise your hand, Faye," Miss Brett said, emphatically. "For goodness sake, if you know something, tell me."

"He wanted our flying machine," she said, feeling a bit self-conscious at how self-important that sounded.

"Your what?" Miss Brett's tone was incredulous.

"The flying machine," Wallace said. "Reginald Roderick Kattaning wanted our flying machine."

"I heard what Faye said, I . . . I . . ." Miss Brett was utterly confused. "He wanted *what*?"

"Our flying machine," said Faye. "We're calling it an aeroplane."

"Your flying machine? What does it fly?"

"It flies itself," said Lucy.

"Are you telling me you have a machine that flies?" said Miss Brett. She felt as if her brain was about to fall out of her head.

"Well," Faye said, "my first model was a disaster. I'd been working so hard and I really felt like I had the whole thing, but . . . . well, I hadn't. You see, it was really just a glider. It had no power and I realized..." Faye looked around at the faces of her classmates. Her fellow inventors. Her friends.

Yes, she realized. They *were* her friends.

"Something like this needs teamwork." She smiled awkwardly at her classmates. Lucy put her hand into Faye's and smiled up at the older girl. Faye squeezed Lucy's hand. "So everyone helped .. . and, well..."

Wallace looked down. "Not me, I only—"

"Everyone." Faye took a gulp and her breath caught. "It's just big enough for one child. And it flies. Right now, it can really carry no more than ninety—"

"Faye," Miss Brett said. "Dear, listen, men have been trying to invent a flying vehicle for hundreds of years."

"It's true, Miss Brett," Lucy said excitedly.

Jasper cleared his throat. "Imagine what power someone would have if they could make a whole fleet of flying machines," he said. "That has to be why he wants it."

"They could take over the world," Noah said. "One giant evil empire."

"Even one bad man with an aeroplane could do any number of horrid, beastly things," said Lucy.

"Do you think that's what he wanted? And for some diabolical plan?" said Miss Brett.

"What else could it be?" asked Noah. "Your biscuits are wonderful, but stealing recipes hardly seems likely."

"And he knew about the pieces, the thing, and the machine," said Lucy, in horror. "He must have seen us when he was the birdwatcher."

"I told you I didn't think it would be safe to drive with him," Noah said.

"We've been so foolish," said Faye. "We did all of our

experiments out in the open. At our homes, in our secret meadow, and out here. We were so stupid."

"We..." Jasper gulped and took a second to get the words out. "We almost walked right into the hands of the enemy."

The children were silent a moment, contemplating their narrow, inadvertent escape.

"At least I managed to place a call," Miss Brett said. "Of course, I don't even know to whom I spoke, but someone on our side, someone wanting to help us."

"If you mean one of the men in black," Jasper said, thinking of the man jumping on his parents' bed, trying to fool him and Lucy, "how can we be sure they aren't doing something awful? We still don't know whether or not they've kidnapped our parents."

"Children," Miss Brett said firmly, "we have been through this all before. We simply do not know. We can only judge by the fact that they have not harmed us—"

"They've stolen our mummies and daddies!" cried Lucy.

"They almost hurt me," said Faye. "They dragged me into one of those carriages."

"And our aeroplane will save everybody," said Lucy, her expression as full of hope as fear.

Miss Brett looked into the faces of her wards. "Were you planning to use the aeroplane to find your parents?" Whatever the children thought of Reginald Roderick Kattaning flying their machine, nothing could compare to the visions of mayhem, death, and destruction that came to Miss Brett's mind at the thought of these children flying in the sky.

"Children, my stars, don't you know how utterly dangerous this would be?" said Miss Brett. "Beside the absolute horror of crashing or exploding, don't you think that, even if you survived, someone would notice you? Someone who might be just the wrong person to notice you?"

"But…" said Faye.

"Children, we simply do not know enough to do something that would only create more danger. It's too much of a risk, in more ways than one. It's too dangerous to try to find people who could be anywhere. We don't even know if they want to be found."

All five children were caught on the sharp hook of her words. Jasper immediately thought of his mother's letter. He looked at Lucy, who had obviously thought the same thing.

"Don't want to be found?" said Wallace, thinking of how his father had just driven away and left him.

Miss Brett realized she had now come face to face with the darkest part of her job description. It was the one thing she had not even thought about herself.

"Listen to me," said Miss Brett. "We all need to be better at telling each other more than we have. I wish you all had told me about your plans, because then I would have told you something I wished I'd not have to." She sighed. "I'd have told you that when I took this job, I was told to keep you from distracting your parents. I never thought … I thought it could do nothing but hurt your feelings—"

"Who told you to keep us apart from our parents?" asked Faye. "Was it one of *them*?"

"Well. To be frank, yes."

"But what about Mummy's—"

"And how do you know your *mummy* wasn't forced into writing that letter?" said Faye to Lucy. "Why do we trust these lunatics?"

"But we don't have a choice, do we?" Jasper said softly. "We have no one else. We know that Reginald Roderick Kattaning is definitely not on our side. We don't have to trust the men in black. We're their captives and we don't even know why. But we have to assume they are not going to attack us, at least for now. Not immediately."

"Well, the flying machine—"

"Faye," Miss Brett said, looking right at the girl, "tell me, do you have the blueprints for your invention here?"

"Um, yes," said Faye. "We have them in the Guild journal."

Miss Brett looked confused. "The what?"

The children explained how they came to find the green leather book that wasn't a book, which had belonged to that mysterious organization of long ago, the Young Inventors Guild.

"And you are the new Young Inventors Guild?" she asked.

"I suppose we are," Jasper said, tentatively, looking at the others one by one.

"I told you! I told you!" cried Lucy.

"But you have a book with the details of your invention?" asked Miss Brett. "All the notes? Everything together?"

For the first time, these very clever children felt quite stupid. Lucy and Wallace had been keeping a meticulous record of all manner of brilliant inventions. Wallace's excellent penmanship and language made for clear explanations of everything. And with Lucy's sketches, it was easy for anyone to see exactly what they had planned. No one would have the slightest problem understanding their designs. No one.

"We'll have to figure out a way to keep all of your notes and drawings and inventions safe." Miss Brett had an idea of what needed to be done first.

Ignoring all other concerns for a moment, Noah looked up at his friends, a small grin at the corners of his mouth. "Are we really the new Young Inventors Guild?"

Miss Brett was caught off guard. She smiled. "My clever, clever, clever children. My wonderfully clever young inventors.. . of course you are."

"I think it's safest to hide the notes from everyone—from those men in black, too. Faye does have a point, doesn't she? We just don't know, do we?" Jasper's cheeks went red as Faye caught his glance. Jasper quickly looked away.

"We did create the aeroplane to use against *them*," said Noah. "It's only fair, after all, to keep it from them."

"Look!" said Lucy, who had been looking forlornly out the window. They followed her finger to the distant road. They could all see a small cloud of dust moving along. Lucy took out her spyglass and handed it to Miss Brett.

Miss Brett could see quite clearly. A large black carriage was ambling down the road, pulled by four powerful black stallions.

"They're coming to help," Miss Brett told them. "See? They're coming in response to the call."

"They're coming to fetch us for the weekend, more likely," Noah said. "This we do not need right now."

"What do we do?" Lucy asked.

Miss Brett watched as the carriage came closer. Handing the spyglass back to Lucy, she made her decision. If she wanted the children to trust her, she would have to trust them. "All right," she said, "we only have a few minutes before the carriage comes for you. Go now and collect your things. Faye, can your larger model be dismantled?"

"It's already taken apart."

"Good. Now, you must take the sections and wrap them up so—"

"Um, we've already done that, Miss Brett, ma'am," said Wallace. "They're wrapped in blankets."

"Right, excellent. How about your smaller models? Well, you'll need to pack all of your smaller models as well. Jasper, get any other drawings you might have, and Lucy, make sure you have that journal."

"I will, Miss Brett," said Lucy. She seemed to stand taller with the heavy responsibility placed upon her shoulders.

"I want you all to act calm," Miss Brett said, "and do not discuss what has happened here."

"The journal," Jasper said. Concerned about his little sister carrying the book, he added, "I'll go fetch it."

"It's mine!" Lucy called after him as he went into the house to get it. "I'm the one who gets to carry it."

"We have too much to carry," said Faye. "Maybe we should hide the book here."

"With Reginald Roderick Kataning, the crazed birdwatcher of Dayton, on the loose?" said Noah. "We'd probably be safer handing it over to our ever-present blackbirds. At least we know they already know it exists."

"Yes, but with our notes in it, they might do something terrible."

"We need to disguise it somehow," said Wallace. "That way, we can just carry it and not worry about trying to pack it or hide it."

Jasper, returning to the classroom, agreed, handing the book he carried to a very demanding Lucy.

"Wait, just a minute," said Miss Brett, running into the house. She was back before they really had a chance to wonder what she was doing. With her was her mother's copy of *Alice's Adventures in Wonderland*.

"You want me to take that, too?" asked Lucy. "Two books will be even heavier than one."

"No, darling," said Miss Brett, removing the dust jacket from the Lewis Carroll book. "I want you to look like you are taking it." And with that, she wrapped it around the journal. It was a perfect fit.

"Goodness, Miss Brett!" Lucy said with a gasp. "Even I'll think I'm carrying your mummy's book."

"Now, about the aeroplane..." said Miss Brett.

"The men in black most likely don't know about the flying machine," Noah said. "And Reginald Roderick Kattaning doesn't know where it is. I mean, he doesn't know we've got it here or where it is exactly."

"I want you to find a good place to hide everything pertaining to your invention," said Miss Brett. "Keep the pieces apart, in separate houses, so if any piece is found, its brothers will remain hidden and the whole machine will still be safe." Miss Brett looked each child in the eyes to be sure they understood.

"What about saving our parents?" Faye asked. Her heart fell as she asked it.

"Well, I don't know how you were planning to do that," Miss Brett said calmly, "but it certainly is not safe to do anything of the kind now. Perhaps it's something we can talk about and work on together. But for now, there are more pressing, real, and present dangers."

"She's right," said Wallace, and his heart fell, too.

Miss Brett put her hand on his shoulder. "I think it's best that you keep the pieces with you and—"

"But Miss Brett," Lucy said, "how do we know they won't find it at our homes? Even in pieces, the pieces are still with us."

"Nowhere is safe," Wallace said. "We need to hide everything somewhere else."

"But we don't know anywhere else," Miss Brett said. "It will have to be—"

"Cousin Katharine," said Faye.

After only a few seconds, they remembered Faye's cousin. The children nodded. It was the one place they could go where no one would ever look.

"How will we get there?" asked Wallace. "We'll have a mighty difficult time getting past the men in black."

Faye smiled. "We'll have well over nine and a half minutes, remember? During the day, the patrol is not as tight."

"Forget the men in black," Noah said. "What about the nannies?"

"We'll figure a way around them," Faye said, but about this she did not seem quite as confident.

"I'm worried about Rosie," cried Lucy. "I'm afraid to hurt her feelings again."

"I'm afraid of being strung up in a secret trap by the men in black," added Noah, to no one's delight.

"Children." Miss Brett could not help but worry. "Please. I don't want you to put yourselves in harm's way."

Jasper smiled. Miss Brett sounded like a mother. "We'll be all right, Miss Brett. This is the best thing we can do."

Soon, the black carriage pulled up in front. The driver wore what appeared to be a black nightshirt and black night cap and larger woolly slippers—black, of course. Beneath his nightshirt, one could see his very bony knobby knees. He had a large, black, fuzzy toy bear tucked under one arm. His nightcap was pulled down low on his nose, covering what looked to be the kind of blindfold people wear when they suffer from a headache or need darkness in order to slumber deeply. He looked as if he'd be more at home in a bed than in a car. He must have been able to see through the blindfold, though, since he was, after all, driving.

"Come along, children," Miss Brett called in a lighthearted sing-song voice.

The children all came skipping out of the farmhouse, imitations of smiles and careless merriment plastered on their faces. Each carried one of the bundles. All placed their bundles on the ground by the carriage and set off back inside to collect more. They were bringing the extra parts and anything else they did not have time to dismantle—wing parts, engine parts, propellers, tails, and rudders—all wrapped in blankets and carpets.

"What is all of this?" the driver asked, shifting his bear to the other arm, looking at the growing pile. "Again there is the work of school?"

The children smiled and nodded. Miss Brett followed their lead and did the same.

If the man did not believe them, he said nothing about it. He took the satchels and piled them up with the other bags onto the top of the carriage. There was quite a load when he was finished.

Lucy hugged Miss Brett. "What about you?" Lucy asked, concern flashing in her sweet eyes.

"I'll be fine," Miss Brett said unconvincingly. "Don't you worry about me."

Lucy climbed into the carriage and began her ritual of waving. Miss Brett waved from the doorway as the carriage took the children away, trying not to show the horrible worry she felt not knowing how things would be when next they met.

CHAPTER TWENTY-THREE

Decisions Can Be Relative

OR

 THE RIGHT BROTHERS FOR THE JOB

A quiet ride takes longer than a happy chatty ride. A near silent ride takes forever. Unlike most Friday and Sunday rides to and from Dayton, the children did not chatter or chat, nibble or laugh. They all sat very still and said nothing. The fact was there was an awful lot to say, but there was infinitely more to think about. What to believe? Who to trust? How to proceed? Where to go?

Though they had managed what no one else in history had managed to do, they realized they still might be very wrong about many things—things they believed with all their hearts. Even Faye, the champion of the cause of rescuing their parents, was suddenly faced with the possibility that their parents didn't want to be rescued and, in fact, wanted the children to stay away.

When the carriage finally turned onto Maple after going around the block twice, all of the children got out at once. Jasper climbed up and tossed all of the luggage off. Everyone grabbed their bags and ran to their respective homes. The driver exited the carriage, stood for a moment, and put his thumb in his mouth. He switched his teddy bear to the other arm before climbing back in and driving away.

"Well, look at you," said Rosie when Jasper and Lucy came running in. "You look all in a state."

"We're just, um, excited to be home," said Jasper, taking Lucy by the hand.

"And what is all of this?" Rosie asked, reaching out for the clumsy satchels that Jasper and Lucy were carrying.

"Oh, don't worry," said Jasper, stepping back out of Rosie's reach. Dashing past her, he shouted, "It's just a project—just a fun thing, really!"

Rosie looked down at Lucy, who also hugged her satchel tightly.

"Yes, it's loads of fun," Lucy said, running off after her brother.

"But the two of you, you need some eating. What about food? I've made—"

"We're not hungry!" Jasper lied, but then added, "But we will be."

Jasper and Lucy ran up to their rooms and dropped off their bags. Looking around for a place to put their satchels, they opted to shove the lot under their beds.

"That's as good a place as any," said Jasper, pulling the edge of his quilt down so the satchel was completely hidden.

"I really think it's just awful keeping all these things from Rosie," said Lucy, "and from Miss Brett and . . . It makes me feel like a naughty girl."

"Well, you're not a naughty girl. None of us is naughty. And we're not telling lies either. Not really," he said. He stopped rushing for a moment and looked Lucy in the eyes. A sneaky smile spreading across his face, he said, "It *is* terribly exciting, isn't it, Lucy? I mean, it's exciting as well as dangerous, amazing, historic, and brilliant, and, of course, terrifying, and horridly worrying. Still, all said, it is frightfully thrilling, isn't it?"

Lucy smiled. "Yes," she said in earnest. "Frightfully."

—————

When Jasper and Lucy emerged from the house, Wallace and Faye were already there in the meadow, standing next to each other, looking down at Noah. Noah sat on the grass, staring down into his lap. He looked up for a moment, then back down again.

In his hand he held a stack of cards, tied together with a pale blue ribbon that Noah seemed not yet to have untied.

"What's wrong, Noah?" said Lucy. Noah looked up at her and then back down again. There was no funny joke or silly response. He just stared at the bundle of cards.

"What have you got there, in that ribbon?" Lucy asked. She loved ribbons.

"Postcards," said Noah. His voice cracked mid-word.

"Where did you find them?" asked Jasper.

"They're mine," said Noah in a very weak voice.

"Where did you find them? They look lovely with that ribbon," said Lucy.

"They just arrived."

"And they were sent here?" said Jasper. "To your house?"

Noah turned over the stack of postcards. The bottom card

did not have an address. It simply said, "Noah Canto-Sagas." "No, just to me, just my name," said Noah. "And they came like this, all together in this bundle with this ribbon."

"Just your ruddy name?" Faye grabbed the bundle. "What are you? The King of England?" But there it was, his name and no address, yet the stack of postcards had made it to Noah anyway.

"Why didn't you open the package, Noah?" Jasper said.

"I just…" But he didn't really know why he hadn't opened the bundle of postcards. His whole life had been made up of postcards, and whenever he received them, he would immediately run to the postman and read his mother's words, drinking up everything she said. "Okay…" said Noah. He untied the ribbon.

"Where has she been this time?" asked Jasper as Noah perused the first postcard.

"She was in Moscow, singing for the Czar and his family," said Noah, looking at the first one. He flipped to the next. "Then in Prague, and then somewhere in Austria." He flipped to the next. "Then she took a royal coach to the south of France…" He flipped again. "…and was riding gondolas along the waterways of Venice with Princess Elena of Montenegro earlier that month. 'Oh, silly me, Lennie has been the Queen of Italy for three years now since she married that teeny-tiny Victor Emmanuel'…and then the Duchy of Liechtenstein, where Prince Johann II and apparently the entire population came to hear her in the park." A smile spread over his face. "And apparently Fifi ran away and the entire population, including all members of the police force, searched the country until they found her."

"Oh, read one to us, please, Noah! Please!" said Lucy, desperate to hear a mother's words, even if they weren't those of her own mother.

"He might not want to," Jasper said.

"Very well," said Noah, clearing his throat. "'Darling Noah,'" he read, speaking in a high, breathy voice that everyone assumed, correctly, to sound like his mother's, "'I am off to Bohemia for a most deliciously romantic engagement. Remember, I sang at the affair when the Archduke Franz Ferdinand married the Countess Sophie Chotek von Chotkowa und Wogninon? That was on the first of July three years ago. I shall never forget it. It caused a terrible stir, inasmuch as they are very much in love, and the emperor was quite livid. Sophie, you see, is from old Bohemian nobility, but not as exalted as the Hapsburgs, so she had to endure a terrible social strain in order to marry the man she loves. And the archduke would not have survived a long bout with the dreaded consumption had it not been for the ministrations, in secret of course, of his adoring Sophie. And now I shall sing for them again! It is a secret from Sophie, who knows not a thing. I will descend upon the affair from a hot air balloon! How fabulously novelesque! Long live romance! Yours ever so—Mother.'"

"Goodness, so much traveling," Lucy said, looking at the picture of the palace on the postcard Noah handed her.

"And that's just what she wrote on that one card," said Noah, with decidedly less enthusiasm than Lucy. He flipped to another. "'... and such a lovely visit with the five sisters of Greiz. Emma's wedding was a lovely affair, and I was asked to sing a cappella...'" He handed the card to Faye, flipping to the next.

"Is she really gone so often?" said Faye.

"Yes, she is," said Noah. "In her own way, she's missing in action, I suppose."

"Um, I don't want Daisy to worry, and I'm a bit hungry and …" Wallace looked a bit anxious. He swallowed hard and quickly added, "Daisy made hot-crossed buns and apple tarts. I just don't want her worrying."

"We should eat," said Noah, who knew very well that hungry was not the only thing Wallace was feeling. Noah suddenly felt foolish and selfish for complaining about his mother. At least he had a mother. And whatever complaints Noah had about his mother, her postcards were at least a reminder that she was somewhere. "Sorry, Wallace, I mean, because you're hungry. I should have—"

"I am," Wallace said defensively. "I haven't eaten since Miss Brett's breakfast."

"Wait!" Faye grabbed Wallace's arm. "Noah, this card was sent in August and it's already October. What are the dates of the other postcards?"

Noah flipped through. "August 17, September 1 … Here's one about presenting a bouquet at the opening of the Constantinople-Baghdad Railway in Ankara. That was September 5."

"So someone has been holding these cards," Faye said with great suspicion. "Someone prevented these from being mailed—or, at least, prevented them from being delivered."

"You mean someone is keeping Noah's mummy, too?" asked Lucy.

"Well, they know she's trying to contact Noah," said Faye, determination in her voice. "These postcards are proof that your mother doesn't know. She doesn't suspect foul play."

"But if they don't want me to know, or her to know where we are," Noah said, "why do I have these now?"

"And how did he get them?" asked Lucy.

Faye was about to give an answer when she realized she didn't have one. "He received them, but someone had held them," said Faye. "He received them, even though his mum never put his address on the card. That doesn't make any sense."

"It makes me dizzy," said Lucy.

"That's because you haven't eaten," said Jasper.

"None of us has," said Noah.

"So let's decide what we're going to do," said Jasper.

"Well," said Faye, indignantly. Even her stomach was betraying her. "I'll just have to walk to Cousin Katharine's and explain."

"We're all going," Jasper said, putting his hand on her arm. "We're not going to let you go on your own." Faye looked into Jasper's eyes and he let go of her arm—not because she glared at him, but because she almost smiled.

"How would you carry everything?" asked Lucy.

"You'll need our help," said Noah.

Faye had to admit she would need help. "Well, all right. We'll think better after we get some food in our noisy bellies. Who can think with all that racket, anyway?"

"After we eat, we should all meet here with our satchels," said Jasper. "Do you have the address, Faye?"

"Yes," said Faye, rummaging in her pockets. She pulled out an old yellowed card. "This is from Aunt Susan. She sent it years ago for my mother's birthday. I kept it because of the painting on the front. It's an eagle soaring on the wind. The address is Seven Hawthorn Street."

"A hawthorn is a tree," said Lucy, excitedly. "It can't be far."

After filling their bellies, the children set about devising their plan. They were going to find Seven Hawthorn Street and talk to Faye's cousins. But first, they had to be sure the nannies would not follow.

"You'll have to do it," moaned Lucy. "I can't bear to do it myself." Her fingers, nails nibbled to the quick, received the brunt of her anxiety.

"I'll do it," said Jasper.

The plan was simple. Each child would tell their nanny they were going to the other's house. Faye would say she was going to Noah's, Noah would say he was going to Wallace's, and Jasper would say he and Lucy were going to Faye's.

But Lucy was miserable. Having a memory like hers, Jasper often thought, was like carrying the truth of the world in your head. Lucy could not bear dishonesty. And it especially pained her to fib to people she loved.

Even so, the children went ahead with the plan. Soon, with great care and sneakiness, they all met, hidden by some of the shrubbery near Noah's house.

"Do you think the men in black know that your cousin is in the neighborhood?" asked Jasper. They were counting down the minutes until the next black carriage would pass. They wanted to know exactly how much time they had, because they were not moving very fast with all of the bundles.

"They could not know," said Faye. "We haven't seen them in years. We have different names. My mother probably has a relative in every city in the world."

In one fell swoop, the children made a dash as soon as the black carriage turned the corner. They ran until they were hidden by the trees lining the street of the next block.

"The houses look empty," Jasper said as they walked more slowly down the next block. It was true. There were no signs of life in any of the neighboring houses.

Most of the journey was spent running and dropping and reorganizing the blanket-wrapped packages. They were heavy and awkward and cumbersome to carry. The house was about seven blocks away, but it felt a lot farther. At least Lucy knew exactly where the street was.

It took all of nineteen minutes.

"That was easy," said Jasper, catching his breath, letting his package rest against his legs. They stood in front of the house.

"And I thought I was the funny one," said Noah, leaning over to catch the stitch in his side.

Faye hurried up to the front door. She knocked. And waited. Then knocked again. A small boy of about four years old answered the door.

"I didn't know Katharine had any children," Faye said, bewildered. "In fact, I didn't know she was married."

"Mommy!" the little boy screamed. "There are very big children at the door and they don't know me!"

A lovely woman in a bright yellow dress came hurrying out from what was most likely the kitchen. She wiped her hands on her apron, her face dusted with flour.

"May I help you?" asked the woman in a pleasant voice. The little boy hid behind her skirt, thumb firmly planted in his mouth.

"You aren't my cousin Katharine," Faye said.

"No, I am not," the woman said, still smiling.

"I'm very sorry," Faye said, collecting herself. "I was looking for—"

"Of course," the woman said, smiling. "I'm sorry, Katharine does not live here."

Faye's heart sank. *How stupid*, she thought. How could she have been so foolish as to expect her family to still be living there? It had been her fault, leading them here, giving them hope, making them believe. It had been her stupid pride that had made her believe she would be the one to save everyone. Now they were standing there with nowhere to go.

And they felt helpless. Would they be captured by Reginald Roderick Kattaning? Would they ever see their parents again? Heads down, their burdens suddenly impossibly awkward and unbearably heavy, the children turned to leave.

"Wait, dears," called the pleasant lady. "You're looking for *Seven* Hawthorn, aren't you? You see, this is *Nine* Hawthorn."

Five hearts skipped five beats.

The woman smiled and continued. "Many people make that mistake. I keep meaning to fix our address plate. That English ivy is a terror. I can never keep it under control. It grows over everything, including the address and, on top of that, one of the numbers is broken."

Faye looked at the house number and saw that, indeed, the ivy was covering part of the number, and the big chip really did make a "7" out of the "9."

"So, there still is a Katharine?" asked Lucy. "And a number

seven?"

"That's the house there, next door," the smiling woman said, pointing. "There is indeed a Katharine. She's a teacher, I believe. Is that who you're looking for?"

Faye nodded again.

"Well, I saw her not long ago, watering the daffodils in the front garden. She should be home, dear."

They all thanked the woman and, carrying the suddenly less awkward and quite manageable bundles, hurried next door.

On the porch was an elderly man in a large chair. The man was snoring away, emitting large snorts, his chin moving his white beard as he mumbled, and his great moustache fluttering in the wake of his snorfling, threatening to find its way into his mouth.

Faye ran up the steps to the porch and knocked loudly on the door. Noah walked over to the man, curious to see whether or not he would in fact inhale his grand moustache.

The door was opened by a very elderly woman. Faye knew this was not Aunt Susan, because Aunt Susan had died years before. She also knew it was not Katharine because Katharine was not at all an old lady.

"Yes?" the old woman said.

"I'm looking for my cousin Katharine," said Faye.

"The bishop ain't to be disturbed," she said, wagging her finger inches from Noah's face. Noah sheepishly returned to the doorway, having clearly invaded the space of the sleeping old man.

"That's Uncle Milton!" said Faye with excited recognition.

"The bishop'?" Jasper asked Faye softly.

"Uncle Milton was a bishop," she whispered back. Louder, she said, "I'd like to see Cousin Katharine, please." She tried to give a smile to the grumpy old lady. It didn't seem to work.

"Not here," said the woman with a prominent Irish lilt. "You her students?"

"No, I'm her cousin," said Faye.

"Don't look like her," the woman said, suspiciously.

Faye's hand went to her face. With her dark olive skin and, of course, her accent, colored with Indian and British pronunciations, she really didn't look or sound anything like Katharine.

"My mother is Gwendolyn—"

"Ah, the one what's gone and moved across the sea," the woman said knowingly. "Went and married that foreigner, ain't it?"

How this Irish woman, with a voice like a grouchy leprechaun, could consider someone *else*, *anyone* else, a foreigner was beyond Faye's understanding.

"Yes," Faye said, now anxious. "Do you know where my cousin is? How we might find her? It's rather urgent."

"Course I know," the woman said. "I'm the housekeeper. I keep the house. Course I know where everyone is."

"Lovely," said Faye. "Would you be so kind as to tell us?"

The old woman gave them a piercing stare, looking each one of them dead in the eyes. Then she turned to Faye.

"Thems with you?" she asked, nodding toward the others.

"Yes," said Faye.

"Well, Miss Katharine's with her brothers at the shop." With that, the old woman began to close the door.

"Wait, the shop? What shop? Where is it?" Faye asked,

grabbing hold of the door.

"Twenty-Two South Williams Street," the woman said, again trying to close the door.

"Where is that?" asked Faye, again stopping her.

"You go right a few blocks, left, then west up and down that way." The old woman pointed this way and that, and then she peeled Faye's fingers from the door and closed it with a decisive bang.

"Actually, it's left three blocks and then right," said Lucy, looking up at the others with an almost apologetic grin.

"Well, if I had to pick between Lucy and that old woman as the one to follow," Noah said, stepping over to stand beside Lucy, "I'd pick Lucy, any day." Lucy beamed.

With that, the children picked up their satchels and headed in the opposite direction from where the old woman pointed. After several left and right turns, they found themselves on a rather busy street.

"We passed South Williams loads of times," said Lucy, "and I've seen the shop at number twenty-two."

"Even if you hadn't, Lucy," said Jasper, pointing across the street, "how many shops on South Williams could there be?"

"It's her!" said Faye, jumping up and down. There, on the corner, was a shop, and in the front, bending over a bicycle, was Cousin Katharine. Faye rushed across the street, minding the traffic, with the other four quickly, but carefully, following.

Faye shouted, "Katharine!"

Katharine stood up. Her dark hair was pulled back and mostly hidden beneath a light hat. At first, she did not seem to recognize Faye, but then, all at once, she grew a marvelous smile that lit up her whole face.

"Is this my little Faye?" she asked, hugging her cousin tight. Faye was almost as tall as she was.

"Oh, I'm so glad to find you," said Faye from the depths of Katharine's embrace.

Katharine looked around. "Where are your parents?" she asked. "And who are these fine young people?"

"These are my schoolmates. Mother and Father... well, they're working on a project. But we must talk ..." Faye looked around, then whispered, "And we must talk in private."

"All right." Katharine thought for a moment. "Come with me," she said.

———◆———

The bicycle shop was full of gears and drawings and parts, as well as finished bicycles. They looked lovely. There were even a couple tandems—bicycles built for two riders. Several men were working at benches and testing wheels. One sketched something at a drafting table.

"I thought you were a teacher," Faye said.

"I am," Katharine said, "but I help my brothers out here at the shop when I can. I love to ride and tinker. Mother always taught us the pleasures of working with our hands."

The children followed Katharine to the back room and closed the door behind them.

"Right," Katharine said. "Tell me, what is going on?"

It took several minutes to explain to Katharine what had transpired. They left out several details. Many, in fact. They divulged no information about what their parents were doing.

They didn't know anyway. About Reginald Roderick Kattaning, they said simply he was in pursuit of their creation and that he was not a very nice man. Of the Young Inventors Guild, they told her nothing.

"We've been led to believe our project would be dangerous if it fell into the wrong hands," said Faye, cryptically. "It might bring about problems for those closest to it, and to our parents, if it were discovered."

"What are you saying, Faye?" said Katharine.

"It's just that we've created something very powerful, and it must be kept secure," said Jasper. "We can't keep it where we're staying."

"And what is this invention?" Katharine asked, looking worried. "A weapon?"

The children looked at one another, and then at Faye.

"Faye, you should do the honors," said Wallace.

Faye slowly unwrapped her satchel. The others followed.

———

Forty minutes later, Katharine opened the door to the room, flushed with excitement at what she had heard and seen. She went over to the man working at the drafting table and whispered in his ear. He stood abruptly, spilling his pencils onto the floor.

"Ed," he called to the man aligning a set of wheels on a bicycle, "please get my brother."

The man hurried through the door that led to the back porch. He returned almost immediately with another man, younger than the draftsman, with a dark moustache and a wrench in his hand. Both the draftsman and the younger brother with the moustache followed Katharine into the back room.

There they found five children standing around a small contraption obviously built to fly. Faye stood up.

"This is Faye, Cousin Gwendolyn's daughter," said Katharine.

The two men didn't look up. Instead, they walked around the small craft.

"Gentlemen," coaxed Katharine, "please stop drooling for one moment and greet Cousin Faye."

"Little Faye?" asked the draftsman, looking around as if suddenly aware that others were in the room.

"Well," Katharine said with a smile, "she's not so little anymore."

The two men seemed taken aback at the sight of Faye. They studied her, as she studied them. "You've grown, Little Faye," said the younger brother with the moustache.

"And you've grown a moustache," said Faye.

"This is some machine," said the younger brother with the moustache.

"Who built this?" the draftsman asked.

"We all did," said Faye.

"But it was her idea," Noah said.

"No, it wasn't," said Faye. "I know when a thing is my idea. This was all of ours."

"It's wonderful," said the younger brother with the moustache.

"It's a fantastic design," said the older brother.

"And it flies," said Katharine.

The two men looked at Faye. She nodded.

"It flies?" they both asked in unison.

Faye's smile broadened. "Yes, it does."

"It truly flies on its own power?" the younger brother with the moustache asked, looking at the engine.

"Yes, although it depends on wind for lift," said Wallace. "And you have to—"

"You've got to keep it for us," said Lucy. "Faye says you're the only ones we can trust."

Faye started to explain, but the younger brother with the moustache cut her off with another stunned sputter. "And you say it really flies?"

"Yes, although we haven't built a larger-scale craft yet," said Faye.

"We've been working on our own designs," said the draftsman, running his hand along the wing of Faye's craft.

Faye said, "We've worked out that the wing-warping—"

"Wing-warping? Of course!" said the younger brother with the moustache. "We've been working with kites and found—"

"Yes, kites!" exclaimed Faye. "That would have been an excellent way to visualize, to get a real, solid handle on—"

"Faye," said Jasper, catching her by the sleeve, "who are these fellows? How do we know we can trust them?"

"I'm terribly sorry," said the younger brother with the moustache, kneeling down and looking Jasper right in the eye. "Terribly pleased to meet you," he said.

"This is Lucy, Jasper, Noah, and Wallace," said Katharine. "They're friends of Cousin Faye. Children, these are my brothers, Wilbur and Orville."

"I can see the similarities between your creation and our most recent design," said Wilbur, still examining the aeroplane, "but you've done a much better job with the engine, the propeller, the wings, and—"

"You need to take this working, half-scale prototype," Faye began, but Orville cut her off.

"What do you mean 'take' it?"

"We need someone to take it from us," said Faye. "In fact, it would be best if the full-scale model was completed and made public. Someone else is bound to be close, and it's safer to have it out there than hidden and at risk of finding its way into the wrong hands."

The children all looked at one another. They had not counted on Katharine's brothers being interested, let alone knowledgeable and, in fact, working on the same thing. They had come seeking a place to hide their invention. What they'd found was a place to launch it.

"May we have a moment?" Jasper asked, but the brothers only nodded, enthralled as they were with the aeroplane.

"Are we just going to give them the aeroplane?" asked Wallace, incredulous. "These guys aren't going to want to simply hide it. And we don't even have a patent."

"We have no choice," said Noah. "We'll just have to be the silent geniuses who changed the world."

"And we do want to change the world, don't we?" asked Faye. "We don't want to destroy it, and chances are we may never have a chance to let it fly it ourselves."

"We can let them finish it," said Jasper. "Then, when it's safe, we can let the world know it's ours."

"Even if that's not until we're dead," said Noah.

"Noah might be right," said Faye. "With everything going on, who knows if it will ever be safe to be in the public eye?"

"Are you saying you think I'm right?" said Noah.

"Me? Say you're right?" said Faye in mock indignation. "I won't say you're right even if you are."

"I'd love to see it fly with a real person in it," said Lucy.

"And what am I, Lucy?" asked Faye.

"I mean so that a real *big* person could fly it," Lucy said.

"Right. Is it settled?" Faye looked at her friends. They nodded. "My cousins can complete it and release it to the world. We can claim credit when it's safe."

Five hands went into the center. The Young Inventors Guild had made a decision, and while they knew it was the right one, they all felt a little sad just the same. It felt a bit like a mother bird watching her baby bird fly away. "Well, we'll always have our journal," said Lucy.

Orville cleared his throat. "You were saying…?" he said.

"You need to build the full-scale version," said Faye. "We can't do this ourselves and, for now, we cannot take credit. You will have to do the calculations for the full-scale version. It will be you doing all of the work from here on out."

Faye looked at the others. This was suddenly more difficult than any of them had thought. It had been theirs. It had belonged to them all. They had succeeded where all the adults before them had failed.

Faye took a deep breath. "You will be the inventors of the world's first aeroplane."

Wallace wrote in the journal frantically. "I need to know the name of the shop again, please," he said.

"For the record," said Jasper. "Wallace and Lucy have been keeping a journal of all of… all of our notes."

"Then we'll eat it," said Noah. It took a moment for everyone to laugh.

"The shop is called Wright Cycle Company," said Wilbur. "But really now, are you sure you don't want your names—"

"We're sure," said Wallace, finishing his notes.

"Right now, and I don't mean to sound so secretive, but it really is not a very good time," said Faye. "Our parents don't know and they're … working on a project … and everything needs to be secret. We don't want you to mention us in connection with this craft. Really, absolutely no mention until we say otherwise."

Wallace mumbled to himself, jotting down figures and rereading his notes. He pulled out a separate piece of paper. "I'll give you some measurements," he said, handing the paper to Lucy, who added a few quick sketches.

"And you'll need a four-cylinder, twelve-horsepower engine," Noah said.

"And two propellers," said Jasper.

"Then," said Faye, "with proper wind to give it that initial lift power, you will, without a doubt, get it to fly—"

"But you'll have to find a windier spot than Dayton, Ohio," Jasper said.

"But you can do it," Wallace said. "It will be a three-axis control that—sorry, I don't mean to … you both seem capable and knowledgeable in the mechanics of it. Your own design sounded excellent, minus a few small flaws."

"I bet you'll be in the air before Christmas," said Noah.

The two brothers looked at one another and smiled.

"But," said Orville, "we can announce your enormous contributions to the future of aviation, after—"

"Only after we tell you it's all right to do so," Jasper said.

"For now, the credit should go to the Wright brothers," said Faye.

Wilbur and Orville both opened their mouths, but were stopped by five emphatic shaking heads. There was a moment of silence. The Wright brothers conceded.

"Can we say that we had great assistance from family . . ." Wilbur looked at Faye. "...and friends..." They looked at the others. "... without whom it would never have taken off the ground?"

"Absolutely," said Faye with a smile.

"Can we call it Faye's Flyer?" asked Orville.

"Just 'Flyer,'" said Faye, although she did like the sound of it.

"Oh, that's a lovely name," said Lucy.

"But you'll let us know if you ever want a ride," said Orville with a wink.

"You know what we *would* like?" said Faye, an idea jumping into her head. "We'd like to borrow some bicycles. Does everyone know how to ride?"

They all nodded, save Lucy. It was getting late, and the night patrol would be coming every forty-five seconds. If they walked, it would be dark by the time they got back. It would be faster with bicycles.

"We have just the thing," said Wilbur, as he, Katharine, and Orville hurried back into the shop. They emerged with four bicycles—three made for one rider and one bicycle, a tandem, built for two riders.

"Consider these gifts," Wilbur said.

Faye put her hand on a smaller, elegant bicycle. "This one's mine."

"That one is built for a princess," said Orville, with a bow, "and until now, we haven't met one to bestow it upon." Faye smiled and curtseyed back.

Jasper, who'd recently taught himself to ride and was teaching Lucy, chose the tandem for the two of them. Noah took the biggest and Wallace took the smallest.

"Ready?" said Faye, turning to the others. "Let's go home."

"Home?" Jasper asked, his eyebrows raised in wonder. Had Faye, the leader of every escape plan, the head of the rebels, actually called her house in Dayton, Ohio, home?

"Well," Faye said, blushing as if caught in the act of something, "besides Sole Manner Farm, where else can we call home right now? Where else can we go?"

Jasper gave her a small nod and a little smile. He understood. They all did.

—————

"Where on earth did you get that thing?" asked Rosie as Jasper and Lucy walked their tandem bicycle up to the porch.

"Oh, we found it . . . at Faye's," Jasper said, smiling up at her.

"Very well, but don't you be getting too many skinned knees," said Rosie. "Those contraptions are dangerous."

"I'm famished, Rosie," Lucy said, rubbing her belly. The smell of roast chicken and gravy perfumed the air.

"Well, of course you are. You'd better get washed for supper," Rosie said, scooting the children in. Taking one more look at the bicycle, she shook her head as she closed the door. "I've made some of your favorites."

The two siblings sat down to a delicious supper, as did their friends in each of their own houses. The food tasted more delicious than ever, now that their aeroplane was safe, and they at least felt a bit safer and more in control of things than they had in a very, very long while.

But they also had given away their only means of saving their parents—assuming, of course, their parents needed saving, and assuming the aeroplane would have helped save them. They would worry about new plans of escape and for finding their parents tomorrow. Tonight, they ate and breathed deeply and, even for just one night, it felt good just to be home.

CHAPTER TWENTY-FOUR

A Bicycle Built For Five

OR

 THE LONG AND WINDING ROAD

By Saturday, with no invention to protect and nothing else they could or had to do, the children spent a normal childlike afternoon riding their brand new bikes. Later, they had a picnic in their meadow, and thoughts turned to Miss Brett.

"I never had a proper picnic before we met Miss Brett," said Lucy, fondly.

"Neither had I," Faye said, suddenly feeling less hungry.

By the end of the day, Miss Brett was on their minds, and they'd become anxious about returning to her classroom.

Sunday brought more worries. Was Miss Brett all right? Had Reginald Roderick Kattaning returned? They worried all the more when, by two o'clock in the afternoon, the carriage still had not arrived. The carriages had always arrived just after lunch.

"How very odd," mumbled Rosie, wringing her hands and clucking her teeth. She had been sitting with Jasper and Lucy on the porch for hours.

Faye walked over to Jasper and Lucy's house. She carried her bag and concern.

"This has never happened," she said to them. "Everything has always run like clockwork with these fellows."

"Oh, dear," Lucy said. "I do hope the clock hasn't been broken." Her fingers went to her mouth and she began to nibble.

The three children left their bags on the porch and walked around the block to Noah's, where Myrtle was pacing and twirling her hair around her fingers. Then the four walked to Wallace's.

"Well, I never," mumbled Daisy, cracking her knuckles.

"What do you think is going on?" Wallace asked in a whisper.

No one knew.

"Let's just wait for one of the patrol carriages or motorcars," said Wallace.

No one had seen a patrol that day, and that was not unusual. But as the clocks ticked and tocked, and hours passed, it was strange that the men in black were nowhere to be seen.

By four o'clock, the children decided they needed a plan. All five of them and their nannies were pacing and worrying on Jasper and Lucy's porch. Daisy was cracking her knuckles, Myrtle was twirling her hair, Camellia was tugging at her ear, and Rosie was clucking her teeth and shaking her head.

"We need to do something," whispered Noah.

"We need to get out there," said Faye.

"I think we should go to your cousins and ask them to help," said Jasper.

Faye agreed. "Maybe they can help us get out to the schoolhouse," she said. "Mother told me Orville has a motorcar."

"I don't think we want to get him involved," said Wallace.

"If he did take us, we couldn't exactly tell him to leave us in the lap of danger and run on home," said Noah. "No law-abiding, kind, generous cousin would do that. Besides, I'd like to keep my head attached to my body. I saw the gleam in his eye when he saw the aeroplane. A ride with your cousin Orville might not be the best thing."

"But we do have to go somehow," said Wallace.

"Maybe the funny men don't want us to go," said Lucy.

"I don't care," Faye said. "Lucy, Miss Brett is there. What if she needs us?"

"She does!" cried Lucy. "She does need us!"

"How do we get there?" said Wallace.

"We don't know where it is, let alone how to get there," Noah said. "Those crazy coachmen always seem to go a different way. Who on earth could ever remember which direction to take or where it, or any other road for that matter, actually—"

"I can," said Lucy, blushing under the gaze of the four others. She looked at Jasper and stopped her little finger from finding its way into her mouth.

"Of course you can," said Jasper. He beamed at his sister. Of course, Lucy would remember. "And I know just how we're going to do it."

———◦◦◦———

"It may take us a month to get there," groaned Faye.

"It won't," Jasper said. "We won't have the packages, and we can ride directly there. Our bicycles are almost as fast as the carriages."

"What are we going to tell the nannies?" asked Wallace.

That was going to be a big problem.

The nannies were already pacing and worrying on Jasper and Lucy's porch, and when the children began to explain the plan, there was not much enthusiasm. Daisy once again cracked her knuckles, Myrtle once again twirled her hair, Camellia once again tugged at her ear, and Rosie once again clucked and clucked like a mother hen.

"Oh, goodness, oh, dearie me," Rosie said, shaking her head, close to tears.

"We don't have a choice," Jasper said, patting Rosie gently on the back.

"We must get out to the schoolhouse," said Faye. "There's no one here to take us and no one coming to get us. We're on our own and we have to go."

The four nannies were persuaded to go inside and have a cup of tea, but not before Rosie gave them some sandwiches and water in canteens. Then the five children mounted their bicycles. Lucy's feet hardly reached the pedals on the back of the tandem, but she was determined to push along and help her brother.

But almost the moment they left their neighborhood, Jasper shouted to get down. Quickly, they all ducked into a toolshed at the edge of someone's property.

Silently, they watched as a man wearing a black beefeater's cap nearly twice the man's own height, a black military suit the likes of which none of them could recognize, and boots that reached nearly to his thighs rode by on a giant unicycle.

"He's got to be one of ours," said Noah, shaking his head.

"Shouldn't we tell him? Shouldn't we let him know?" asked Lucy.

"Absolutely not," Faye whispered loudly. And they watched

as the man, full speed, rode past them.

"He's headed toward our house," said Lucy. The man was gone before she finished her sentence.

"No!" warned Faye in her most dangerous voice.

"Why not?" begged Lucy, picking at a bit of sticky tar stuck to her shoe.

"Because," Faye said, her voice deep and soft, "this is our chance to get back at them, to get away, to rescue our parents."

"Get back at them?" asked Jasper.

"They stole our parents and ruined our lives," said Faye, quietly.

"So this is all about getting back at them for taking our parents?" Jasper said, looking accusingly at Faye.

Her devious expression dropped from her face. She suddenly realized what she had just said and how it sounded both to her and the others.

"I didn't mean … that is, I …" She didn't know what she meant. Did she truly feel that the men in black were kidnapping evil-doers? Or did she just hate them because her parents were gone?

"Whatever Faye may or may not be feeling," Noah said, "we have got to get going now. Whatever the men in black want, they don't want us to get to the schoolhouse today, and we've got to get to Miss Brett. With all the danger in this crazy place, she could well be in the middle of some herself."

<hr />

After that, Lucy's instructions led them in a perfectly straight line. By going straight instead of in circles, Lucy got them to the edge of Dayton in fifteen minutes instead of well over two hours.

"What's that sound?" asked Wallace. He heard a hissing noise as they rode along the quiet road.

Stopping, they saw quickly that Noah had a flat tire.

"It's a shoe nail," said Jasper, pulling out the culprit. He quickly put his finger against the hole to keep the air from seeping out.

"We'll never make it with a flat tire," groaned Faye. She bent over to look at the nail. Lucy slipped and fell into her.

"Sorry, Faye," said Lucy, pulling tar from the bottom of her shoe. A truck with roofing tar must have recently passed.

"I can ride with you," Noah said to Faye. But his gangly legs were an impossible fit for Faye's bicycle to hold them both.

"Can we switch the tire with Faye's?" suggested Jasper. Since Noah's bicycle was bigger, they could both fit on Noah's bicycle.

"The tires aren't the same size," Faye said as she shoved Noah off her bicycle, "and we have no tools to change them."

"There's got to be a way to fix this," Noah said, looking around.

"If we can't, we're doomed," Faye said.

"Oh, no, we can't be doomed!" cried Lucy.

"Just hold on, there's got to be something…" Looking around, Jasper began to feel hopeless.

As Wallace watched Lucy pick at the tar stuck to her shoe, an idea hit him. "Lucy, let me have that tar," he said. With the help of a small bit of dirt from the side of the road and the magnifying glass he kept in his pocket, Wallace melted the tar with the magnifying glass and mixed it with the dirt and sand. He then plugged the hole with the mixture.

"We'll need to let it set," said Wallace, but the hole plug was holding well.

Faye put her hand on Wallace's shoulder. "Well done, Wallace."

"Where to from here?" asked Noah as they waited for the plug to harden, nibbling on Rosie's sandwiches and drinking some water. It was not very warm, as autumn had come upon them, but they had been riding hard and fast and they were feeling warmer than the weather.

"Oh, it's just straight up the road," said Lucy, pointing to the middle of three roads leading out from Dayton toward the fields and farms of the countryside.

"Amazing," said Jasper, putting the cover back on his canteen. "It really was a straight road, nearly, from our homes to the farm."

Suddenly, they all realized what that meant. The beefeater on the unicycle might well have been on his way to their homes and now knew they were not in them. The men in black might be along any second. Which could be one of two things—good, if they were coming to take them to the schoolhouse, or very, very bad.

Without a word, the five children scrambled onto their bicycles and sped down the center road as fast as their bicycles could carry them. They'd have to hope Wallace's plug would hold. With luck, it would get them to Sole Manner.

CHAPTER TWENTY-FIVE

AN APPLE FOR TEACHER
OR
 WALLACE EMPTIES HIS POCKET

The rest of the trip back to the farm would have given the world's calmest person the jitters. They rode as fast as possible, only to fly off the road and hide in a ditch every time a cart, horse, or tractor came by. They did not encounter a single member of the men in black brigade, but they could not tell for sure until the farmer or milkman or traveler passed them. Only then did they drag their bicycles up onto the road again and resume their lightning-fast ride. They didn't know which was more tiring—the racing or the constant stopping.

After about forty minutes, Jasper was exhausted. Although Lucy pedaled when she could, she was small and her legs were only so strong. The others were tired, too, but Jasper was determined not to show how beat he really was.

"We're nearly there!" he called, without a clue whether this was true or not.

Suddenly, Lucy called out, "Look, look! It's the twirly-twisty-birdy-boxy thing!"

"Lucy, what are you talking about?" Jasper asked.

"It's the, you know, where they live and people feed them, only this one has that twirly-twisty thing upon it."

With no clue as to what she was talking about, Lucy's four mates looked around until they saw it. Indeed, there was a twirly-twisty-birdy-boxy thing. In English, it would be called a barn, with a tall wrought iron weathervane with a large hummingbird on the tip.

"Ah, but of course," said Noah in his best French accent. "Eet ees the traditional twirly-twisty-birdy-boxy thing. What fools we be, *n'est-ce pas?*"

"And what, pray tell, does it mean now that we see the twirly-twisty-birdy-boxy thing, Lucy?" asked Faye.

"It means we'll be at the farm in about five minutes." True to Lucy's word, the beehives at the edge of the apple orchard were soon in view.

———⟡———

Not knowing what they might find, the children decided not to patrol the property once they arrived. Instead, they climbed down from their bicycles and walked them over to the drainage ditch. There, they lay their bicycles down behind the beehives, leaving them out of view of the road and out of view of the farmhouse.

The apples from the nearby orchard were still quite small and hard as a rock. Luckily, the leaves on the trees were plentiful, and that helped to hide the children as they sat on a branch and searched for any movement in the schoolhouse.

"I can't see a thing," said Jasper, looking through Lucy's spyglass. "We've just got to get over there and get inside."

"Get inside?" Noah asked.

"Yes," Jasper said. "We'll have to figure out a way to do it carefully."

"What should we say?" asked Lucy.

"We should act normal," said Wallace.

"Normal?" Noah said. "Normal? You mean we should come in wearing black rubber flippers and black wooly mittens on our noses? Or perhaps a black sombrero and a pair of black stilts?"

"I mean like we've just come back after a weekend at home," said Wallace, not finding this funny.

"I don't know," said Jasper. "I think we should be quiet and sneak inside."

"We don't want to appear to know anything is wrong in there," said Wallace. "We don't want Reginald Roderick Kattaning to *do* anything."

"I think you're both right," said Lucy. "We should come in quietly, but if someone sees us, act as if we're coming back as always."

Approaching the schoolhouse, they couldn't help but notice how quiet it was. Usually, they could hear Miss Brett humming, or they could smell whatever she was cooking for supper. This time, even the birds and the clouds and the trees seemed to be silent, except for one bird nearby making a strange, eerie cooing sound.

Jasper took some time to reattach the hanging, twisted wires so the telephone would work. He had to untangle the wires before he could reconnect them.

Walking around to the front, the children found the door slightly ajar. Lucy peeked through the crack and put her hand to her mouth to stifle her gasp.

The whole classroom had been ripped apart. The desks seemed to have been systematically shredded into tinder. The test tubes and beakers were crushed. The drawings and sketches were crumpled and torn to bits. Miss Brett's desk was overturned and broken nearly in half. All her desk drawers, now mostly broken, were pulled out and strewn about the room. It was as if some giant fiend had trampled everything. Even the blackboard was torn from the wall and the slate smashed.

Wallace quietly stepped into the room before anyone could stop him. He lifted a bottle that still contained a clear liquid. He tilted it. There was a crack, but it seemed otherwise to be fine. He placed the bottle on the table. He then bent down and picked up something from the rubble—a small glass vial. This, too, was cracked, except the bottom was broken clean off. Wallace panicked for a moment, then reached into his pocket, pulling out a vial of his own—intact, corked, and sealed. The vial contained a gold, viscous liquid.

It had remained in his pocket since the day Miss Brett helped him clean the blackboard. Wallace now returned it to his pocket, where the vial seemed to fill the emptiness left by his lucky coin.

It would have taken years to recreate his experiment had he lost this vial and the catalyst he had created to combine with it.

Amidst the strewn pieces of the destroyed classroom, it was impossible to tell if anything was missing. There was, however, one lone and blatant exception.

Miss Brett was definitely not in the classroom. She was not among the wreckage. And the door to the kitchen was closed.

Not daring to enter through the kitchen door, the children

ran around to the side of the building and hid.

"Why are we hiding?" whispered Lucy.

"Because he might still be in there," Jasper whispered back.

"He broke our everything," whimpered Lucy.

"What did he think?" Faye grumbled, pointedly but quietly, her anger simmering. "That we were hiding the aeroplane in our pencil boxes?"

"He was probably looking for the plans," said Noah, picking up a beaker from the grass. It must have been thrown from the window. He set it on the window ledge. Faye grabbed his hand and pulled it back down.

"I'm going to look and see if the birdwatcher's truck is there," said Faye. "Then we'll know."

"No, I'll go," Jasper said, unconsciously rubbing his legs, sore from the long hard ride.

"You won't!" cried Lucy, grabbing his hand.

"He is the fastest," Wallace said, matter-of-factly.

Jasper looked over at Faye. She nodded.

Stealthily, Jasper edged along the wall and disappeared around the corner.

"What do we do now?" Lucy said softly, chewing on her nails and leaning against Faye.

"If we just barge in there," Wallace said, "we may cause a whole lot more trouble for everyone."

"Sometimes we have to barge," said Lucy, who had no other point to argue. New tears burned her cheeks.

Two very long minutes passed.

"I feel like barging," Lucy said, trying to put a brave smile on her face. Jasper was still not back and she was beginning to fear he had been caught. Lucy's fingers were bleeding as she continued to gnaw on them.

Wallace placed a hand on Lucy's shoulder. "We have to *think*," he said.

"And think fast," said Noah. "And think quietly. We can't be heard."

"And we can't be seen," said Jasper, reappearing suddenly, out of breath from running. "It's there. The truck. I saw it from the other side. And I could hear him in the schoolhouse. I think Miss Brett is in there with him. We have to stay hidden. We're no good to Miss Brett if he catches us."

"We have to get her out of there," said Faye.

Most of all, they had to find out if Miss Brett was in the clutches of Reginald Roderick Kattaning. Inching along the side of the building, they reached the first window. Lucy peeked in, her nose resting on the window ledge. Nothing. Only the devastated classroom.

Ducking even lower, they crept along to the next window, the one above the kitchen sink. Jasper knelt so that Lucy could climb up on his knee. Faye reached for her pendant but grabbed only its chain. Wallace twirled the vial in his pocket. With Lucy's head barely above eye-level at the bottom of the window, she could see.

Miss Brett was sitting in a chair facing away from the window.

"I see her," said Lucy.

"Shhhhh," hissed Jasper. "If Reginald Roderick Kattaning is in there, he'll hear you."

Jasper lowered Lucy back down.

"What do we do?" Lucy said. "Oh, please, let's do something."

Deciding it was best to get Miss Brett's attention so she would know they were there, the children went slinking off to the other side of the building like some ten-footed, five-headed, slithering ferret. When they almost reached the kitchen window on the opposite side, Noah nearly knocked over the bushels of apples piled next to the window. Before he could let out a yelp, Faye covered his mouth.

They found the kitchen window already open, so they slowly raised their heads and peeked into the room.

They did indeed catch Miss Brett's attention. But Miss Brett was in no position to do anything. She was not merely sitting in the chair—she was tied to it, wrapped with rope from her shoulders to her ankles. Her hair was a mess and her face . . . well, her eyes were red and one seemed swollen. She saw them, but frantically shook her head at the children, motioning over her shoulder.

That's where they found Reginald Roderick Kattaning, rubbing his pointed little beard, looking up toward the ceiling.

In one quick movement, the children ducked, staying below the edge of the windowsill.

"He's got her captured!" said Lucy in a quiet whisper.

"We've got to save her," Wallace said in a whispered blurt, his voice cracking.

"Oh," Lucy said, biting her fingers as if Miss Brett's life depended on it, "I hope she isn't terribly, terribly hurt. I hope that horrid, horrid man hasn't terribly, terribly hurt our Miss Brett." Though she tried not to, Lucy was crying.

"She seems to be all right, Lucy," said Noah, not believing it himself. "She's a bit mussed, but she's all right."

"Oh, that bad man," Lucy said. "I want Miss Brett to be all right. I want—"

"We're all worried, Lucy, not just you," Jasper said, turning to his sister. "You have got to be quiet. Do you hear me?"

"Jasper—"

"No, Faye, she's always—" But Jasper caught himself. He didn't even know what he was going to say. As Lucy's big brown eyes gazed up at him, pleading, the feeling turned into something else. "I'm sorry, Lucy, I . . . I just . . . I suppose—"

"It's all right, Jasper. You're scared, too." Lucy tried to stifle her sobs. She touched the tear that had come to rest at the tip of Jasper's nose. Jasper took his sister in his arms, this time as much for his own comfort as hers.

"But what do we do?" Lucy chewed on her fingers to fight her tears.

"Shh. We don't want to make it worse for Miss Brett," Faye said. "If he thinks someone's out here, he might make a move."

They heard a sickening thud. A collective gulp and a collective peek through the window was followed by a collective sigh. Reginald Roderick Kattaning had not hurt Miss Brett but thrown a chair across the room. The chair hit the pile of firewood, knocking over the pan Miss Brett used to make her pancakes. Lucy remembered that first morning.

"We need a secret ingredient," Lucy said with conviction.

"Like cannonballs," Noah said, "or an army."

"Or something to make him stop—freeze, so he can't do more harm," said Jasper.

Yes, thought Wallace. They *did* need a secret ingredient. A secret ingredient would make all the difference. Wallace suddenly stood up, out of the window's view.

"What are you doing?!" Faye whispered loudly.

"I'll be right back," Wallace said. Faye grabbed his arm. "Give me twenty-seven seconds," he said.

She let go with a knowing nod. "I believe in you, Wallace," she said.

As Wallace left, Faye looked at Lucy. "He's got the secret ingredient," she said with a reassuring smile.

Then came a sound that made all four remaining children jump. It was followed by a moan from Miss Brett.

"He's hurting her!" cried Lucy.

Faye peeked in. Miss Brett's chair was on the floor. As Faye watched, Reginald Roderick Kattaning kicked the chair, and his foot connected with Miss Brett's hand.

"She's ... she's all right," Faye told Lucy, but her eyes did not deceive Noah and Jasper.

As Lucy popped her head up to see for herself, Reginald Roderick Kattaning pulled the chair back up.

"Come on, Wallace," Noah said to himself.

Wallace, hands shaking but moving as fast as he could, found the burette and the clear liquid, still in the basket Miss Brett had insisted remain outside the classroom. Both sat, untouched, on the window's ledge.

Back in the kitchen, Reginald Roderick Kattaning's voice rose yet again. He seemed to be getting more dangerously abusive as he shouted at Miss Brett. The four children cautiously slid their noses up the outside wall to peek in the window.

Facing the other way, Reginald Roderick Kattaning leaned all too close to Miss Brett. "For the seventy-ninth time, Miss Brett," he growled, "you had better tell me where the *thing* is. Do you hear me? We have the children locked away and we will not release them until we have it."

"I don't know what you're talking about," said Miss Brett defiantly. She looked over at the window, where four foreheads and eight eyes peered in at her.

"YOU KNOW EXACTLY WHAT I AM TALKING ABOUT!!!" roared Reginald Roderick Kattaning, pounding his fists on the table.

Menacingly, he leaned right into Miss Brett, his face mere inches from hers. He grabbed the arms of her chair and shook it violently.

"No, he'll hurt her!" Lucy cried softly.

Reginald Roderick Kattaning kicked the leg of Miss Brett's chair, arms flailing, feet stomping like an angry spoiled child. "I WANT THE THING, MISS BRETT!!!" he shouted. "I WANT THE THING AND I WANT IT NOW!!!" He stood up straight and stomped one more time. "YOU WILL REGRET THIS! YOU WILL FEEL PAIN, MISS BRETT!" And he raised his fist.

"No!" shouted Lucy, and before anyone could stop her, the littlest among them grabbed an apple from the bushel and threw it at Reginald Roderick Kattaning.

Instantly, Reginald Roderick Kattaning looked around, distracted, wondering where the apple had come from. Then, new fury in his eyes, he turned back to Miss Brett.

Suddenly, a spray of tiny rock-hard apples came raining in through the window and onto Reginald Roderick Kattaning. Stumbling, he fell onto Miss Brett, but then he stood with a "GRRRRRROAAAAARRRRR" and turned around.

As he searched for the source of the attack, Reginald Roderick Kattaning growled like an angry tiger, swatting at the continuous apple spray. He crushed apple after apple beneath his feet, batting others out of the way as he looked toward the window, but the children ducked in time.

Then, Lucy grabbed a very small apple that had remained on the window ledge. She peeked up just as Reginald Roderick Kattaning turned in her direction. She pulled back her arm and threw it as hard as she could. It hit Reginald Roderick Kattaning right between the eyes.

His eyes crossed and moved around as though searching for that little unripe piece of fruit that hit him, believing it still lodged right in the middle of his forehead. He staggered, haltingly, as if trying to remember a dance he once knew.

Then, without as much as a tweet, a bird flew over and perched on the window ledge.

"You've come back!" whispered Lucy, much to the confusion of the others. "It's Samson!" The bird turned to Lucy and seemed to purr at the sight of her.

Samson, the little bird that had flown into the carriage window, who Lucy had nursed back to health, turned back to face the room and hopped from foot to foot, agitated, making quick sharp chirps.

Faye, without being seen, tried to shoo the bird away. "Get that thing out of—"

But suddenly, Reginald Roderick Kattaning lunged for the bird, as if it was the feathered creature which had been throwing the apples at him. The bird flew out from his grasp, into the room. It circled overhead in short, angry circles. Then, as it swooped by and gave out an angry "caw!," the bird clipped Reginald Roderick Kattaning hard on the left ear.

Lucy reached up as if to give the bird safe purchase on her arm. But it was Reginald Roderick Kattaning who found the arm first, grabbing it and yanking Lucy away from the now empty bushel beneath the window.

"No!" yelled Jasper, but Reginald Roderick Kattaning swatted him down before he could reach his sister.

"I'll give you whatever you want!" cried Miss Brett, but Reginald Roderick Kattaning just kicked her chair over, knocking her to the floor again.

Samson dive-bombed Reginald Roderick Kattaning again and again, circling and cawing and leaving little bird droppings on Reginald Roderick Kattaning's head and shoulders, but still the man clung to Lucy, who screamed trying to break free. Neither the terrified children nor Miss Brett knew what to do.

Then Wallace appeared, running toward them, the vial in his hand. Wallace had spent a year creating this chemical. He'd made a promise to his mother. None of that mattered now.

The moment he saw Lucy in peril, Wallace wound up and threw the vial hard onto the floor. It crashed, splashing all over the floor and upon Reginald Roderick Kattaning's feet.

Reginald Roderick Kattaning took a step, then another, but then he could not gain purchase from the wide glassy patch on which he had stepped. His legs seemed suddenly stiff, as if his trouser legs had turned from linen into glass. As he slipped, he released Lucy, who ran quickly to Miss Brett, moving her teacher's head from off the hard floor and into her lap.

"He's getting away!" cried Faye, sure that if Reginald Roderick

Kattaning stepped onto the regular floor, he would take off like the wind. But Reginald Roderick Kattaning was not getting away. He was trapped, flailing his arms and spinning his feet on a friction-free section of the floor that happened to be made of a totally different molecular structure. His skinny legs now looked like a blur. Wallace stood frozen, his arm still raised in the throwing position. The children all held their breath.

Like an utterly graceless ballerina, Reginald Roderick Kattaning did a glissade and then a pirouette and then fell, face first, onto the floor at Miss Brett's feet.

In the few seconds they stood there staring at the sight of their fallen enemy, covered in bird poo, Wallace knew, for the first time, that they could not have done this without him.

Noah took Wallace's hand and shook it. "Never a dull moment," Noah said.

CHAPTER TWENTY-SIX

THE BACK OF KOMAR ROMAK

OR

THE MAN WHO WASN'T THERE

The children climbed into the kitchen and ran to Miss Brett.

"That was marvelous, children. You're all so brave," Miss Brett said as they untied her from her chair.

"Wallace was the real hero," said Faye.

"You were all heroes," said Miss Brett.

Wallace said nothing as he continued to untie the ropes.

The ropes, once unknotted, fell away easily, and once Miss Brett was off the floor, the students and their teacher all clambered to tie up Reginald Roderick Kattaning before he came to.

"For such a skinny man, he sure is hard to move," Noah said as the six of them dragged Reginald Roderick Kattaning's unconscious bulk across the kitchen floor.

"Let's put him in the telephone room," Miss Brett said. "It's the only room that can be locked from the outside."

Folding their gangly burden, they managed to get Reginald Roderick Kattaning into the tiny room, shutting the door just before they heard a low groan. Miss Brett turned the lock and put the key back on the shelf where she kept it.

"He's likely to wake up any minute," said Miss Brett. Then she turned to look at her five charges and gathered all of them into her arms. "I was so worried."

"We were worried about you," said Lucy, wiping her eyes.

"Worried about me? I was fine," she said, a bit too quickly. "Well, I was all right until last night. When he didn't come back Friday evening, I thought he had gone for good. I tried to reconnect the telephone wires."

That explained why they had been so badly twisted when Jasper went to reattach them.

"Saturday, for most of the day, I tidied the kitchen and cleaned the house," Miss Brett said. "I wanted to alert the people in charge of all this that we might have trouble, but they should already have known. I told them on Friday, before Reginald Roderick Kattaning cut the telephone wires."

"We never saw any of those men in black hanging around our houses," Faye said. "If they were supposed to be helping us or protecting us or keeping an eye on things, they never checked on us."

"They gave us Rosie," said Lucy, "and Rosie could lift a horse if she wanted, all on her own, I bet."

"They never even came for us," Wallace told Miss Brett.

"They probably wanted to keep you from coming back here, in case our unwanted visitor returned," Miss Brett said.

"Well, I … it does seem … Well, you might be right," said Faye. "It seems like they may have wanted to protect us. Perhaps."

"But what about you?" asked Lucy, mortified, tugging at Miss Brett's sleeve. "Didn't they want to protect you?"

"Well …" Miss Brett considered her words carefully. "I don't think they didn't care about me. I'm sure they were planning something," Miss Brett said. "Saturday night, as I was sitting at the kitchen table here, I heard all manner of noises coming from the classroom. When I went to look, Reginald Roderick Kattaning grabbed me and tied me up with that rope." She rubbed her wrists and stretched her neck.

"You spent the night sitting in that chair?" Faye asked.

"Yes, and my neck is quite stiff." Miss Brett rubbed her own shoulders. "He just ranted and raved at me until, well, until I fell asleep. When I woke this morning, he was still pacing and grumbling and screaming about some *thing*. 'The THING!' he kept shouting. It must have been the aeroplane," she said. "My goodness, he was at it all night."

The children looked at one another—all except Lucy, who instead looked out the open window. In the distance, she could see a cloud of dust along the road. She pulled out her spyglass to get a better look. Everyone stopped talking.

"What is it, Lucy?" asked Noah.

"It looks like a big black automobile. No, two. No, wait— there are at least six motorcars coming down the road," she said, counting clouds of dust.

"Well, it's probably the directors or whoever those men in black are," said Miss Brett, straightening her skirt. "Thank goodness. Now we can turn over that awful Reginald Roderick Kattaning and find out what all of this means. And I want to ask what that gibberish meant that they were saying over the telephone."

"Gibberish?" said Wallace.

"Yes, they said something like 'crowbar roback' or 'gomart lotack' or—"

"Komar Romak?" said Lucy.

Everyone looked at her.

"Yes," said Miss Brett excitedly, "that's what they kept shouting. What on earth does that mean?"

"And how do you know about it?" asked Jasper.

"It was written on the envelope Reginald Roderick Kattaning had in class. I saw it when he dropped it. It just said 'Komar Romak' and nothing else."

"What does it mean?" asked Miss Brett.

"I don't know," said Lucy. "I only saw it written on the envelope."

"Is it a place?" said Wallace.

"It could be something in another language," said Miss Brett.

"Or a code word," said Jasper.

"They're coming!" Faye exclaimed, pointing out the window. "The nannies must have turned us in."

"Don't be silly. They'd never turn us in," Noah said, "unless they thought they were helping us."

Six motorcars drove up the long road to the farmhouse, followed by several now familiar black carriages.

They all hurried toward the door. Miss Brett stopped only to check that the lock on the telephone room was secure.

Miss Brett and the children stood on the front steps of the schoolhouse and waited as the large black motorcars came to a halt in front of them. Each motorcar contained four of the men in black, all of whom emerged at once, like a river of black seeping through every car door.

Miss Brett and the children recognized many of the men, although not all. There was the man in a lady's bonnet and the man in the inner tube. There was the man in the black nightie and the man with the black beret. There was the man in the black fur coat and the man with the wooly jumper, as well as the man in the lady's floral hat.

"That's the man who was jumping on Mummy's bed," Lucy whispered to Jasper, pointing to the man in the velvet hat.

There were several men in black bowler hats and long coats and three in top hats. To her surprise, Faye saw the man in the turban.

The man in the black fur coat walked up to Miss Brett. "Where is he?" he asked in a deep, accented voice.

"Reginald Roderick Kattaning?" she asked.

"Who?" the fur man asked.

"Reginald Roderick Kattaning? The man who was here?"

"Yes," the fur man answered gruffly, "the man who was here."

"We've locked him in the telephone room," she said, stepping aside.

"Locked him?" the fur man asked in surprise.

"Yes," said Miss Brett defensively. "He had me tied to a chair all night and was very rough with the children. We had to protect ourselves."

"He is locked?" the fur man asked again. Then, with a grunt, he pushed past Miss Brett. "We shall see," he said.

Miss Brett and the children followed the fur man to the telephone room door.

"Open, please," the fur man said.

Miss Brett took the key from her apron pocket and unlocked the door.

The room was totally empty. A pile of rope sat in a heap on the floor. Lucy pointed at something beside it, which looked very much like a small caterpillar. Upon closer inspection, however, it was half of a brown moustache.

"But...but...I...I..." Miss Brett stammered. "Children, you saw...you were there...we all...he was—"

"Yes, we all saw," said Faye, reaching for Miss Brett's hand, giving it a gentle squeeze.

"How is this possible?" said Wallace. "We haven't had the door out of sight for a minute."

Miss Brett looked up. About nine feet up on the wall was a tiny window.

"Not even Lucy could fit through that," said Jasper. "Even if she could reach it."

"This is impossible," said Noah, shaking his head.

"Komar Romak," said the man in the black swimsuit who had come to see.

"Komar Romak," said the fur man.

"Komar Romak?" asked the bonnet-wearing man.

"Komar Romak," said the man with the black inner tube, looking up at the impossibly small window.

"Komar Romak?" said Miss Brett. "What on earth is Komar Romak?"

"What Komar Romak is not," said the man in the bonnet.

"What it is not what?" asked Noah.

"Not what," said the bonnet-wearing man.

"*What* is not what?" said Jasper, now utterly baffled.

"It," said the fur man.

"What?" the children asked at once.

"Not it," said the inner tube man.

"I am asking what Komar Romak is," Miss Brett said, calmly

315

and slowly. "Does it mean something in another language? What is it?"

"Not *it*," said the fur man, rather more emphatically than before, looking at the other men in black, clearly as frustrated as the children and Miss Brett.

Miss Brett took a deep breath, and was about to start again when Lucy asked, "*Who* is Komar Romak?"

"Yes," said the bonnet-wearing man. "Yes, who."

"All right," said Miss Brett, addressing the fur man, "*who*, pray tell, is Komar Romak?"

All of the men in black standing near the doorway looked up in unison, pointing to the window above.

"Him?" Miss Brett pointed up. "Reginald Roderick Kattaning?"

"No," said the man in the black nightie, "Komar Romak."

"Who is he?" asked Noah.

"We cannot say," said the nightie man.

"We mustn't," said the fur man. Miss Brett could see fear in his eyes.

"Is he really so very bad?" asked Jasper.

"So very bad," said the inner tube man, adjusting his inner tube as one might adjust a collar growing too tight under pressure, "and what is not alone." The inner tube squeaked like a duck as the man shifted under the immediate gaze of his comrades.

"What is not alone?" asked Wallace.

"No!" shouted several men in black.

"But what can we—"

Miss Brett was cut off immediately by the bonnet-wearer, putting a finger to his lips. "We must go now," he said. The fur man picked up the telephone and spoke in whispered tones, inaudible to Miss Brett and the children.

"Everything must go now," said a bowler hat-wearing man. "Now, we go now."

Miss Brett and the children scrambled to collect their things. Within minutes, the children were all in a large car, once again headed somewhere. Miss Brett was in the car right behind. The children thought they must be going home, at least to one home or another. But they had been wrong before.

CHAPTER TWENTY-SEVEN

The Young Inventors On The Move

OR

 THE FIRST CAR AND WHAT THEY FOUND THERE

The children had taken many a roundabout route to their Dayton, Ohio homes. But the roundabout route they took that Sunday was, without question, totally different. They first drove the entire perimeter of the city. Then they drove through the city, and back out. They inched farther and farther from their neighborhood.

"We're not going home, are we?" Lucy asked her brother, hoping for an answer she knew she would not get.

Jasper pulled her close. He had nothing to say. No one in the back of the car was in the mood to talk.

Lucy turned around to wave at Miss Brett's car behind them, and she continued to wave as the car followed them through several twists and turns. As they cut through town, though, Miss Brett's car turned left while their own car continued straight. Lucy waved frantically, as if this would bring her back.

"Is Miss Brett going somewhere else?" Faye asked the driver.

Either he chose not to answer the question or the large, fuzzy black earmuffs he wore made it impossible for him to hear. So the five children, once again knowing not at all what was in store for them, could do nothing but watch as Miss Brett's car disappeared around the corner.

Lucy, unsure if Miss Brett saw her wave, tried to stifle a whimper. Jasper hugged his sister and handed her a handkerchief when the tears came down.

Resting in the back of the car as it motored bumpily along, was not easy, but they were all tired and worried and tired of worrying. After what seemed like hours, they dozed off.

⊷⊶

"It's getting late," said Faye, who was the first to wake. She looked at the last remnants of light in the waning sky. She guessed it was long past supper.

As the rest of them, awakened by Faye, stretched and wiped the sleep from their eyes, Noah, yawning, asked, "Are we anywhere yet?"

Looking out the window, none of the children recognized where they were.

Except Lucy. "This is the way to the train station," she said.

The view, though, was of a street that looked just like any street—until the car took a sharp left, and then another left, and then a right. There, in front of them, was the train station. The car stopped behind three other black cars.

"Out," said the driver. He spoke very loudly. Jasper assumed this was because he could not hear himself with those fuzzy black earmuffs covering his ears.

All of the children piled out of the car. They looked around to see if Miss Brett was anywhere to be seen. She was not.

"Do you know where—" Faye began, but she was cut off with the swish of an arm in front of her nose. The driver pointed to the train yard.

"But is Miss Brett—" Lucy tried to ask, but the driver again swished and pointed.

"The blackguard," mumbled Faye, helping Lucy out of the car.

The children walked slowly toward the train. As they got closer, wondering what direction to take, a man in a large black conical hat and dark oval glasses appeared, pointing in the direction of the outbound trains. Another man with a black eyepatch over one eye and a dark monocle over the other, wearing a black sea captain's jacket and cap, followed several yards after him, pointing toward Platform Seventeen. There, they found just one train, of a shiny green and gold color, that appeared as if someone had just polished it, engine to caboose.

"It's beautiful," said Lucy. And it was. There were four long cars, all sparkling green with gold trim. The windows reflected like mirrors so the children could not see inside. A man in a black conductor's suit, a black conductor's hat, and dark spectacles looked at his shiny black conductor's watch. He pointed to the last car, and the children gingerly stepped up and aboard.

The inside was even more beautiful. The aisle of the last car was carpeted in beautiful floral patterns, and the walls were papered in deep green and gold. The doors were made of maple, and stained a deep reddish brown. Instead of compartments, there was a lounge and a cozy salon, with thick soft chairs and ornately crafted tables. Toward the middle of the car, the aisle led into a large room with a tall glass dome ceiling. It was like no observation room any of them had ever seen.

"You can see the sky," said Noah. The glass was perfectly clear—it was like looking out of a giant bubble. A stairway led up to a thin balcony that went around the perimeter of the dome. The children walked up and wandered around the circle of glass. They could see everything.

"Look at all the people rushing around down there," said Noah, pointing down. It felt as if they were two stories up.

"A train can't be this tall," insisted Faye. But it was, or seemed to be.

"Look at the sky," said Lucy, pointing up. She waved, but no one outside seemed to see her. "It must reflect like the glass of the windows. No one can see in, but we can see out."

"It's like we're invisible," said Jasper, watching as everyone rushed back and forth along the platform.

"It must be beautiful looking out of there when the train is moving," Faye said. "I'll bet it feels like...like—"

"Like you're flying?" said Noah.

Faye blushed.

"Come on," said Jasper, descending the stairs. "Let's see what else is here."

They left the dome room, moving toward the front of the train, through a set of stained glass doors that led to the third car. They found themselves in another aisle, this one lined with paintings in between the windows. The windows were on one side, and on the other was a row of big wooden doors. Assuming these must be the compartments, Lucy turned the knob on the first one. It wasn't locked.

"Go ahead, Lucy," said Noah, "Open the door."

The fact that the room was empty of people was a surprise to no one. What was a surprise, though, was that it was nothing like any cabin in any train the children had ever seen. The cabin was furnished like a fabulously luxurious bedroom. In the middle were a large four-poster bed with a lace canopy and two small beds that closely resembled the large one.

"Look," said Jasper, walking across the room. He picked up the small glass jug of water that sat on the bedside table. "That reminds me of Mummy."

Lucy walked over and held her brother's hand.

"Where is everyone?" asked Lucy, concern creeping into her voice. "Why have they left us here alone?" Jasper kissed the top of her head.

The children opened the next door. It, too, was beautifully furnished, with two identical and very beautiful beds right next to one another. The whole room was filled with bouquets of flowers.

"That makes me think of *my* mother," said Noah with a sigh. "Someone is always sending her flowers."

The next room had beautiful Asian art and a satin spread over a large bed in the center of the room. A smaller day bed covered in red and orange silk pillows stood against the wall. The room smelled of sandalwood and jasmine incense. Faye was reminded of her own room back in New Delhi.

In the fourth room, Wallace saw the glass slides mounted on the wall between the two beds and thought of his father.

The last room was smaller, with one bed in it, covered with a soft peach-colored cotton quilt. The window had lace curtains.

The room smelled of lavender, but was empty of life. There were no people to be found anywhere.

"What do we do?" asked Lucy as they reached the end of the car.

"We should be used to being abandoned by now," said Faye.

They pulled apart the train car doors and crossed from the third car into the second. The second car, they quickly discovered, was at least as remarkable as the third.

At the end, where they entered, there were several desks against the walls—five to be exact. These were great wooden desks with chairs, pens, writing blotters, and microscopes. The desks were just the kind one would find in an inventor's laboratory.

"Are these for us?" Wallace asked.

Lucy sat in one of the seats. Her feet didn't even reach the ground, and she could hardly see the top of the desk. "The size is all wrong for me," she said, jumping down.

"You're like Goldenlocks, sitting in Papa Bear's chair," said Jasper, laughing.

"Look at me," said Noah, laughing. "They got my size wrong!" He sat at a very small desk, his knees right up to his chin. Lucy pulled him from the seat and took his place. He sat down in the chair that Lucy had been sitting in.

"This one is just right," said Lucy. "I'm Goldenlocks!"

"And I'm the Mama Bear!" said Noah.

They all found a perfect desk for each of them. Thoughtfully, Faye looked at the others and said, quietly, "We'd never have known that story if it hadn't been for Miss Brett."

"I hope she's all right," said Noah.

"Where do you think that leads?" Wallace asked, pointing to

the large wooden door on the far side of the room.

"Might as well go and see," said Noah. "No one's here to stop us."

Opening the door and stepping through, they found themselves in a beautiful dining room, like one might find in the fanciest chateau or hotel. There were two chandeliers and a long, elaborately laid table down the center. Although there was only warm bread in baskets and fresh fruit set out in bowls, they could smell the aroma of roasted meats and grilled vegetables. There was just the faintest hint of a blueberry tart, and perhaps a bit of treacle, cinnamon, and vanilla.

"I'm getting hungry just looking at it," said Jasper.

"Someone has to be cooking all of this," Wallace said.

"Probably a man with a black chef's hat. And a black apron," said Noah.

"Whatever he's wearing," said Jasper, "he sure can cook."

———————

But there was still one car left to explore. When the children stepped into it, they were struck by two rather remarkable things. The first thing was the size of the room. The entire car was one grand space. There were two fireplaces with roaring fires, and several couches and chairs that looked comfortable enough to be beds. There were bowls full of oranges and apples and grapes laid about the room. The walls that were not covered in soft blue silk were lined with books like the grandest of libraries. The ceiling seemed impossibly tall and arched at the center. But for the windows, one might never even know that one was on a train.

The second thing was even more remarkable. In fact, it was more amazing than anything else they had ever discovered. It was so amazing, none of them felt the train begin to move. There, right in front of the roaring fire, the children, the inventors, those brilliant scientists, discovered what they had been wanting most of all.

Their parents.

———

Drs. Isabelle and Tobias Modest and Gwendolyn and Rajesh Vigyanveta sat with Dr. Ben Banneker IV and Dr. Clarence Canto-Sagas. The children stood frozen for a moment, a thousand things running through their minds, but questions and accusations flew away like bats from a cave, and all five children came running into the outstretched arms that awaited them.

Then Noah, hugging his father, heard it first, and recognized it immediately: the gargling singing exercise emerging from the powder room at the rear of the library. It was a sound he always heard after a long voyage.

"Mother!" cried Noah, flying from his father's arms into his mother's as she exited the powder room. Turning back to his father, Noah was caught instantly in a double embrace.

———

Faye was in the warmest arms she could remember. "We've missed you so much, my little *marmelo*," Rajesh Vigyanveta said, holding his daughter close. Somehow, it was that term of affection that reignited her anger. She opened her mouth, ready to accuse, ready to demand if he had missed her, had even thought about her and, if so, why had he not come back for her or made contact with her? But instead, Faye let herself be held, and the warmth of her father's embrace tempered the cold hard anger she felt toward her parents, even if only for the time being.

———⋙●⋘———

"Where have you been?" Jasper asked his mother.

"We've been working very hard," she said, but that was all she offered.

"We've wanted to see you," Tobias Modest said, holding tight to Lucy.

"We ... well, we were just unable to do so," said his wife.

———⋙●⋘———

"Son," Dr. Banneker said, trying to offer a stiff chin but unable to keep it from quivering, "it's so darn good to see you." Wallace wrapped his arms around his father's neck.

"I've missed you, Father," Wallace said.

"I have something for you," his father said, opening Wallace's hand and putting something into his palm.

"My lucky coin!" Wallace exclaimed, squeezing the familiar object in his hand. "Did it work?"

"Work?" His father looked taken aback.

"Did it bring you luck?"

Dr. Banneker laughed, and his whole demeanor seemed to change. He relaxed and breathed a deep sigh. "Yes, son, it did," he said. "And I am surely going to be needing that luck again. But you keep it for now."

And he held his son tight.

⸻◈⸻

"It's been something of a mystery to me, too, luvvie," Noah's mother said, caressing Noah's hair and looking at her husband.

"To me, as well," Dr. Canto-Sagas said. "We haven't been told very much, either. But we were totally secluded and the work is very, very important."

"Don't tell me," Ariana said, covering her ears. "I don't want to hear anything about it. It will frustrate me to no end to hear you are doing something worrisome."

"I don't think Father could tell you anyway," said Noah, reaching for his father's hand. "Could you, Father?"

With very sad eyes, his father nodded. "I'm so sorry, both of you. There's so much ... Well, it's just good to be together."

"Where's Ralph?" Noah asked.

"Glenda is taking great care of him," Ariana said. "In fact, Fifi is staying at home as well. It seems the two little creatures have struck up something of a friendship."

Noah found this hard to believe, but it didn't matter. He was glad to hear about Ralph. And his mother had, after all, left that dog of hers behind to come here and be with him and Father.

The car door opened.

"Miss Brett!" Noah heard Lucy shout.

And there stood Miss Brett in the doorway between the first two cars. The children rushed to greet her, and suddenly, everyone was talking at once. "My angels," Miss Brett said, returning the kisses and embraces of her students.

But between the animated chatter lay great mounds of hesitation. Happy though they were all to be reunited, it felt like they were all standing behind fences they were not at liberty to cross.

CHAPTER TWENTY-EIGHT

MUCH ADO ABOUT NOTHING
OR
THE MYSTERIOUS BEYOND

Soon, the children and their parents followed Miss Brett into the dining room. As Jasper had predicted, there *was* a man in a black chef's hat, and he was ladling soup from a huge terrene into large bowls on the table. The soup smelled of roast garlic and vegetable broth. The chef was assisted by a very, very short man in a long black stocking cap, who wore pointy black shoes with little bells upon the toes, wearing a suit that could only belong to one of Santa's helpers—but black, of course. He had a pair of black spectacles perched on the end of his nose, steamed up from the hot soup.

As the second course of roast beef, fried potatoes, and grilled leeks was being served, and the soup bowls removed, conversation returned to common ground.

"We were all worried about you," Dr. Banneker said to Wallace. "We heard that there had been trouble."

"*We* were worried about *you*," Wallace said. "All of you left us without saying a word. We didn't know a thing. We thought the men in black kidnapped you."

The parents laughed.

"Kidnapped us?" Faye's mother said. "Well, that *is* funny. Really. You see, the men in black—"

"Gwendolyn." Faye's father stopped her gently, taking his wife's hand and shaking his head ever so slightly.

Faye's mother put her hand to her lips. "Well, let's just say we were not kidnapped."

The children all sat, waiting to hear more. But clearly, more was not forthcoming.

"Well?" Faye said. "What happened, then? What was so important that abandoning your children was worth it?"

"Dear…" her mother began.

"You all just left us," said Jasper. "And what's even worse, you tried to pretend that you hadn't."

"We…" the Modests began in unison, but there wasn't really any argument they could make.

"We were not at liberty to say," said Dr. Banneker. "We still are not."

"You couldn't tell your children?" asked Wallace.

His father turned a shocked face toward his son. "Wallace, I.. . well, you needn't—"

"You all left us, without warning, without word," said Jasper. "We're only children! We have feelings and we worry. And we're not just any children, we're *your* children!"

Wallace turned and looked his father right in the eyes. "Father." Wallace spoke firmly, surprising both himself and his father. "It was…very unkind." Wallace knew this was not enough to describe what he felt. Bravely, he added, "More than that, it was horridly cruel." The vision of his father driving away as Wallace stood on the side of the road punctuated his words and made his face feel hot.

"I ... I'm sorry, son." Dr. Banneker had nothing else to say. The other children got similar looks and declarations from their own parents, but still no further information.

Lucy cleared her throat. "Can you tell us about Komar Romak?" she asked.

The parents gave a collective gasp, with forks dropped, water sipped, coughs coughed.

"How on earth do you know about Komar Romak?" Faye's mother asked, recovering first.

Not knowing how to answer, the children all looked down into their plates. Gwendolyn Vigyanveta continued, "Even we were never told much about ... I mean ... Well, how do you children know?"

"Because ..." started Jasper, but then he thought better of it. "Nothing," he said instead. "We just thought we'd ask."

The five children looked at one another. They didn't want to tell their parents, for five very private reasons—Faye out of spite, Noah out of protection, Wallace out of fear, Jasper out of concern, and Lucy out of confusion. They also knew that after all the worrying they had done, they didn't want anything more to worry about.

"I think it is safe to say," Dr. Banneker said, looking at the other parents as if checking whether or not it was, in fact, safe to say, "I mean, what I can say—and I speak for all of us—is that, from what we have heard, Komar Romak is, we believe, a very bad man."

Dr. Banneker looked at the children, who looked back, unsatisfied. He cleared his throat again. "All I know, and I don't think it is saying too much ... that is ..." Dr. Banneker seemed to consider his words carefully.

After what seemed like ages of silence, Miss Brett asked, "What *do* you know, Dr. Banneker?"

Dr. Banneker cleared his voice. "Komar Romak, as I have heard—as we have heard—was, I believe, originally . . . from Transylvania."

"I am sure you mean Australia," Gwendolyn Vigyanveta said. Then, blushing, she said, "I mean Austria, don't I?"

"We know that his parents were in the circus," said Dr. Canto-Sagas. "Or was it the symphony?"

"I had come to believe they were sailors," Dr. Banneker said. "And they had joined the Spanish—no, it was the French Navy."

"No, that isn't what I heard," Gwendolyn Vigyanveta said. "I am almost positive that his mother was a contortionist and his father, well, at least I am certain that they both were involved in a plot to steal the Crown Jewels. But that might have been ages ago."

"Yes. Yes, indeed, there was a plot," said Dr. Banneker, "but it was the emperor's gold in China. And it was Romak's mother, I thought, who had disguised herself as an acrobat in the caper."

"No, not an acrobat. Komar Romak's mother was disguised as a dancer," Dr. Canto-Sagas said.

"No, that was his father," said Isabelle Modest. "The mother was something else. A seamstress, I think. Or maybe a milliner."

"I am sure I have heard the name in theatrical circles," Ariana said, sipping from her flute of champagne. "I was under the impression that Komar Romak was the great Czechoslovakian escape artist. Yes, he was a teacher to that young American who is so famous in London right now—you know, they call him the

King of Handcuffs. Now, what was that young man's name—ah, yes, Houdini. Yes, Komar Romak was the teacher of young Harry Houdini. Komar Romak the escape artist, that's what he—"

"Nothing," said the man in the black chef's hat.

Everyone turned, surprised to hear him speak.

"Komar Romak is that," he said.

"He is what?" asked Ariana.

"He is what," said the man, serving helpings of sweet potatoes smothered in butter and maple syrup.

"What is he?" Miss Brett asked. "Komar Romak is what? What do you know of Komar Romak?"

"Nothing," said the man.

"Nothing?" Ariana said. "But that's impossible. You must— someone must know."

"Two," said the man.

"Nothing, too? Two? To what?" Miss Brett asked, leaning forward in her seat.

"Changes, escapes, but steals," the man in the chef's hat said. "And we fear him. Two. Always fear. Two. Always." He then walked back into the kitchen.

There was silence for a while after that, until Faye, glaring across the table at her parents, finally said what had long been on her mind. "Was Komar Romak someone you knew might be around?" she asked. "Someone you knew might harm us?"

Her parents denied it instantly.

"We had no idea..." Dr. Canto-Sagas said. "We had no idea that he would—"

"He would what?" demanded Wallace.

"So you *did* know he might do something?" Lucy asked, her

eyes wide as saucers.

The parents all became quite interested in what was on their forks, and the whole set of them fell silent again.

The children, too, fell silent. It was difficult even to lift their eyes to look at anyone else.

Faye felt the burning anger rising in her face. She wanted to shout and accuse all of their parents of putting them in danger and not caring at all about any of them. She tried to breathe deeply, but her breath caught in her throat and anger was not the only thing that burned her cheeks. The sting of unwanted tears could not be wiped away by a mere napkin.

Noah could not believe his father could have known, but Dr. Canto-Sagas was looking down as well. Even Noah's mother seemed unable to face her son.

Wallace leaned against the table with the arm that held his fork. His hand began to shake, although he didn't know if it was from fear, hurt, or anger.

Jasper felt the weight of the world shift awkwardly on his shoulders. Once again, he carried the crushing fear of being the only one there for Lucy, and for the second time today, he felt it was she who was there for him.

Lucy was the only one who looked from face to face. Mystified and utterly confused, she did not know what to think and suddenly felt a stranger in the presence of her parents.

After several heavy moments, the silence was broken.

"Sweet Lucy, and all of you children," said Dr. Tobias Modest, so softly his words seemed to carry on the silence. "You have been inadvertently, without your consent and without our desire, brought into a strange world. It is a world that remains a mystery, even to us. The word magic comes to mind, but only in that things we do not understand seem to be magic. Things that have not yet been invented seem mythical and things first discovered seem... well, they can be terrifying, exciting, and miraculous."

The children shot looks at one another. They understood all of this very, very well.

"It was never our intention to lead you into harm. It was, in fact, our intention to lead you out of harm's way. This will be the course taken always. Please understand that there is much we cannot tell you right now, just as, it seems, there is much you feel you cannot tell us. We must tell you that some of what you hold secret is not unknown to us."

Faye threw a look toward Jasper. But none of them would have, and certainly none of them had, any opportunity to tell anyone.

"There will be a time, perhaps very soon and perhaps not, that you will need to know all we know, and by then, you may know all the more. Until then..."

For the first time in Jasper and Lucy's life, they saw tears form in the eyes of their father. Isabelle Modest placed a hand on her husband's cheek and caressed it softly. "Until then," Tobias said, "please know that we love you."

Tobias Modest buried his face in his wife's shoulder. Lucy and Jasper stood and embraced their parents.

⎯⎯➤◆◆◄⎯⎯

As the inventors dressed for bed, there was much to think about. But as four of them finished dressing, a sound came through the halls that brought a strange calm among them.

Noah had found, lying on his bed, his violin. The bow was rosined and the strings tuned. Gingerly, he picked up the bow and found it taut and ready for use. He plucked the strings and found them in perfect tune.

As his mother began to hum Bach's *Zerreißet, zersprenget, zertrümmert die Gruft* from her dressing room in the bathing area of the cabin, Noah picked up the violin that felt, even after all these weeks, so natural beneath his chin. Plucking the string part he knew so well, Noah joined his mother so that voice and violin blended into perfect harmony.

Throughout the train, the sound of this lilting music filled the air and, as music does, it served to bring forth all the joy and sadness and triumph and defeat and pleasure each person on that train had ever felt, budding in each of them a strong, indistinct, but deeply personal blossom of emotion. The sound of Noah and Ariana flowed through the train, seeping into restless minds and pounding hearts.

That night, five young inventors were tucked into five warm, cozy beds. They were each kissed on the forehead by their parents. There had been moments of doubt and fear, not only about their safety, but also about their parents' love. But there, in the close comfort of their cabins, they all did feel loved. Unquestionably loved.

Noah fell asleep to the sound of his mother's voice. Faye rested comfortably as her parents fussed over her pillows and blankets.

And Lucy and Jasper went to bed wondering what the future held. Jasper felt under the pillow where Lucy always kept the journal. It wasn't there.

"Where's the journal?" asked Jasper.

"I gave it to Wallace to keep for now," said Lucy.

Jasper was surprised. Lucy had always felt it was hers. "Why did you give it to Wallace?" he asked.

"Because I thought he should have it for now. For tonight," said Lucy. "He needed it because he needed to know he was a hero."

Jasper did not really follow the whole path of Lucy's logic, but he understood the kindness his sister had shown Wallace. True, they were a team, but it was Wallace who had, in the end, saved the day—and saved Lucy. And he'd sacrificed the most important work of his life to do it.

Jasper reached his hand out to his sister. "Don't be scared," he said. "Whatever happens, we have each other."

"I know," Lucy said, reaching for Jasper with one hand and wiping her tears with the other. "But I'm afraid of Mummy and Daddy leaving us again."

Jasper wanted to make her feel better, but he had no idea what tomorrow would bring.

⟫●⟪

As he lay on his bed, Wallace turned the last page on his last entry in the Young Inventors Guild journal. He smiled as he thought of Lucy's funny gesture, offering for him to keep the journal. Lucy had an uncanny kind of honesty that held wisdom in its innocence. Wallace had decided to fill in the final notes from Sole Manner Farm, and when his work was complete, he placed in the book another page, a blank white page, waiting to be filled. *What goes there?* he wondered.

Smiling to himself, he tied the string around the book, placed the journal in his bag, and climbed down. Something came to him as he was pushing the journal under the bed. "Did mother sing to me, Father?" he asked.

He looked over at his father, who had fallen asleep still wearing his spectacles. Wallace got up and leaned over the edge of his father's bed. He took off his father's glasses and folded them, placing them on the bedside table.

Wallace yawned and felt the weight of sleep upon him. He was about to climb back into bed, but instead climbed in with his father. Cuddling close, he turned out the light.

———————

Faye had a moment of uncertainty as she drew closer to slumber. She worried, just for a few moments, that maybe, just maybe, she had been prideful and wrong to believe it was the aeroplane that Komar Romak or Reginald Roderick Kattaning or whoever he was, wanted. In those twilight moments between awake and asleep, she considered that Reginald Roderick Kattaning had demanded the *thing*. "The *thing*," he had said precisely, the "*thing*" and the "*pieces*." Reginald Roderick Kattaning had indeed mentioned the aeroplane, of that she was sure, but did he actually ask for it?

That's just silliness, she thought, yawning and feeling sleepily reassured. And as real sleep pressed its advances upon her, she smiled. *What else could he possibly have wanted?*

———————

The last pair of eyes closed, and Miss Brett fell soundly into slumber. Deeply relaxed, she slept easily now that her charges were safely present. The green and gold train ambled on into the night. All aboard slept soundly, as the mysteries that were to come tomorrow lay just beyond the horizon.

— Book Two —

P R O L O G U E

The following article appeared in *The New York Times*, fall, 1903 (actual date withheld).

FOUND DEAD IN TUNNEL

Body of Italian, Full of Stiletto Wounds, Near Jerome Park Reservoir

The body of a murdered Italian was found yesterday by John Martins, a foreman of the Jerome Park Reservoir, in the new tunnel which, when opened, will connect the reservoir with the High Bridge Aqueduct, within about 100 feet of the opening.

The body of a young man in his early 20s was in an advanced state of decomposition, although a scar was evident across the eyelid of the victim's left eye.

Martins notified Policeman Bailey of the King's Bridge Station and telephoned Coroner O'Gorman. When they examined the body, it was found that there were nine stiletto wounds in it—six in the back, two in the breast, and one in the stomach . . .

Near where the body had been there was found a long and murderous stiletto, with strange signs carved on the handle . . .

The police came to the conclusion that the young man was Italian. his was because Italian coins were found in his jacket pocket, and ecause his rather worn clothes had tailoring marks in Italian. The ousers, it was noted, were made in *Italia*.

But in truth, these were not such terribly mysterious or important ues. In truth, the fact that the murdered man was Italian would matter ttle to the police of New York City. In truth, they would never know what ad happened in that tunnel or why.

The article did, however, fail to mention three terribly mysterious ad important clues. First, in the right hand of the victim was a corner a map showing a sliver of the Apennines mountain range. Second, in e left hand of the victim was a fistful of black feathers. Third—and e absence of this clue from the article was in no way the fault of the urnalist, his editors, the coroner, or the police investigators at the scene, ecause this terribly mysterious and important clue was gone by the me any of them found the body—hidden by a rock, down the tunnel, in e shadows, there was a crumpled envelope with a broken wax seal and torn note inside that, when it was intact and legible, read simply, "They ill be on the train."

ACKNOWLEDGEMENTS

Mom, Dad, Nate, Lu, Jeffrey, Jules, Lyric, Cyrus, and Jill

To the wonderful friends and readers from all over the world:

lexander Carlsson
lexandra Curtis Boyer
ndrea Spira
ndrew Ferguson
pril Sugarman
arbara Price
ernie Schwartz
huchi Oka Zeh
lare Fleishman
yrus Unger Bowditch
ff
liodhna Noonan
anny Neville
avid Bredin
oris Bowman and
er friends up in Scotland
r. Brandon Canfield
r. Dorothee Heisenberg
r. Gavin Rae
r. Trent Pomplun
lizabeth Bredin

Ford Duvall
Gabriella Gensheimer
Innes Wyness
Jane Cowper
Jason Williford
Jennifer Fugate
Jorge Verlenden
Joseph and Rosie Pearce
Josh Dalsimer
Julius Unger Bowditch
Kate Bowditch
Laura Bradford
David
Lavanda Davis
Lisa Dalsimer
Lukas Hager
Lynn Towart
Lyric Unger Bowditch
Madeline Cowper
Dr. Marla Friend Hartzen
Mary Bauer

Maya Rinehart
Mia Dixler
Michele Carlsson
Mohini Kumar
Nate Unger Bowditch
Ned Oldham
Pascale Rozier
Patrick Ervin
Polly Thomas
Rachel Tunis
Randi Danforth
Sandy Allen
Sebastian Bauer
Shireen Akram-Boshar
Sih Oka-Zeh
Sonali Edwards
Stephen Bredin
Steve Parke
Tracy Copes
Wendy Vissar
Michael

the incomparable Harrison Demchick, who has an eye and an ear capable of knowing ore than the rest of us. I wish you were not always right. It would have been so much eas- r. And to Bruce, who never wavers when he finds something he trusts—and then works endingly to make it the best it can be.

Jonathan Scott Fuqua, who has the brilliant habit of standing when all the world is tting down and for speaking out when all the world doesn't seem to bother. I can never ank you enough.

r my children, Julius, Lyric, and Cyrus, who showed me where "magic" falls short and at real magic is something we can touch.

nd to the love of my life, without whom I just wouldn't be—Nate.

ABOUT THE AUTHOR

Eden Unger Bowditch has been writing since she was very small. She has been writing since she could use her brain to think of something to say. She wrote at the University of California, Berkeley, and she wrote songs as a member of the band enormous.

She has written stories and plays and shopping lists and screenplays and dreams and poems—and also books about her longtime Baltimore home. She has lived in Chicago and France and other places on the planet, and has been a journalist, as well as a welder, and an editor, and other things, too.

The *Atomic Weight of Secrets* is her first young adult novel, and she has been as excited writing it as she hopes you are reading it.

Presently, Eden lives with her family (husband and three children) in Cairo, Egypt. But that's another story entirely...